ᴊuffolk Cou

GW00692307

THE
CHINESE THEOREM

THE
CHINESE THEOREM

Leo Heming

The Book Guild Ltd
Sussex, England

This book is a work of fiction. The characters and situations in this story are imaginary. No resemblance is intended between these characters and any real persons, either living or dead.

The Book Guild Ltd
25 High Street,
Lewes, Sussex

First published 1998
© Leo Heming, 1998
Set in Baskerville
Typesetting by
Keyboard Services, Luton, Bedfordshire

Printed in Great Britain by
Antony Rowe Ltd,
Chippenham, Wiltshire

A catalogue record for this book is
available from the British Library

ISBN 1 85776 341 6

1

Hong Kong   September 1988

Typhoon Wanda came rolling and smashing her way up the South China Sea. She had already left Manila and a great deal of Luzon shattered and battered in her wake, and was now venting her furious spleen upon Her Majesty's Colony of Hong Kong, the Pearl of the Orient.

Derek Harwood had been through many typhoons in his time in the East, but Wanda seemed to be the worst he had experienced. There could be no question of going to work with signal number eight up, and the radio forecasting a direct hit. The weather observatory had left that warning until almost the last minute as typhoons are notoriously unpredictable and frequently veer off course without warning, in a way that leaves meteorologists looking like fools.

He stretched luxuriously in his bed and peered out of the picture-window beside him, already protected by typhoon bars he'd put up as a precaution when he'd gone to bed.

From his tenth-floor apartment at mid-levels on Hong Kong island, he had a panoramic but murky view of the harbour below him in the pale, early-morning light. The sea was a maelstrom of tossing, white spray, and totally empty of ships that had fled out to sea well in advance of the typhoon's arrival. Through the heavy, driving rain which had been pouring down for the last 24 hours, he could just

1

discern the glow of lights in Kowloon and the loom of Tai Mo Shan mountain in the background, beyond which lay the limitless lands of the People's Republic of China.

He turned the other way and looked at the young girl beside him. She lay in an abandoned sprawl, the sheet tossed carelessly away below her waist, her high-cheek-boned, delicately-chiselled, northern Chinese face framed in a mass of thick, black hair, spread across the whiteness of her pillow.

Her arms were long and slender, her breasts small and neat, and what could be seen of her belly was flat and well-muscled, accentuating the graceful curve in and down from the rib cage. As a ballet dancer she had the body of an athlete, and her beauty was only marred by the fact that her long, beautifully-tapered legs ended in typical ballet dancer's feet, distorted by the cruel pressures of her trade.

But at this moment Harwood wasn't thinking of her feet. He reached out and tentatively placed an enquiring hand upon her taut, young breast.

'Ho nushi nin zao.' 'Good morning, Miss Ho,' he murmured.

She opened one slanting, jet-black eye. 'Don't hairy barbarians ever sleep?' she grumbled.

'This one finds it difficult when he is sharing a bed with a prima ballerina of the Beijing Ballet Company.'

She put up a long-fingered hand, and taking hold of his hair, almost as black and thick as her own, pulled his face down towards her. 'Be patient, my lover, I have to do something first.'

She slipped out from the bed and walked naked to the adjoining bathroom. Harwood ogled her joyously all the way.

What a lovely ass, he thought happily, stretching his large, heavily-muscled body in eager anticipation of what was to come.

There was a sudden terrifying blast of wind and the building swayed with an unexpectedly violent motion that caught the breath in his throat. An anxious squeak emanated from the bathroom.

'It's alright, darling,' shouted Harwood.

Such buildings were designed to sway in typhoon conditions, but nevertheless he had been surprised by the suddenness and extent with which it had moved and waited nervously for any repetition. None came so he relaxed and lay back. The fish tank across the room caught his eye. The water in the tank, complete with goldfish, was sloshing gently back and forth as the building continued to move, although in a more moderate way. This was something he had never noticed before and a touch of disquiet stirred again in his gut.

She returned then, hair brushed, silk kimono half-open, slithering lasciviously against her undulating body so that Harwood began to twitch uncontrollably, his fears swept aside. She came round to his side of the bed and leaned over him so that the gown fell open exposing her breasts and belly.

He was rampant, now, and hungry for her. His large, muscular arm pulled her slim body easily over on to his own, and with one movement he slid the gown from her and held her tight and close, loving the feel and smell of her.

'Easy, my darling, easy,' she murmured breathlessly in his ear. 'A little rape goes a long way.'

His heart stilled.

The Bedouin girl-woman, lower half naked, legs astraddle, blood gouting from her, eyes rolled up in the trauma of death. The mercenary grinning, pulling up his shorts, licking his lips with pleasure. He'd shot the bastard on the spot.

He groaned, lust lost with the recall. He loosened his grip, but remained holding her fragrant perfection tenderly.

'You alright, darling?' Concern in her voice.

'Couldn't be better,' he murmured, desire returning, to the accompaniment of the wind shrieking and wailing about them.

They both gasped in shock as the earth suddenly moved. Literally.

* * *

At the weather station placed 2000 feet up on the top-most ridge of Tate's Cairn, almost directly north of the international airport of Kai Tak, the screaming wind and vertical monsoon deluge beating against the observatory windows made verbal communication almost impossible.

The young duty 'met' officer and his colleagues were coming to the end of a long, tiring 8 p.m. to 8 a.m. shift. To make matters worse the appalling conditions had called for a tremendous increase in communications traffic.

The usual hourly wind force readings to be taken from the anemometer had, on orders received, been increased to four an hour, which had to be reported back to Observatory HQ in Tsim Sha Tsui, together with observations of local conditions, such as cloud cover, barometric pressure, wind direction and a mass of other general details. These were then assimilated with reports from the other stations, all round the colony at Green Island in the harbour, Cheung Chau at the western approaches and Waglan Island to the south, so as to provide an overall picture of the situation for the emergency services, if called upon.

Winds gusting up to 177 mph had been recorded. The Marine Department had reported that at least 20 ocean-going vessels, that hadn't fled the storm in time, had been beached or were in the process of going ashore. Many thousands would undoubtedly be made homeless, and the young man himself wondered how on earth he would get back to his own home that morning. Wearily he rubbed his sleep-hungry eyes and lifted the heavy high magnification binoculars for possibly the hundredth scan of his watch. To his right, through the driving rain, he could just make out the catchment area, on the shoulder of Tai Mo Shan mountain, which drained the run off from the mountain

4

into the Shing Mun Reservoirs. As he looked he noticed a huge chunk of rock dislodge and slide down the slope to disappear out of sight.

Christ, he thought, if there had been any houses below that instead of just a reservoir, it would be splat city. Definitely something to report in.

Wide awake now he arced his binoculars back to the left and gradually brought Hong Kong island mid levels into focus. Plenty accommodation there, he thought and moved the viewing slowly up the sheer cliff face towards Victoria Peak.

At first he couldn't really see a thing so he continued on to his left. And then a sudden quirky gust produced a temporary break in the murk. Just for the hell of it he swung back. High up on the reinforced face, directly above the myriad apartment buildings, he saw a powerful jet of water, almost like the controlled jet from a hydro-electric dam, suddenly shoot out into space. For sure he knew that it wasn't controlled. He also knew exactly what it was.

'Holy shit,' he shouted and grabbed the phone.

To give the authorities their due they tried to avert catastrophe but it was too late. The roads had already been choked by falling trees and other debris which prevented police vehicles from getting through and at the crucial moment, to fatally compound the problem, transmission aerials blew away and the phone lines on the island went out. A quarter of a million people lay in their beds, cut off from the rest of the populace and ignorant of the appalling danger that hung over them.

* * *

The block in which Harwood had a flat was well enough built. The foundations were deep and true. But there was one fatal flaw with Golden Lion Mansions.

The land-hungry property tycoons, anxious to save every square foot of the immensely valuable area, built the enormous edifices very close together on extremely steep slopes,

5

which meant deep-cutting into the hillsides to provide the site. Thus each building had virtually overhanging it a precipice of rock and earth reaching up to the top of Victoria Peak, well over a thousand feet above.

The reinforcement of the soil behind and above these tower blocks looked firm enough on the surface, but had definitely been skimped. A combination of 20 inches of lashing rain and ceaseless buffeting for 24 hours by winds of over 150 miles an hour, had weakened the thin, outer layer of scrub and cracked the concrete facing, enabling vast quantities of water to seep through and build up into an enormous, unstable reservoir behind it.

First one boulder started to move down hill and then the next, accompanied by tons of earth and sludge, until, within terrifyingly few seconds, a vast slip had been generated gathering momentum and further débris until thousands of tons of roaring destruction came crashing down upon the buildings in its path.

And there was no notice. The howling of the wind and the hissing of the deluge drowned out the rumble of the earth-slide.

One second Derek Harwood and Ho Ching-hua were shivering with delight in each other's arms, the next they were tumbling through hell. Shock provided merciful numb-ness. Both were clamped immobile. A faint speck of light and air was filtering through the dust. Enough to keep a faint flicker of hope alive. Then from all around came a cacophony of terror, agony and despair as the occupants began to truly appreciate this was not a nightmare. Harwood was only able to move his left arm and hand a few inches. Their naked bodies had remained entwined and locked face to face, breast to breast in a ghastly parody of intercourse.

He was barely conscious, hardly able to breathe and hurting like hell, with the abrasiveness of shattered concrete on his naked body and countless other injuries. He made a feeble attempt to clear his throat and nose, and inhaled the stench of burst sewage pipes like an open drain in a Yemeni bazaar, concrete dust dribbling from his nose. Ching-hua's face was at a level just below his chin and slightly upturned. Her eyes were closed, and even in the dimness he could see the waxen pallor of her skin and the gash across her right temple.

His own breathing was none too stable, but he could feel the hurried broken wisps of her breath against his neck. At least she was alive, he thought gratefully, but for how long? A trickle of blood was oozing from the corner of her mouth, which could mean anything.

He began to realise how much this woman meant to him. 'For God's sake, open your eyes, Ching-hua,' he said, then repeated the request again, louder.

Nothing.

Don't panic, Harwood, he said to himself, and moving his left hand the trifle possible, he cupped it under her chin and stroked her throat.

Nothing.

In a kind of resigned despair he let his hand fall away and heaved a sigh. Pain shot through his side. He grunted with the agony of it, then felt himself drifting in a nebulous sort of way, seeming to rise above the pain and the smells, viewing it all dispassionately from a different plane.

His thoughts flicked back rapidly, in and out of focus. My God, is this dying, and is that corny old saying about life flashing before your eyes true?

He was a soldier. In the constant, grating, sandy grit of endless desert, with the SAS. Soaking up the heat and the harshness of the place, doing dirty work for the crumbling empire by killing the enemies of the Sultan of Muscat. Then to the rotting mangroves and sweating jungles of Borneo. Different enemies from across the Indonesian border but they died just as easily.

The excitement was a turn-on, but eventually there was too much death for him. Too much death among the innocent, the women and children caught in the whirlpool of hatred that seemed to always surround him. He couldn't go on living like this. He needed something more cerebral.

7

A leave in Hong Kong made up his mind for him. That was the place he wanted to be.

A gloomy, rainy day in London. Resigning his commission at the Ministry of Defence, a mind-crunching year at the School of Oriental Studies, learning Mandarin. It seemed the obvious thing to do with his golden handshake, though so few Kwai Lo – foreign devils – took the trouble.

China fascinated him. The Chinese, in their turn, appreciated his being able to speak Mandarin, their official language; and the fact that he was 'sympatico' in his dealings with oriental peoples soon came through to them.

His language skills made him a natural for the China trade. His employers valued him greatly and paid him accordingly. He was going to make his fortune well before the treaty agreement with China ran out in 1997, some ten years hence, and even after that those in the know could continue to make their own opportunities. He was 40 years old, fit and keen. There was still plenty of time.

Being a bachelor, and a presentable one at that, considerable opportunities for dalliance came his way. Not least from the married women, oriental and occidental. Many were bored with their luxurious, over-indulgent life-styles and were looking for excitement to break the monotony of the endless round of entertainment, bridge, mahjong and being waited upon by numerous servants. Not infrequently, they were married to husbands who in the ceaseless quest for riches, or sometimes with affairs of their own, came home late if at all, and much too tired to provide that which was expected of them.

Such ladies gave their favours without strings, and certainly did not want involvements that might endanger the enviable security they presently enjoyed.

But in this regard he was unusually reserved. Only under extreme provocation did he take advantage of the possibilities that came his way. The moral line drawn by his Catholic Irish mother was seldom crossed and then only with considerable anguish. Prude he was not, but neither was he a philanderer.

His contacts in Hong Kong were with China Resources, who worked out of the fortress-like Bank of China building next to the

Hong Kong Shanghai Bank, but he frequently visited the mainland with trips to Canton for the trade fairs, and occasionally Shanghai and Beijing when business warranted.

The hideous creak of settling masonry brought him back and caused further cries of fear from those entrapped about him.

His eyes strained to assess how ominous the sound might be. Christ, he thought, what's it matter? Can't get worse than this. He peered awkwardly down his nose in the gloom. There came a flicker of the girl's eyelid.

'For God's sake, speak to me, darling,' he pleaded, but without reply.

He was too tired to try any more, much too tired, and lapsed back into his painless shadow world.

On his last visit to Canton he had stayed at the Dong Fang hotel near to the Export Commodities Fair building.

Despite it being a spring fair, the mercury was already into the high eighties, with a humidity to match. He had taken off his clothes, and putting on a sarong, which he always used since Borneo days, he lay on the bed. His first appointment was not for two hours. There was no hurry. As he drifted on the edge of sleep he heard a quiet tapping on the door.

'Jinlai.' 'Come in,' he called.

There was a rattle of keys and the door swung open. The girl stood there looking at him, her arms full of towels.

'Baoqian.' 'Sorry,' she said, and, with a half-inclination of her head, sidled toward the bathroom.

She was dressed in the white coat and wide black trousers of the Chinese amah or servant girl. But this was no amah. Harwood became wide awake and stared at her. Her carriage so erect; the head proudly held; the thick, glossy hair, sleeked into a heavy pigtail that flowed down her back to the minute waist.

She isn't even Cantonese, thought Harwood, noticing the coppery glints in her black hair and the fine northern bones of her face, very different from the round, flatter features of the southern

Chinese. And that walk. The slightly splayed feet, the athletic undulation of her firm posterior.

No doubt about it. The girl came from Beijing or thereabouts, and was, or had been, a dancer. Harwood felt pleased with his detective work and intended to find out if he was right. But he was here for at least ten days. There was no rush and he had no wish to embarrass her.

As she had her hand on the door, preparing to leave, he'd said 'Wo zenme chenghu ni ne?' 'What should I call you?'

The delicate hand hovered over the door handle, betokening her confusion as to whether or not she should answer. Familiarity of this kind could lead to trouble.

'Wei shénme?' 'Why?' she asked, head averted.

'Please,' he said, in a low voice.

She turned to him then.

He was smiling and appealing at the same time.

'Ho Ching-hua.' And the way she had said it sounded like water running over smooth stones.

'Thank you,' he replied, and she was gone.

He started to choke. Water was running down his throat. He returned to his dreadful prison. A trickle of foul water was falling on his head, entering his mouth. It was still raining.

He could sense water covering his legs. So cold, so desperately cold. How long had he been unconscious? Were they now to be slowly drowned? Dear God that would be too cruel.

Through the blur of wetness over his eyes that he was unable to wipe away, he saw the pale oval of Ching-hua's face, eyes still closed. Even near to death and despite his hazy vision, her face was perfection.

Why aren't they digging us out? Why no noise?

The bastards were going to leave them here to die. That was the only explanation. The steep angle of the rubble was too damned dangerous for the rescue services to risk their precious lives on a bunch of no-hopers.

He drew a breath and opened his mouth to shout for

help, but the burst of pain from his chest was followed by a repetition of the previous floating state of self-anaesthesia and recall.

Over the next few days he'd made a point of striking up a casual friendship with Ching-hua. The room-girls also doubled as waitresses in the large dining room, and he'd always sat at one of the tables which were her responsibility.

He had a good idea of the times when she would come to make his bed and tidy his room. If it did not interfere with his business appointments he would come into his room when she was there, on the pretext of picking up some papers he had left behind. Never once did he endeavour to touch her or frighten her. She began to accept him now and no longer showed any sign of confusion at his presence.

He learned that she had indeed been with the Beijing Ballet. Their work, despite some loosening of official constraints, was still aligned to 'correct thinking', which meant a great deal of propaganda and virtually no time for classical ballet as known in the West. Harwood did not consider it politic to ask why she was now working at menial tasks a thousand miles from her home, but he had a good idea.

One day he came in and found her at the desk gazing at the entertainments section of the South China Morning Post, *Hong Kong's English language paper, which was delivered daily to Harwood's room. So engrossed was she that he was almost upon her before she was aware of his presence.*

'What are you looking at?'

She turned her head away from him but did not rise.

He saw the half-page photo of the Dance of the Cygnets in Swan Lake *from the recent Royal Ballet production that had taken place in Hong Kong.*

The girl still sat, face turned away from him.

Very gently he placed his hand under her chin and turned her head toward him. Her eyes were closed, the tears sparkling on her lashes. Her generous, moist lips tremulously parted. He simply could not help himself. He lowered his head and softly kissed her.

At that she came to her feet and, flinging her arms around his

11

neck, cried, 'I would do anything to dance again. Anything. Not the stupid, ugly rubbish the party still wants us to do, but real ballet. Giselle, Swan Lake, Romeo and Juliet. Such things we have not been allowed to do for so long.'

He held her as the tears flowed, murmuring endearments, his lips brushing her cheek and neck. Slowly she recovered herself, accepting the offer of his handkerchief to dab her eyes, as if it were the most natural thing in the world.

'Are you here doing this work as punishment for voicing these sentiments?' he'd asked.

She raised her face and kissed him on the mouth, then leaned back in his arms pressing her lower body against him.

'We must labour to help the people,' she intoned. 'They are the blood of China and they rejoice in the greatness of our beloved leader's thoughts.' She broke free from him. 'You are a kind man, sir, but I must go before there is much trouble.'

His feelings were so inflamed his senses left him. He had to have her.

'If ever there is anything I can do to help you, let me know.'

She had taken his hand with both hers and kissed it, then, giving him one last searching look, slipped away.

That evening he had been disappointed to note she was not serving in the dining room. Casually, he'd asked her replacement, a dumpling of a girl, where Miss Ho might be, only to be met with a blank stare, followed by a nervous and barely perceptible shake of the head. Derek's heart sank, she'd gone or, worse, had been taken away.

He joined some of the other businessmen in the rather garish bar set aside for foreign visitors, and sank a couple of Tsing Tao beers with an Australian friend, but found he could not join in the general conviviality. He went to bed at ten but could not sleep.

He kept thinking of the girl and kicked himself for being so cautious in his approach towards her, particularly after the experience of their last meeting when she had shown such warmth.

Just as he began to drift off there came a gentle scratching at the door. It was far too timid to be officialdom. (It was a habit of the really keen cadres, and most of them were keen, to come in a mixed bunch and knock on guests' doors at any time of the day or night to announce the glad tidings of some totally boring victory of the proletariat.) With more curiosity than expectation, he had quietly opened the door. Swiftly the girl had slipped past him and into the room, immediately shutting the door behind her.

'They are after me,' she'd whispered. 'Please help me.'

The terror in her voice brushed aside any hesitation that prudence might have dictated. He'd placed his arms around her and held her tight in an endeavour to comfort her. She in turn had pressed herself against him, seeking every ounce of reassurance that this large, powerful man could give her, until the wild beating of her heart lessened.

At that instant there had come a loud, peremptory banging on the door. Ching-hua gasped. Derek pushed her toward the cupboard. Where else was there? He waited.

Another series of loud bangs.

'Mr Harwood, Mr Harwood, wake up, we must talk to you.'

'OK. I'm coming. Is there a fire?'

'No fire, just open door.'

Outside had been two men and a woman of the People's Liberation Army. He allowed his sarong, loosely tied about his waist, to slip lower. He saw the woman avert her eyes, and stretched grotesquely, sticking out his hairy chest, and ended up this pantomime by scratching himself, then peering at them myopically.

'Wassa matter?' he'd queried, scowling ungraciously.

The male guards had stared at him in fascination, apparently more interested in the delicate status of his covering than their reason for visiting him.

'Well?' growled Derek.

The senior of the guards started, and came back to the business at hand.

'A dangerous female revolutionary has escaped and is thought to be in this hotel. If you see anyone suspicious you must report it immediately, Mr Harwood.'

'Do you think she might be in my room?' Derek asked incredulously. He'd stepped out into the corridor closer to them. They'd moved nervously back from the hairy foreign devil. 'Come in and have a look,' he said, bowing graciously, and this time the sarong

13

slipped well below the level of decency so that the woman hurried away, followed smartly by her two companions.

Derek allowed himself the luxury of a long expulsion of air and re-entered his room, closing the door and locking it with the safety chain.

'That was a damn stupid thing to do,' he'd muttered to himself. 'Now where's my little ballerina?' Keeping the light off he'd opened the cupboard door. 'Mei you le.' 'They're all gone,' he whispered.

No reaction.

He'd put his arm into the cupboard and touched her. She gasped and shuddered under his hand.

Very gently, he drew her out and carried her to the bed. He put her down and lay beside her with his arms still around her, until she ceased to tremble. Secure in his hold, her breathing evened into sleep. Strangely satisfied by this, Harwood followed suit.

When he awoke she had gone. There was a note on his dressing table.

'I will never forget you, my very dear barbarian.'

2

Women and danger make a heady combination. Ching-hua's beauty and apparent vulnerability touched a chord in his heart, so it was some time before the memory of the incident faded to the back of Harwood's mind. She had disappeared from the hotel, so either she had been taken by the security police or successfully gone to ground.

It was July before he saw her again. He had gone to the Hong Kong Arts Centre to see a rendition by the Hong Kong Ballet Company of Giselle. His lady companion was a keen advocate of the ballet, Harwood less so.

He was sitting in a semi-torpor when, part-way through the second act, the dramatic entry of the spirits jerked him to attention, particularly the dancing of the Chinese girl taking the part of Myrta. Not only was she lovely, but even as a layman Harwood was struck by the amazing extension of her beautifully-moulded legs, the arch of her feet, the languorous posing of her arms and her impressively bright footwork.

He realised he was watching a performance that soared above the norm and from the rapt attention of all around him it was obvious this girl was the spirit of dance itself.

He was so moved he found his eyes were moist with emotion, and at that crucial moment she turned and gazed straight towards him, and despite the make-up he recognised her. Quite spontaneously, he rose to his feet and led the roar of applause that shattered the hitherto tense atmosphere in the auditorium.

His initiative had, for a second, caused him to stand out from the crowd around him, so that with equal spontaneity Ching-hua

15

blew him a kiss of appreciation. He could not deny the receipt of the compliment, nor did he wish to, but sat down highly elated.

'Well, well,' said his companion coolly, 'you're quite a connoisseur, and if I didn't know better I would almost believe you knew the girl.'

'I do,' he answered shortly. 'I'm going round to see her after the performance to congratulate her. You come too,' he said, boldly.

Ching-hua's pleasure at seeing Harwood again was clear. As they left, he handed her his business card and said, 'Do call me when you can, and tell me all about yourself, and how you got away.'

'I am sorry my English not so good yet, but hope we meet again.'

'I look forward to that,' he said sincerely.

His companion's comment later was direct and to the point. 'I would approach that one with utmost caution. She has the look of the siren about her. I expect she can sing as well as dance.' The words were prophetic.

Within days, unable to wait, he had contacted her. He arranged their first meeting in a hotel of sorts in North Point, which rented rooms by the hour. He arrived early and stood around in the foyer of a nearby cinema looking at advertisements for coming attractions to pass the time. He was as nervous as any adolescent on a first date, and jumped when a hand touched his elbow.

'What are you doing in this dump in the middle of the afternoon, Harwood?' The voice was a near-bellow, the face puffed and red-veined, the breath stinking of drink.

Michael Jones was the last person Derek wanted to see. He was a colleague of some seniority and, worse, a great gossip.

'An assignment with one of your commie friends, eh?' he persisted, tapping his nose knowingly.

Derek's position as the company's departmental head for China was, at times, cloaked in undeserved glamour. Mainland business agents in an effort to maintain some semblance of independence from their Beijing control, sometimes requested meetings in unexpected places away from their Hong Kong headquarters in the Bank of China.

16

'Keep it down a bit or you'll frighten him away, Michael. In fact, I'd be glad if you'd move along,' said Derek, taking up the cue offered.

Jones was instantly apologetic. 'Sorry old boy, I'll be on my way,' he replied, and almost tiptoed off in an exaggerated parody of secretiveness that made him look comically furtive.

'Come to think of it,' muttered Derek, 'what the hell is he doing here? The dirty old sod's probably had his fun already.' He grinned wryly. Who was he to talk?

Instantly he regretted the whole plan. Why had he decided to meet her in an area like this? Because he did not want his acquaintances to know of it? Surely she deserved better than this? He cursed his lack of tact and prayed Ching-hua would not take offence at his gaucheness.

And yet at the back of his mind was a small black cloud. The security guard at the Dong Fang had described her as a dangerous revolutionary. If it got back to Beijing that he was having a relationship with her, what then?

Oh hell, he thought, in the cleft of his dilemma, but just then he saw her. The whole seedy ambience changed magically and his doubts were swept away in a torrent of desire that left him quite breathless.

She wore a close-fitting, pale blue silk cheongsam, that sets off the Chinese figure so well, with the high, tight collar accentuating the proud tilt of her pretty head. The natural turn-out of her high-heeled shoes displayed her balletic training as she walked, as did the grace of her carriage. That this girl, now smiling and hurrying toward him, had eyes only for him created such a surge of anticipation that Derek could barely restrain himself from shouting out loud with delight.

In the privacy of their tawdry hotel room, with its obvious sexual overtones of mirrored walls and ceiling, and huge waterbed with a large erotic picture of an orgy in intimate detail hanging at its head, he wondered if she might turn on him in disgust. But not a bit of it.

She insisted on examining everything, including the picture, and demanded that they bathe together in the sunken bath provided in the corner of the room before proceeding further.

17

Until that moment she had been all naive appreciation and girlish chatter about the fittings provided, but when she began to strip herself prior to entering the water and saw Derek staring at her half-clothed figure in dumb admiration she became quiet at last, and taking his face in her hands she kissed him softly.

'My darling hairy barbarian,' she murmured, 'let us love each other.' And her hands disrobed him as her lips moved about his body in a way that brought him close to frenzy. They shared the bath, each delighting in the caresses of the other, then, unable to refrain any longer, went to the sensuously rolling water bed where she took him into herself, both of them gasping with the pleasure of it.

After that he visited her in the small flat she had rented in Hung Hom. Parking a car in the narrow, crowded streets of the area was virtually impossible, so invariably he took the ferry across from Central on the Island, to Tsim Sha Tsui at the point of the Kowloon peninsular.

The short trip across the busy, narrow neck of Victoria Harbour was a time for him of heightening anticipation. Nevertheless at the other side, so as not to arrive in a muck sweat, he forced himself to saunter along the seafront, through the scurrying throng of intensely earnest Chinese, no matter what the hour. He would savour the delicious aromas at a food stall, and perhaps buy some dimsum, to tempt the appetite, a bottle of Chinese Sam Su and a small bunch of flowers.

With these he would climb the three floors to her apartment and as if by second sight she was invariably on the other side of the door so that it opened before he had even taken his finger off the bell.

By incredible luck or charm she had obtained one of the few flats that looked directly out over the harbour from the tiny back verandah and it was there that she told him of the hell she had suffered in China, hiding in terror from the security police, who never gave up in the intensity of their search.

'You must understand,' she explained, 'that to lose a peasant refugee to Hong Kong is one thing, but a prima ballerina of the Beijing Ballet was intolerable.' She put on a solemn face and intoned: 'The modern revolutionary dance drama Red Detachment of Women warmly praises the surging revolutionary

18

*struggle waged by the masses under the guidance of communist
thought, and is a paean to the People's Army and People's War.'*
She blew a most forthright raspberry.

Harwood felt like smiling at her little act but the melancholy
coming through sobered him.

'Tell me,' he asked, 'what had you done to be sent south to work
as a maid in a hotel in Canton; you, a prima ballerina?'

'I had publicly expressed my dislike of the régime and supported
the democratic movement.'

'You must have known you would be punished?' said Harwood,
amazed.

'Someone had to do it,' she replied grimly, 'and people listened
because it was me and the movement flourished accordingly. I was
stupid enough to think I would get away with it because of my
position.' She gave a sardonic laugh. 'After all, the party was
trumpeting its new liberal policies.'

'You were lucky to get away with simple banishment,' Harwood
intervened.

She went quiet suddenly. 'That was not all they did to me,' she
whispered. 'They forced me to recant.'

'How?' he asked, dreading the answer.

'They kept me without clothing in a place with no light. An
underground cell. There was nothing there. Just the stone floor and
walls, and a stinking bucket emptied once every three days, that I
had to find by touch and, of course, smell.' She pulled a wry face.
'Every day I had what they laughingly called an exercise period.
They dragged me to an interrogation room where they strapped me
to a chair in a most undignified manner.'

Harwood growled in his throat.

She looked at him quizzically. 'They never left a mark on me or
assaulted me sexually.' She shook her head. 'Oh no, they were most
careful about that. They simply drowned me.'

'Drowned you?'

'Yes. They wrenched my head back, put a towel over my face and
poured water on it until I lost consciousness.' Her eyes were blank
now, recalling the past. 'It was a difficult choice,' she said, matter-
of-factly.

'What was?'

19

'Whether to hold one's breath and try to retain consciousness, which was agony, or just let go and be suffocated as quickly as possible, which was no fun either.' She looked at Harwood. 'They left the choice to you,' she said, straight faced.

'Then what?' he asked.

'Why, then they brought you to, and proceeded to repeat the whole procedure, maybe three or four times.'

'Sadistic bastards,' he said, clenching his fists.

'Indeed they were but they were very methodical. They even arranged for a doctor to check you out between drownings to ensure you were able to take another dose, and all the time they were shouting party rhetoric at me.'

'Were there many of you?'

'Yes there were, but they paid special attention to me because I had once been the Chairman's favourite. He came to many of my performances and even had the nerve to try and give me advice on my dancing.' She gave a snort of contempt. 'It took seven days of this treatment before I gave in. They say it's the longest anyone has stood out. Towards the end the doctor was pleading with me to recant, with tears in his eyes.' She said it with a certain amount of pride in her voice. 'The doctor even perjured himself after four days and lied that I could take no more, but they would not believe him and replaced him. Whatever happened to him the gods alone know.'

'You recanted and that was it?' asked Harwood, fascinated despite himself at her outpouring.

'Oh no. They fed me up for a few days so I looked better. Up till then it had just been a tiny bowl of watery rice and gristle once a day, which I had to eat like a dog because my hands were kept tied behind me. I had to get down on my knees and pick it up with my mouth and lap the liquid with my tongue.' She covered her face with her hands. 'Then they pumped me full of drugs and propped me up in the dock at a show trial, where I muttered a few chosen phrases of regret which they recorded on a video, and I was sentenced to three years at a correction centre in Canton. I got off easily because the Chairman interceded for me. When they thought I was properly broken I was allowed to go to work as a chambermaid at the Dong Fang hotel serving foreign devils like you.' She

20

laughed quite genuinely. 'They thought that was the ultimate degradation.'

He kissed her and held her close. 'Are you tired or can you tell me more, like how you got to Hong Kong? I want to know everything about you.'

'Everything?'

'Everything you want to tell me,' he replied. 'You've been pretty close-mouthed about yourself up to now, and I want you to feel you can trust me.'

'In Canton when I met you I had been in contact with the local democratic party head, and obviously the government's spies had found out. Somebody warned me they were after me so I had to make a break for it. That's about it.'

'And the journey here?' he prompted.

'Ah, the journey.' Her eyes were far away, her mind cast back to the scorched heat of the Kwantung rice plains nearly a hundred miles west of the mountains of the New Territories.

'I was thirsty all the time,' she said, 'and when I did find water it was mostly foul and passed through me bringing pain. Kwantung always has an excess of rain or drought.'

'But you survived,' said Harwood, admiringly.

'Yes, but I saw others die of thirst and starvation. Even those with money who paid huge sums to the snakeheads were tricked and taken in the wrong direction until they fell by the wayside. The snakeheads were evil men who took the refugees' money with a promise they would get them into Hong Kong and through the wire, but led them in circles to their death or back into the hands of the police. And then,' she continued, 'at the mountains the wind came, and with it rain so that it became precarious and one slip might mean death. The rain flooded down the tracks and drains, roaring off the hillside above us then cascading over the precipices to the flatlands below, taking with it not only the topsoil but the unwary, particularly the weak and very young.'

She started to cry then and Harwood held her close, rocking her back and forth to comfort her. She clung to him. 'I do not wish to tell you more. It is not nice.'

She raised her face. In her eyes was such complete trust and

21

*longing that he felt a great surge of tenderness. Love was some-
thing Harwood did not particularly wish to know about. He'd
certainly never experienced it before, but now this rather waif-like
creature seemed to be changing the whole scene. She wasn't giving
herself to him for the excitement of it, nor, as far as he could gather,
for what she could get out of him, although one could never be sure
of that, but he hoped it was because she genuinely needed him. For
Christ's sake, he was beginning to feel protective of her, which was
a novel sentiment for someone who had never really thought of
anyone but himself.*

*'Tell me, I will understand,' he reassured her, and felt faint
surprise at such self-commitment.*

*She nodded. 'Alright, but I will not look at your face while I
speak. If after I have told you it is to be the end, you will just go. I
will understand.'*

Harwood waited for what was to come, his belly in turmoil.

*Ching-hua pushed her face against his chest and held him
tightly. 'When I finally came to within a mile of the fence at Sha-
Tau-Kok, I could see, through the wire, soldiers patrolling. Small,
brown men whom I was told were very fierce.'*

'Gurkhas,' said Harwood.

*'I could not see very well as it was getting dark and I lay down
and went to sleep intending to search for a gap somewhere in the
morning. When I awoke there was a man standing nearby staring
at me. He was squat and heavily-built, and of middle age. When
he saw I was awake, he grinned at me showing great gaps in his
teeth. He was very ugly, unshaven and dirty.*

*'I tried to scramble away because he frightened me, but in a
second he straddled me like a filthy toad and in his hand was a
knife which he held to my breast. I screamed. He laughed at me
and said, 'Scream away, little bird, no one will hear you.'*

*Ching-hua was breathing rapidly now and was obviously in
distress. Harwood tightened his hold on her.*

'No more, my dear, I think I know what happened.'

*'You do not know. There is more I must tell you or I will not
rest.'*

'If you must,' he replied.

'At knife-point he made me take off my clothes, then, revealing

22

his revolting body, he pushed himself into me grunting and slobbering with lust like a wild boar. As his climax began he lifted his head in ecstasy and let go of the knife, which fell by my hand. Whilst he was in the midst of his ejaculation I took the knife and drove it into his belly.' She started to shake with the horror of recall. 'The surprise and rage on his face is something I will dream about all my life. He tried to strangle me but I stabbed him again and again until he collapsed in death on top of me.'

She stopped then to regain control of her voice, which was rising in hysteria. 'After that I took from him a hundred Hong Kong dollars that he had in a pouch at his belt, then went and washed in a nearby stream. Getting into Hong Kong was surprisingly easy. The hundred dollars paid my way through a border post. I had the telephone number of a European lady in the Hong Kong ballet world whom I had met when she had visited Beijing. She took me in, looked after me and got me a job.'

She sighed and looked at him. Her eyes were questioning and bright with tears. 'Now you know everything.'

She said it almost as if she was expecting him to give her absolution. Instead he leaned toward her and kissed her gently on the mouth.

* * *

They spent all their spare time together. Harwood had a boat at Sai Kung in the New Territories. He would anchor off an isolated beach on one of the outer islands and there they would swim and water-ski and make love as the spirit moved them, in the idyllic setting of the South China Sea.

One day, Harwood, who had a private pilot's licence, asked her casually if she would like to go flying.

Her reaction was one of sheer delight. 'You can take me in the air? Just the two of us?' she had asked delightedly.

'On a magic carpet, my princess,' he said gravely.

'I would much prefer an aeroplane,' she replied seriously.

He laughed with pleasure at her dubious expression and hugged her close. 'Alright, then, an aeroplane,' he replied.

'When?' she asked immediately.

He looked at his watch. It was noon. 'Now,' he said.

It was a perfect day for flying. Blue sky with wispy white cirrus clouds at great height, and a gentle three-knot wind straight down the runway. Harwood glanced at his companion. She was trembling, eyes wide, fists clenched.

'Relax, darling,' he said, 'there's nothing to be frightened about.'

'I'm not frightened. Just excited,' she replied. 'Do we go now?'

The crisp tones of the aircraft controller came over the speaker. 'Cessna Hotel Papa you are cleared to threshhold.'

'They must have heard you, girl,' said Harwood.

And then, 'Hotel Papa you are cleared for take off.'

In no time at all they were airborne, climbing up to the craggy prominence of Lion Rock that guarded the North Pass exit from Kaitak airport. Once over the summit, the earth dropped sheer away two thousand feet into the Shatin valley, and he heard Ching-hua gasp with the surprise of it.

To the left towered Tai Mo Shan mountain and before them the sparkling waters of Tolo Harbour surrounded by craggy bare hills burnt brown by the blazing tropical sun, in strong contrast with the bright green of the carefully irrigated fields below them.

Throughout the flight Ching-hua's attention to what lay about her was absolute. She hardly spoke but just occasionally turned to smile at her companion as if she were coming back from some reverie and sought reassurance that this was real.

He said nothing, leaving her to it, until he noticed the glint of a tear upon her cheek. Putting up his hand he placed it gently against her face.

She took it in hers and kissed it. 'Can we fly into China?' she asked.

'We could,' he replied, 'but we would probably be shot down for our troubles, so don't even think about it.'

'I think about China so much,' she said. 'One day I may have to die for her.'

He gazed at her appalled.

He was struggling to breathe, taking small, short gasps to avoid a repetition of the awful pain.

His eyes focused. She was gazing back at him. For the first time since the collapse there was the light of reason in her eyes, and with it the accompanying terror as she appreciated the situation. A surge of optimism ran through him. At least she was conscious.

'Oh, my darling, you're alive,' he said desperately, hoping for a reaction.

She started, gave a tremulous smile, then screwed up her face in agony. 'Oh, the pain; the pain. I cannot stand it.'

'This will pass, dearest. They will come for us, I'm sure.'

Hollow words he thought, helplessly, but he could not let her drift away into death.

Suddenly she moved her head slightly. 'I think I can hear people talking,' she croaked.

'I'll shout,' replied Derek, the possibility of rescue overcoming the thought of the agony which ensued every time he filled his lungs.

'No don't,' she hissed. 'They're talking in Cantonese. You can't understand but I can.' She frowned again in concentration, trying desperately to pick up what was being said.

'What is it for God's sake, girl?' he asked anxiously.

'One says they know the concrete had too much sand in the mix and they think it's a great joke that white devils paid out far too much for their own tomb.'

'Bastard,' said Harwood through gritted teeth.

'The other says that it's too dangerous to dig into this to save fat cats who are probably dead anyway.'

Just as I guessed, thought Harwood grimly. He moaned in frustration.

'The first man says that if they hear anyone they should pull down more débris to finish the job and then they can rob the dead when the stuff settles more securely.'

'Son of a bitch,' whispered Harwood, now fully aware of the danger they were in. 'How can anybody be so callous?'

'Easy,' Ching-hua replied, with Manchu directness. 'They're Cantonese.' And then, 'Derek, I feel water round my body up to my breasts,' she moaned. 'Oh God, I am so cold.'

It was still raining, water pouring in little rivulets through the shattered tons of masonry between them and freedom, and still the pervasive stench of sewage.

'It's alright, my love. Someone will come soon, I'm sure. They must.' They must indeed. The water had risen perceptibly since the last time he had taken note.

Ching-hua's eyes had closed again. Her face was a pale mask, with the dribble of blood from the corner of her mouth glistening in the wetness. There came a creaking groan overhead and a patter of falling pieces of masonry, followed by a further rush of water which was now quite clearly up to Harwood's chest. Ching-hua stirred and shuddered uneasily as the water lapped just under her chin.

Despite his early upbringing, Harwood had found it difficult really to appreciate the power of prayer, but right now it was all he had to cling to.

'Anything, God. Any damn thing you want but for Christ's sake save her,' he groaned.

And God appeared to hear and particularly liked the selflessness of his plea.

'What the bloody hell are you lazy bastards doing?'

The bull-like roar of the very angry, very English voice of Police Superintendent Heaviside, above, strengthened Harwood's conception that God must be an Englishman.

'Fuck all!' he shouted upwards with all his strength, oblivious to the frightful spasm of excruciating pain that convulsed him into total blackness. It was enough to ensure Heaviside set the wheels in motion.

* * *

They both survived, scarred and with ribs fractured to a degree that entailed weeks in hospital, but they came through it virtually unimpaired. Physically, that is. Mentally, it was a different story.

They could not bear to be separated and Harwood insisted and they were given a room together, their beds within touching distance. They both suffered dreadfully from nightmares and comforted each other when the horrors assailed them, which was frequently in the early stages.

Ching-hua, who was young and in fine physical condition, was back to taking ballet classes in four months and Harwood, who was tough, worked from his hospital bed before dragging his battered body to the office within a similar period. As one friend put it, he had a craggy face like the map of Ireland anyway and a physique to go with it, so the only outward change was a touch of white at his temples and a slight loss of muscle tone, which he set out to recover with grim intensity as soon as he was able.

The really positive thing that came out of the experience was that he and Ching-hua had more than fallen in love. They were now totally as one in their affection and need of each other.

They decided to stay temporarily in Ching-hua's rented apartment. There was no hurry to move into something bigger, and keeping a low profile for the time being to see how the land lay, vis-à-vis China, was something Harwood wanted and Ching-hua understood.

One evening when they returned to her place there was a young, well-built Chinese man squatting patiently outside her door. As they approached, he bounced to his feet with the movement of a trained athlete and smilingly extended his hand.

'Mr Harwood, I am pleased to meet you. Ching-hua has told me how you so bravely assisted her in Canton. It is good to have an Englishman fighting for our cause.'

So this is the downside of our relationship, thought Harwood, wryly. I suppose after what she has been through there must be some doubtful characters in the picture. No fault of hers.

He turned enquiringly to Ching-hua.

'This is Kwan Yue Ming. He danced with me in Beijing and does much work for the democratic movement in China.'

Harwood looked back to Kwan. The man seemed pleasant enough but his smile appeared to stop at his eyes. He was also handsome and seemed to behave familiarly with Ching-hua which put Harwood on the defensive. To put it simply, he had taken an instant dislike to the man. A gut feeling said that he should not be trusted, but for Ching-hua's sake he had to handle this carefully.

'Mr Kwan, I am of course very glad to meet any friend of Ching-hua's but you have exaggerated with regard to what I did for her in Canton.' He paused picking his words. 'It may sound old-fashioned, but she was a lady in distress, a very beautiful one, as you will agree, and what I did was for her. There was nothing political about it I assure you.' He looked keenly at the other man. 'In fact, I have excellent relations with the government of your country. I have to, I earn my living doing business with various mainland corporations, as I expect you already know, and I want it to stay that way. Do you understand?'

'Of course, Mr Harwood.' Kwan put up his hands apologetically, but the smile had left his face. 'Is it permitted to speak to the young miss?' There was a touch of cynicism in his voice.

'It's not up to me,' said Harwood irritably. 'Ask her.'

Ching-hua soothed him. 'It's alright, darling. Kwan goes in and out of China frequently and sometimes brings news of my mother.'

'I see,' said Harwood. 'Of course you must speak to him. I will go out for half an hour. I have something to do anyway.' He realised he was being churlish but could not help himself. Kwan was someone he could not take to.

That night as they lay in the dark together, fingers entwined, he said, 'I'm sorry if I was unpleasant to your friend, but I don't trust that man. Is the only reason for his coming to tell you about your mother?'

'He is a man of courage, Derek. He fights for freedom, for civil rights, which is surely what you too wish for China.'

'Maybe, but because you mean so much to me, I am fearful that you will become involved in something that takes you into danger.'

28

'Is it that, or is it because you do not wish to become involved yourself?' She rose on her elbow and turned with her naked breasts upon his chest. 'You are either for me or against me, there can be no half measures.'

She placed her mouth on his and drawing her nails down his chest and belly came upon his unmistakable answer. 'By the gods I love you,' she murmured in his ear.

* * *

When she put the proposition, his immediate reaction was disbelief.

'You want me to take a briefcase of high denomination US currency to Beijing to help fund a student revolution? You're really telling me that if I want to keep you, which I desperately do want, then I should prove myself in this way. The whole idea is crazy.'

He was angry now, close to shouting and with a tremor in his voice. Whether it was rage, or fear of losing her, he was not quite sure. Probably both, but anyway he was in no mood to be analytical. All his adult life he'd been prepared to stick his neck out. Go in with his men at his back. Take his chances. This was different. This was clandestine stuff. If you got caught there could be no question of fighting your way out.

Ching-hua had waited quietly for him to finish, her face composed. She put out a slim, cool hand, touched his cheek.

'Nobody is forcing you to do anything. Whatever you decide I will understand.'

Now what the hell does that mean? thought Harwood, his anger subsiding only slightly.

'Anyway,' she shrugged, 'it's just one briefcase and it's for the cause and you can get over a million dollars easily into one briefcase. It's not as if you are supplying the money,' she concluded, matter-of-factly. 'That is contributed by Chinese businessmen from Taiwan, and in China you can buy a lot of guns for a million US dollars.'

He didn't really want to be drawn into further discussion

29

but he felt he had to know as much as possible so that he might dissuade Ching-hua from this foolishness and get himself off the hook as well.

'What can even a million dollars' worth of guns do against the People's Liberation Army, and anyway who will sell them to your organisation?'

'You think this is something which is being done on the spur of the moment, that we have not thought it through.'

Who's this 'we' he thought, immediately suspicious.

She moved closer frowning up at him. 'You think the PLA are all happy, earnest patriots? They are deserting all the time. They sell their guns to bandits and robbers and then disappear into the remote provinces to avoid further military service. There are a billion people in China, my darling, and most of them no longer believe the lies the government hands out.' As if to ensure complete attention, Ching-hua took a firm hold of his arm, underlining the significance of what she was about to say. 'You I trust,' she said, 'with my life, my soul, my everything. No one else. Not Kwan. Certainly not Kwan.'

Her eyes were piercing, filled with emotion. She made a movement as if to stamp her foot, to drive her point home, then desisted. 'I must have you do it. Can you not understand?' Her voice was imperious, implying disbelief that he could not immediately see matters as she did.

He wanted time to think. He turned on his heel, strode a few paces one way, then the other, her eyes following inexorably.

How the hell do I get out of this and still keep her? he thought.

'Garibaldi began with one hundred men in Sicily, and united and liberated Italy.' She said it almost triumphantly.

Harwood stopped and turned back to her. 'No comparison,' he said shortly. 'Italy then was nothing compared to the vastness of modern China.'

'True, but our democratic underground movement is also very strong. Far stronger perhaps than any of you in the West may appreciate.'

30

'Hold on, my little firebrand. Let's get down to some important detail first.' Christ, he thought, I'm beginning to discuss this proposition as if it were feasible. 'Supposing, and I make no promises, I were to do this, what would happen if the Chinese customs searched my briefcase?' he asked.

'How many times have they searched it before?' she retorted.

'Never,' he answered. 'Baggage, yes; briefcase, no.'

'They know you and trust you so why should they change their routine now?' she demanded triumphantly.

Harwood shook his head. Obviously the democratic movement had been keeping an eye on him for some time. He wondered how many other organisations might be doing the same thing. 'How long have your people been watching me?' he shot out, hoping to take her off-balance.

'Maybe three years or so,' she answered, without a hint of embarrassment. 'That was long before we met, I promise you, and our meeting was quite by chance. If it makes you feel better, we have our own people in Customs and Immigration who could smooth out any problems you might have.'

He changed tack. 'You trust me with your million dollars?'

'Of course.' The straightforwardness of her reply made him realise how uncomplicated her view of the situation was. 'I've told you I trust you completely.'

'Okay then, but what's in it for me?' he asked, making the question as brutally frank as he could.

She did not flinch. 'Me,' she said simply, and then: 'The undoubted gratitude of the New China in a most practical way.'

'You're conning me, my girl,' he said, 'and even though I know it, I can't say no. I must be nuts.'

'I don't think so,' she replied, coolly. 'It's a small risk, and think of the influence you would undoubtedly wield as the agent that made a democratic government possible in China.'

31

He smiled wryly, but to himself he had to admit the heady thought of the favourable treatment he might receive from a Chinese government he had helped to install was massive motivation.

'I just need you,' she continued. 'You always lean on the ones you love, and I love you with all my heart.'

She made it sound so simple and the way she looked at him as she said it made his stomach turn over.

Harwood had made many calculated decisions in his life, and this was undoubtedly the most important. He looked at it objectively, or so he told himself, and even without his overpowering need for Ching-hua he reckoned the potential return if he was successful, and he saw no reason why he shouldn't be, was so enormous that he had to go for it or regret the missed opportunity for the rest of his life.

* * *

When Kwan next visited them Harwood was cool but nevertheless he was polite and attentive. Passwords to identify contacts were given him to memorise and he was told he should book his room in the Beijing Hotel on Chan'an Avenue looking out on Tian'anmen Square.

'How did you know I was going there?' he asked. He had not yet told Ching-hua.

Kwan grinned. 'We have a friend in the visa office in the Bank of China here. You are leaving in a week. Yes?'

'Yes,' agreed Harwood shortly.

'I will bring you the briefcase with the money the day you go.'

And so it was arranged.

During the days that ensued, Derek found it difficult to concentrate on his work, envisaging the possible risk he might be taking. But at night in Ching-hua's arms the problems seemed to dissolve into insignificance.

On the day of his departure Kwan brought him the briefcase. The two of them were alone; Ching-hua had gone to work. Kwan opened the case in front of Harwood, showed him the money, then shut it and rolled the tumblers so that it locked.

'What is the combination?' asked Harwood.

'There will be no need to open it again until it is picked up in Beijing,' said Kwan flatly.

Harwood felt his temper rising. 'Alright, then, you devious sod. I won't take it, and that's that. You can all go to hell.' He suddenly felt a great weight lift from him. He'd been a bloody fool and he'd drawn back from this madness just in time.

'That would be most unwise, Mr Harwood.' The coolness of Kwan's retort held more menace than a shouted threat.

'Get lost, Kwan. You can't do anything to me. Now get out and find some other sucker.' Then, with his heart breaking, he added, 'And tell that scheming bitch I never want to see her again.' He found his eyes were filled with tears, and turned away, embarrassed that he should show such weakness in front of another man. He sensed Kwan at his shoulder.

'I think you should look at this first, Mr Harwood.'

An eight by eight, brilliantly sharp, colour photo, was placed carefully in his hand. He looked at it and coldness gripped his gut. It had been taken by a zoom lens of high quality, focused on his boat. Both of them were on the cabin roof, in profile, and naked. Ching-hua's head, mouth open, was thrown back in ecstasy. Harwood's face, poised above hers, reflected with blazing clarity such voluptuous intensity as to come close to depravity.

It took some seconds to register with Harwood and he was shocked by such a baring of his soul.

'My God, is that really me?' he muttered.

'That, Mr Harwood, is one of the least outrageous,' commented Kwan.

'Does she know about this?' It was all he could bring himself to say.

'No, she does not,' replied Kwan, but he did not look Harwood in the eye as he said it.

Harwood could imagine what a field-day the more lurid Chinese scandal sheets would have. That by itself was something he need not worry about. European men had affairs with Chinese girls all the time, and anyway there was no question of adultery as far as he was concerned. His board, who appreciated his value, would probably slap his wrist and tell him to satisfy his lusts more privately.

But this wasn't just any Chinese girl. This was a dangerous female revolutionary.

Beijing, too, valued greatly the satisfactory trade he carried on with China, and if the relationship was kept low-profile, which it was so far, a blind eye could be turned. However if it was thrown in their face through the media, that was something else. Face is all to the Chinese. It would be the end of everything. He really had no option. He was completely ensnared. He hunched his body in resigned anger, struggling to control himself.

'Now I suggest you close your suitcase and get ready to leave,' said Kwan. 'I have dismissed your driver and will accompany you to the border. It is not the end of the world, Mr Harwood. Please believe me, we will not use these pictures unless you force such action upon us. We are most grateful to you for your assistance.'

Harwood raised his head and stared at the Chinese.

'We are desperate men, Mr Harwood. Desperate for the future of China, and sometimes this forces us to take unpleasant measures.'

The bloody man almost sounds sincere, thought Harwood.

* * *

As he crossed the bridge at Luohu, with the coolie in front of him carrying his suitcase and two briefcases, he looked over his shoulder and saw Kwan standing at the British end, watching him. Kwan had carried the briefcase with the money all the way in the car and train up to the border, and only handed it over at the last second. Harwood had kept to himself and Kwan, sitting beside him, appeared to respect his silence.

As he approached the customs, he picked out what he reckoned was the least aggressive-looking of the officials and put his suitcase on the counter, leaving his briefcases on the ground beside him.

'Qing dakai bei bao.' 'Please open your case.'

He did as he was told and tried to look bored as the customs man rummaged through his belongings. This completed, he started to close it in order to move on.

The official leaned over the counter and pointed at the two briefcases on the floor, indicating that they should be moved up on to the counter as well. Harwood's heart seemed to stop, and he stood there looking confused.

'Ganjin. Ganjin.' 'Hurry up. Hurry up.' At that moment a round-faced, obviously more senior, man appeared beside the first and, leaning over, grasped Harwood warmly by the hand. Harwood didn't know him from Adam, but accepted the interruption gratefully.

'Nice to see you back, Mr Harwood. How is the weather in Hong Kong?'

His first experience of a password. 'Drizzly,' he said.

The older man turned to the other. 'I'll take over,' he said. 'You can go to lunch.' He smiled. 'I hope you will have good business,' he added, and waved him by.

Weak at the knees, Harwood walked on. The back of his shirt was wet with sweat.

* * *

He had one day and night in Canton at the trade fair to confirm some minor contracts, and the next day flew from White Clouds Airport to Beijing. He was glad he had passed the hurdle of customs in Canton as he knew from experience that the Beijing customs were difficult to the point of being obnoxious.

It was a long, uncomfortable flight in the ancient China Air Lines Trident, which stopped at Shanghai and Tsing

35

Tao on the way to Beijing, so he was relieved to get a taxi without delay outside the airport.

He noticed that the one that took him forced its way in front of another approaching cab to get his custom, which resulted in a great deal of shouting and gesticulation. The driver thrust all his baggage in the boot, ushered his passenger into the back, and was off with unusual alacrity. It meant little to Harwood until on the way along Capital Airport Road to the hotel the driver turned his head and asked about the weather in Hong Kong.

'Drizzly,' he replied, automatically.

'Three men will come to your room in the hotel,' said the driver. 'You will know about this and you have been told the passwords. Please tell them to me.'

'No,' replied Harwood. 'You tell them to me.'

The driver grinned. 'Hen hao Xiansheng.' 'Very good, sir, that is the correct reply.' He passed a heavily laden truck, belching smoke, then said: 'One of them will ask you if you have any English cigarettes. You will reply that you have not, but that you could give him some American cigarettes if he so wished.'

'OK. I've got that,' said Harwood, wishing he would get on with it.

'And that is all. He will open your briefcase, check the contents, then take it away and you will hear no more.'

Thank God for that, thought Harwood tiredly and closed his eyes. At that moment his taxi slammed on its brakes to avoid an erratic cyclist, and the battered old truck they had just passed smashed into their rear at considerable speed.

* * *

When Harwood regained consciousness he was totally at a loss, and his head, which was heavily bandaged, ached abominably. He tried to move his right arm and found it was encased in plaster. He closed his eyes, then opened them again, to assure himself this was not a nightmare.

His vision was blurred but there was some light coming

through a small window set high in the white-washed, rough stone wall to his front. Very gingerly he turned his head, and sitting on a chair beside the bed was a Chinese woman in some sort of white jacket.

'Where am I?' he asked. 'What is happening? This is not my hotel.'

The woman, who was built like a wrestler, did not reply. She rose from the chair and, opening the door, called out to someone outside: 'The foreigner is awake.' Then she left, closing the door behind her with a hollow clang.

What the bloody hell is going on? thought Harwood. The focus of his eyes improved and he saw bars in the window. Barred window. Metal door. Dear God this is a prison.

He lay, heart pounding, trying desperately to recall what had happened. All he could remember was leaving the airport and speaking to the driver.

He heard voices in the corridor. The door opened and a uniformed Chinese came in. The uniform was that of the Chinese customs and in his hand the man carried the briefcase which contained the money.

Harwood felt sick. His mind recalled the myriad reasons he had rehearsed, in case the impossible occurred and he was asked to open the case. He had decided to pay for some Chinese produce in cash to avoid bank charges. He was told he could get a better exchange rate for cash. He intended to open a branch company in Beijing and thought it best to pay cash for everything initially, and so on. Whatever, they all sounded weak.

All he could cling to now was that, to his knowledge, there was no specific Chinese law that stopped one from bringing in US dollars. And yet he was definitely in a prison. They must have guessed the money was for seditious purposes.

He could deny it was his. Yes, that was it. Swear he had never seen it before. His mind continued to race wildly. Attack is the best method of defence.

'Where am I?' he demanded. 'What am I doing here?' Even to himself he sounded hysterical, and he could feel the sweat trickling down his face from under the bandage. He recalled from somewhere that customs officers were trained to watch for people who perspired over much, as it betokened guilt.

'I wish to ask you some questions,' said the customs man without preamble. His expression was totally cold and he completely ignored Harwood's request for information. 'You speak Mandarin, which makes it easier.'

Harwood did not comment. It was a statement not a question. Obviously during his period of unconsciousness they had made enquiries about him.

The customs man held up the briefcase. 'The driver of the taxi in which you had your accident tells me you had this in your possession.'

For a moment Harwood considered a denial, but it was such an obvious lie it would go hard against him. What Beijing taxi driver would own a briefcase containing a million dollars? 'Yes.'

'Would you please open it?'

'I do not know the combination,' he replied truthfully.

The customs officer turned the case around and thrust it almost into Harwood's face. Harwood put up his good arm in a defensive gesture, then saw that the edge of the case was broken and there was a small jagged aperture in the fibreglass.

'That is why you are here in this prison.'

'I do not understand.'

For the first time the Chinese displayed some emotion. He grunted angrily, lifted the case above the bed and, turning it over so that the opening was underneath, gave it one vigorous shake. Out trickled a small stream of white powder, pyramiding onto the grey prison blanket like the evidence of doom.

'What is it?' whispered Harwood. But he knew. That bastard Kwan had done a switch on him. A briefcase full of pure heroin was worth ten times a million dollars. Ten times as many guns.

'The combination,' insisted the customs officer.

'I truly do not know. It was given to me to deliver here in

Beijing. I did not know the contents. Please believe me.' He was babbling now. With a great effort he controlled himself.

The other man looked at him incredulously. 'You are an important business man of great experience and seniority. You did such a thing? Such an incredibly stupid and dangerous thing? Why?'

'For a woman,' replied Harwood brokenly. 'For a goddamned woman.'

The customs officer looked at him with contempt.

When the case was broken open it was stuffed full, with packets of the finest grade heroin and not a single dollar bill.

3

At the trial before the People's court, he told them about the money, the switch to heroin without his knowledge, his complete entrapment and the blackmail photos. He pleaded for leniency, in the light of his previous record of dealings with China, and begged forgiveness for breaking trust in the way he had. He had no option but to grovel and it sickened him. They branded him an enemy of the people, gave him twenty years and told him he was lucky not to be executed as was usually the case for the heinous offence of drug smuggling. When the enormity of it hit him, Harwood almost wished they had.

He had been returned to the hospital until his head had healed, which had taken another ten days, but thereafter, despite his broken arm, he was transferred to the main prison building and was placed in what was virtually a dungeon with several dozen other inmates, most of whom were students. From them he learned of the Tian'anmen Square massacre.

The gaols were full to overflowing with arrested students, and there was no question of being placed in a cell with maybe two or three other occupants until the situation had calmed down and the courts had processed the thousands of detainees from the riots. It was uncomfortable as hell and the food was lousy but the spirit among the students buoyed him up, and he joined in their discussions and felt almost as one with them.

He told them his story and they gave the impression of

believing that he had been used, and praised him for his original intention of smuggling in money to support the democratic movement. One, somewhat older than the rest, who was a member of the students' civil rights committee, told Harwood he was acquainted with Ho Ching-hua and would never believe she could carry out such a perfidious plan.

'Ching-hua could twist men round her little finger, as you well know, but at heart she was sincere and strong for the cause.' He paused and shook his head. 'She is so beautiful. You are truly privileged to have known her in the way you have. Do not believe the worst of her until she has had the opportunity to clear her name with you.'

'Not much chance of that now, is there?' complained Harwood.

'Do not despair, my friend. These old men cannot keep us at their feet for ever. Our time will come and when it does you will be remembered.'

Harwood clung to that sentiment as a ray of hope in an otherwise bleak world, particularly as the diplomat who had visited him during his trial held out little or no hope for British intercession on his behalf. He had been a fastidious young man, who made it clear he considered drug smugglers deserved what they got, and that even if Harwood's story about the money was true then it still constituted a seditious act against a sovereign government, which could hardly be condoned.

The guards were obviously incapable of controlling the unruly mob of students properly. With the massive overcrowding of prisons it was either a case of total enforcement to the point of cruelty or letting a certain amount of self-discipline prevail.

Had it been the warders' free choice they would have definitely gone for the former but the volatility of the situation had shaken officialdom to the roots and, as they were not sure what the future might bring, they played it cautiously. After all, if democracy were to win out their own skins would be at stake. So until they were sure of the outcome certain privileges were granted, especially to those who could pay, such as allowing relatives in to visit prisoners with food and inevitably news of what was going on outside. As a result, the prison was a hotbed of rumour and counter-rumour.

The story went that thousands had been killed and tens of thousands detained, including leading figures in the government who had supported the uprising. One visitor told them a regiment of local militia had joined the students in protest at their treatment and troops from as far away as Tsing Tao and Dairen had been brought in to regain control. Worse still, there was talk that the old Red Guard had been reinstated.

The inmates were only allowed half an hour a day outside their cells to exercise in the prison yard, always under the watchful eyes of nervous guards manning machine guns in emplacements on the top of the prison walls. Their numbers were such that they could only progress in unending circles at a slow shuffle – ideal conditions for the passing on of information.

Here Harwood was told that Xiaoping, who still controlled China behind the scenes, had died from a heart attack, and the country was falling into a state of anarchy. Other great cities such as Shanghai and Canton were ablaze, with rioters in the streets defying all attempts to bring them under control. Even Hong Kong was in tumult and world governments were protesting strongly at China's attitude over the issues of democratisation, human rights and the brutality in Tian'anmen. Most exciting was the tale that students, supported by some soldiers, were actually breaking into prisons and freeing political prisoners.

Most of these stories were close to the truth, except that the old fox Deng Xiaoping was certainly not dead. After curbing the prime minister Li Peng's worst excesses, he set about bringing the country back under control. One of the steps taken was to shift politically sensitive prisoners out of the disturbed areas to more stable backwaters, where they could not provide a focus for revolutionary fervour. Out of sight, out of mind.

Some of the students incarcerated with Harwood had been released due to lack of evidence against them and either at the behest of the students' civil rights committee or on their own initiative, they had taken up the cudgels on his behalf as a wrongly-accused supporter of the cause. They had made him quite a cult figure, and his likeness appeared on many a poster during protest marches.

The fact that he was a Chinese-speaking foreigner of considerable standing, who was apparently prepared to risk his all for their ideals, excited their imagination and created considerable sympathy for him. The question of his possibly being involved in drugs was conveniently overlooked. It was a time for heroic martyrs, and Harwood's status was elevated, in the students' eyes at least, to just such a level, and as a result his name came before the powers-that-were as a possible trouble-maker who should be moved.

He was taken from the prison in the middle of the night and placed on a train eventually destined for Kwangsi province, in the far south, near the North Vietnam border. With him on the train was a diligent member of the PLA to whom he was handcuffed and who did not release him even during their trips to the train's stinking toilet. After days of discomfort and desperate boredom, during which his guard would not talk to him and the other passengers were afraid to, the train entered the station in Canton.

Harwood's sense of despondency was overwhelming. He knew the place so well, and Hong Kong, with all it meant to him, was only a few hours to the east. He had been told of his final destination, and envisaged a hell-hole in a tropical jungle where he would undoubtedly rot away, isolated from everything he valued in life. His melancholy thoughts were disrupted by the bright chattering of a bunch of female cadres, who were climbing into his carriage.

As they passed him to take seats to his rear, his heart lurched as he recognised Ching-hua. He shook his head unbelievingly and looked again. It was definitely her. He was about to show a sign of recognition when she looked directly at him for a second or two with the natural curiosity that a European on a Chinese train might arouse. Then she frowned and imperceptibly shook her head. She was going to ignore him. He was desperate to talk to her to beseech an explanation from her, but something held him in check.

The train began to move, and as she passed him, between the seats, her hand brushed his as if she were a trifle off-balance, but he knew she was warning him – warning him to ready himself for impending action. He was not forgotten after all.

The hollow despair changed to nerve-wracking expectation. He exhaled noisily and his guard turned and looked at him curiously. Control yourself, Harwood, he told himself. For Christ's sake don't alert the little shit.

There was a tinkling of a tambourine-type instrument behind him and, turning his head, he saw that some six of the girls had risen and were now standing in the aisle posing dramatically, Ching-hua among them, in the style of the old Red Guard. With their voices raised to an almost unbearable pitch, in the cacophony of Cantonese-style opera, they pranced down the aisle, cheerfully imitating the bayonetting and shooting of capitalist enemies, and extolling the delights of communism and Deng Xiaoping, their glorious leader. The old-time propaganda was back in full force.

Harwood noticed how impressively like the real thing were the pistols and bayonets they waved about within inches of the nervous passengers' faces, and all the time the horrendous caterwauling went on.

As she approached him, his nerves jangled with anticipation. Those were real guns, he was bloody sure of it.

At that moment everything went black. Jesus, I'm dead, he thought. They've shot me to keep my mouth shut. But he could still hear, and then, near to his face, came the distinctive 'Phut' of a silencer. The guard grunted and fell heavily against him. He could sense Ching-hua leaning over him and fumbling about the body of the dead guard.

44

'We must hurry,' she whispered urgently. 'We will soon be leaving the tunnel.'

There came a faint rattle of keys and his handcuff opened. He raised his arms in the darkness to take hold of her.

'Not now,' she said, and, grabbing his arm, dragged him out of his seat, on the trail of the other girls.

Then they were all gathered in the open on the connecting plate between two carriages of the slow moving old train, puffing its way up what Harwood could tell was a considerable gradient. The girls were silent now waiting for Ching-hua's instructions.

She stepped down on to a platform, holding Harwood's hand. The clouds of coal-smoke in the restricted area of the tunnel made breathing very difficult. He put his hand across his mouth and nose in a vain attempt to filter it. A glimmer of light appeared and then all of a sudden they were out in the open but still enveloped in black choking smoke.

'Now!' said Ching-hua and, letting go of Harwood's hand, she jumped. Hitting the ground she rolled away down the embankment with athletic proficiency.

Harwood wavered. One of the girls behind pushed him impatiently. He did his best but only achieved a clumsy exit, endeavouring to protect his injured arm, and practically winding himself. But the train had been going very slowly and he was not really hurt. The rest followed without hesitation. They all lay prone at the bottom of the embankment, out of view from the passing carriages and still covered by the drifting smoke which was now thinning rapidly. The train disappeared into the distance before Ching-hua allowed them to get up.

'You were wonderful, darling. All of you were wonderful.' He waved his arms to encompass them all, his face shining with pleasure.

They surrounded him giggling and clapping. Harwood marvelled. One minute they were determined killers as dangerous as any commando, the next they looked, and even behaved, like naively cheerful schoolgirls.

Then Ching-hua brought them back to earth. 'When the authorities fully comprehend what has happened they will make every effort to find us. We must get far away from here without delay. Our lives depend on it.'

'Where will we go?' asked Harwood, his excitement dissipated.

'The others will leave us now and go back to their homes in nearby villages. I will look after you by myself.'

'I should be so lucky,' muttered Harwood.

'Please do not shame me in front of the others,' reprimanded Ching-hua speaking in English so her companions could not understand.

He glanced at her sharply.

She spoke to her compatriots in short bursts of high-pitched Cantonese that Harwood could not follow. They turned to Harwood, bowed their heads quickly, then moved away from the railway line to the east at a steady trot that soon caused them to disappear into the heat-haze hanging over the vast rice valley that spread around them.

'Come,' said Ching-hua abruptly.

'There is a great deal I want to know,' he burst out, reaching for her.

'We do not have time now for explanations,' she said.

As if to emphasise her point there came the shrill screech of another train entering the tunnel they had just left. She darted away into the cover of some underbrush.

He tried again. 'I must know,' he repeated doggedly.

She turned her face to his. 'Kwan told me what he had done to you, as if it were a great joke.'

'Switching the money for heroin, and the photographs?'

'Yes. I had not known till then. I swear it on my ancestors' graves. And you thought I had betrayed you. You did, didn't you?'

He just stared at her. Why should I feel guilty? he thought. But he did.

'One of the students, who was in prison with you, escaped to Hong Kong. He sought me out and told me what you had said about me.' She bowed her head. 'I swore then I would free you somehow. I told Kwan that if I could not get you away I would kill him and he believed me. He arranged all this and he is waiting for us now with a boat to take us down the Pearl River to Macao.'

'The bastard. He owes me that at least,' muttered Harwood. 'But that is not important. What about us? You and me, I mean. That's more important.'

'I don't know,' she said quietly.

'That's no answer.' He threw up his hands in exasperation. 'By your actions, you have shown without doubt that you were not party to what happened to me. But now you are questioning our relationship because I lost faith temporarily?'

He grabbed her and shook her roughly. Unexpectedly, she went limp in his arms, head swinging back and forth like a rag doll. Appalled, he let her go, bit his lip, and stood back from her.

'Better you had left me to rot in prison than arrange my escape only to abandon me afterwards. Life without you would be a hopeless, miserable affair.'

She put her hands on either side of his face and looked into his eyes. 'That is really how you feel about us?'

'Of course it is,' he exclaimed wildly. 'Otherwise I'd be getting the hell out of this place, instead of standing here talking about feelings.'

He closed his eyes and sighed. He felt her warm lips on his, her tongue sliding into his mouth. He sighed again. This time with relief.

'Just keep that bastard Kwan away from me,' he growled, when he came up for air.

4

Harwood had to admit the cause was well organised.

They moved at night from safe house to safe house in an ancient, creaking cart, pulled by a water buffalo and loaded with farm produce, some of which was well past the sell-by date. Harwood squatted in a back corner between a pile of rank cabbages and some rather more fragrant greens. There were many other travellers about after dark, anxious to avoid the heat of the day, so they drew no attention to themselves and Harwood, wearing peasant garb with his skin darkened and a wide-brimmed coolie hat, was a barely-noticeable shadow among the vegetables surrounding him.

In three nights they made it to the Pearl River and, to his credit, Kwan had arranged a motor-junk. As soon as they boarded, by a sagging gangplank, the sail unfurled above them and the diesel started in a billow of smoke then thumped steadily away as they drove down past Whampoa towards the estuary.

As if to advertise their clandestine flight the moon came up with silver brilliance, and when Harwood came on deck he found himself the centre of attention of the junk crew's bare-arsed kids who sat and stared with unashamed fascination at this foreign devil in their midst.

Ching-hua came and sat beside him on the hatch-top, talking to the Hoklo children in their own language.

'Where are we going?' he asked.

'Not direct to Hong Kong. The Chinese gunboat patrol

48

boats will be looking for us in the estuary, waiting off Lin-Tin and Lan-Tau islands.'

'How do we avoid them?'

'We head further south for Macau, then take the ferry across to Hong Kong.'

A wind came up from the north east and the frugal owner cut his engine. The junk laid off, and heeled over feeling for the right tack, then settled down and creamed south-east. For nearly six hours they kept on the same tack and, as the moon spent itself, giving way to the faint light of dawn, they could just discern the rough outline of the Praia Grande and the lights twinkling from the temple gardens.

They approached the dangerous but beautiful, phosphorescent surf of Coloane, surging threateningly before them, and slipped between the islands, mingling with the early fishers drifting past in the morning mist. They anchored a short distance off a sandy beach, and were ferried ashore by the junk's sampan.

It was very quiet and the ghostly mist seemed to deaden what little noise there was. They left the beach, climbing up to the road, and paused for breath.

Ching-hua came close to him, put her arms around his neck and kissed him. 'We are safe now,' she said.

The mist lifted as if a vacuum had suddenly sucked it away, and below them the sea sparkled in the early sun. Their junk still lay at anchor and alongside it was the dark, menacing silhouette of a Chinese patrol boat. They could see one of its crew searching the beach with his binoculars.

'Jesus, that was close,' exclaimed Harwood.

Ching-hua took him urgently by the arm. 'Come, let us go from here before they come ashore after us.'

'What happens to the junk's crew?'

'They will handle it,' she said, enigmatically.

The two of them went quickly along the road to Coloane. At the hilltop they turned back and looked down toward the beach where they had landed. The patrol boat had left the scene and the junk was proceeding placidly on its way.

'They are alright,' was her only comment.

They walked easily down the other side to the jetty where the ferry was waiting, the tourists pouring ashore, Americans and Japanese, cameras pointing, swamping the place with their presence. They went into a cheap bazaar shop. Harwood purchased a sports shirt and European type trousers. He kept his prison sandals. Ching-hua paid.

The trip on the ferry was uneventful, but the Chinese immigration officer in Hong Kong was sceptical. Ching-hua had an entry permit, but Harwood had no passport and nothing to identify himself. The Chinese called his superior, an Englishman. The white man, after a muttered aside with his Chinese colleague, asked Harwood to follow him. He waved Ching-hua through.

'I have seen you dancing, miss.' He smiled, apologetically. 'I sometimes go to the ballet when my wife makes me accompany her. The only time I didn't fall asleep was when you were dancing.'

'It is very kind of you to say so,' she replied, smiling falsely at this philistine. At the exit she turned and looked at Harwood, her soul in her eyes. He smiled reassuringly and mouthed a kiss.

The immigration officer thought the Chinese girl's look had been for him and turned back to Harwood, a grin on his stupid face. Then he became all business.

'This way, sir. We have someone coming to my office who probably wishes to speak to you, and then maybe we can get to the bottom of this. If you are who you say you are, you became quite a celebrity here.' He finished on a sour note. 'For a short time.'

He was given a straight-backed chair in a box-like office and told to wait. Not even a cup of coffee. What the hell did they think they were doing? He waited half an hour. Nothing. He became angry and went to the door to voice his displeasure. The door was locked. He rattled the handle fiercely. He looked around. No windows.

The furniture, what there was of it, was solid and basic. A tin ashtray full of half-smoked butts appeared to be the only thing around that he could throw. Other than the chair, of course. He picked up the chair, fury overcoming reason, tensing to throw it at the door.

The door opened. His colleague, Michael Jones, stood there. Beside him was the immigration officer.

'What *do* you think you are doing, Derek?' he asked.

Feeling foolish, he lowered the chair and set it gently back on the floor. 'Bloody door was locked and I've had enough of locked doors.'

'I didn't notice it,' Jones said. 'It seemed to open easily enough from the outside.'

'Must have jammed,' said the immigration officer, a smirk on his face.

What the hell are we doing talking about doors at a time like this, thought Harwood. 'Very glad you're here, Michael.' He moved quickly towards him, his hand outstretched.

Jones ignored it. 'For Christ's sake, Michael, it's me, dammit. Tell him who I am.'

'It's him, alright,' said Jones, woodenly.

'That's alright then, sir. You are free to go,' said the officer.

Harwood ignored him. 'What's going on, Michael?' he asked, turning to his colleague.

'We can't talk here,' Jones said stiffly, 'and we have a great deal to discuss. Let's go to the office. The board want to see you.'

'What a bloody homecoming,' complained Harwood, but worse was to come. Much worse.

* * *

'Surely you don't believe all this crap about drugs,' shouted Harwood.

'Please don't yell, Derek, and tell me, was there not heroin found in your briefcase?'

'Yes, heroin was found in my case, but it was there without my knowledge. The damn case was switched. The court didn't believe me and I know it sounds feeble, but I

51

am totally innocent. For Christ's sake why would I want to become involved in drug smuggling?'

'Totally innocent?' queried Jones, his voice cold. 'Remember your court proceedings in Beijing were translated verbatim in the *South China Post*. And I read it. Every word of it.'

Harwood kept silent.

'You admitted to risking your career, everything, to smuggle a million dollars into China to fund a bunch of crazy seditious students, all at the behest of some Chinese bit you couldn't keep your hands off.'

One of the other directors interrupted. 'We don't expect you to be celibate, for heaven's sake, just discreet. Plenty of attractive ladies in this colony, who would probably have been delighted to pander to your lusts without bringing the whole world crashing about your ears, and to a certain extent ours as well.' He shook his head from side to side. 'But no, you get yourself involved with a flaming revolutionary. We have to sit here and read about it in the papers and listen to all the false condolences of our business associates and friends, so-called, who lapped up the scandal with almost orgasmic delight.' He threw up his hand. 'You realise, of course, you are out of a job. In fact, I doubt you'd be employable again anywhere. You'll get no parting handshake I can assure you. Our China business will take years to recover, if ever.'

Harwood could only admit to himself that in the main he was guilty of the accusations made, and with a muttered apology turned and left with as good grace as he could muster. This was not a time for bluster.

A call to his bank elicited the information that he was not short of funds, so he reckoned he could relax for some time, at least to think about his future, and looking at Ching-hua being happily domestic he realised that there were compensations.

After a few days of delight in their love-nest, the idyll was rudely shattered by two large men coming to see him. One was European. The other a Chinese. They flashed police

IDs and were very sure of themselves. He was required to come with them to answer a few questions.

'What about?' he asked, irritably.

'I really don't know, sir, but I expect you'll find out soon enough,' said the European, stating the obvious. They went out, leaving a worried Ching-hua behind.

'Don't be upset, darling, I'll be back shortly.'

Outside an unmarked car and a driver were waiting. The windows at the sides and rear had dark glass. The three of them sat in the back with Harwood in the middle, which seemed an unnecessary crush.

'I'm not going to try and make a break for it,' complained Harwood.

'It's regulations,' said the Chinese, speaking for the first time. His colleague nodded in silent agreement. Harwood shrugged and tried to relax, but it was difficult. When they came to the cross harbour tunnel entrance, the driver went to the head of the queue of waiting cars and was waved on without hesitation.

'Ah the privilege of rank,' muttered Harwood, trying to make a joke of it. There was no answer.

As the tunnel began to slope up from the river bed to the Hong Kong island side, Harwood noticed the driver move into the left lane to exit.

'Hey, we're going in the wrong direction,' he commented.

The driver took no notice, nor for that matter did anyone else.

'Look here. Central Police Station is to the right. Where the hell are we going?'

'I never told you we were going to the police station,' said the European, a look of innocent surprise on his face.

'Nor you did,' Harwood conceded. 'So tell me where are we going?'

'We'll be there soon,' came the non-committal reply, and with that he had to be satisfied.

They carried swiftly on along the new coast highway until they approached Shau Kei Wan, where they turned off down the road to Little Sai Wan just past the Lei Yue Mun Channel outlet. They came to a heavily-fenced area, within which Harwood noticed an array of radio aerials perched atop a few concrete buildings. He'd seen them before from the sea, when he'd gone sailing through the channel, but had thought it to be associated with purely maritime needs. Now he wasn't quite so sure.

Their identity was carefully checked by a couple of flat-faced security men before they were allowed in, and the gates closed firmly behind them.

'This is the end of the road,' said the European, as they drew up outside a particularly bleak-looking edifice, painted an austere grey.

'I hope not,' replied Harwood.

All he got for that effort was a minimal grunt.

They passed down a lengthy corridor until they approached a heavy, metal door with an entry-phone system beside it. The European pressed a set of numbers, then spoke into the unit. 'Clarke here, sir. I've got Harwood with me.' The door slid silently open and the three of them entered.

The room was full of electronic gadgetry. The man seated behind the space-age desk was of middle age, his fair hair thinning, slender of build with features that were completely nondescript. Only the eyes were bright, and shone with intelligence. Harwood knew him casually as a fellow member of the Hong Kong Club. His name was Brian Summervill, and Harwood had no idea of his occupation or anything else about him except that he was an extremely good chess player, up to international standard. He was also the club squash champion, so it seemed the skinny frame belied his physical potential.

'Ah, Derek, good of you to come,' he said, proffering a chair.

'Didn't appear to have much option,' grumbled Harwood. He sat down.

Summervill turned to the two minders. 'You can leave now.' No more was said, and they turned and left.

Harwood felt uneasy but he had no intention of showing

it. 'Would you kindly explain what's going on here? I have certain rights which you, Brian, seem to be ignoring. I – '

Summervill raised a hand, interrupting the flow. 'That is where you are wrong, Harwood.'

No more Christian names? 'What do you mean? I take it you are running some sort of James Bond set up, with sufficient clout to have the police work for you in a highly suspect way.'

'As a committed drug smuggler you have no rights at all.' That cold statement brought Harwood up short. 'And just to let you know the bottom line of your abysmal situation, the Chinese government will probably apply for your deportation, which request would be legally and also morally binding on the Hong Kong government.'

'But I am innocent,' protested Harwood. 'Taking in money in a moment of madness, yes; but drugs, no way.'

'You know that. I know that. But who else would believe it?'

Harwood almost keeled over with surprise. 'Thank God someone believes me. It's been like a bloody nightmare. I can't tell you how awful it's been. He stopped and clenched his fists. 'But if you know I'm innocent, what are your reasons for bringing me here?' He was beginning to get to the truth now.

'We've been watching Kwan for some time. One of my men even saw him switch briefcases on you. He's a slimy one, that Kwan. Plays the political game and lines his pocket as well.'

'When did he see him? Your man, I mean.'

'He was in the car with you when you went to the station. He infiltrated the Democratic Movement Party some time ago and is an excellent agent.'

'So why didn't you do something about it and save me all this strife?' Harwood was furious now, upset by this man of contrasts who seemed to be playing with him like a yo-yo.

'We're not here to watch over your kind, Derek.' Christian names again. 'If you're stupid enough to get involved in matters like this we simply keep a low profile and watch and wait until we can take advantage of the situation. Rest assured I know intimate details of virtually every European's nasty habits in Hong Kong, and most of the Chinese that count as well.'

'You're a rotten bastard Summervill!'

'I'd go along with that,' was the cool reply.

Harwood gave up. 'Okay. So send me back to China. If the government is going to be so damn moral, there's nothing I can do about it, is there?'

'Officially the Hong Kong government doesn't know where you are. Let's say the immigration authorities have not yet passed on the news of your entry to the central authority. Bureaucracy at its worst.' He shook his head despairingly.

'They'll soon be able to find me if Peking requests a deportation order. You'll just tell them, won't you?'

'Why should I?' Summervill's eyebrows rose as if to stress his point.

'I see. Another of your "low profile and just watch" operations,' sneered Harwood, thoroughly fed up. 'Stop playing games. It's obvious you're going to use me somehow, so let's have it.'

Summervill stood up and moved over to a console covered with a mass of complicated-looking dials and switches, one of which he flicked over. The quiet hiss of a UHF carrier wave came through a speaker above their heads. His long, capable fingers moved across to a nearby control and suddenly, clearly and without interference, a male voice speaking in Chinese came through the speaker. It ceased and another replied, staccato and equally clear.

'That's not a broadcasting station. That's military talk,' exclaimed Harwood, sitting forward in his chair, interested despite himself.

'Absolutely right. We are picking up two tank commanders talking to each other in Shanghai.'

'Really? I'm impressed,' said Harwood sincerely.

'We can do even better than that,' said Summervill and

for the first time there was a trace of enthusiasm in his voice. 'We have radio probes in all parts of China and have a fair idea of what is going on. This miracle of technology brings us transcripts of meetings among the highest echelons.' He patted the console fondly. 'Put a bug in the right place and we could hear the Chairman fart.'

'I believe you,' nodded Harwood.

'Now to your part in this.' He gazed at Harwood as if inspecting a specimen pinned to a board. Harwood felt distinctly uncomfortable. 'Since the Falklands,' he began, and Harwood wondered what the hell tack he was off on now, 'we have owed our American colleagues a great deal, as I am sure you appreciate.'

'So I understand.'

'Since then there have been occasions when we have been able to do minor things for them, but nothing on the same scale which could satisfactorily redress matters.'

He moved back to his chair and sat down, tilting it back with his hands behind his head. He seemed to have dried up completely or else was miles away. Then with a suddenness that made Harwood jump he leaned forward bringing his palms down on the desk with a smack that resounded round the room. 'Now,' he said, 'they want us to do something really important. Not a big operation but one that has enormous emotional content. One that would generate enthusiasm, relief and gratitude in the White House itself.'

'I get the impression that you look upon this from a viewpoint of personal satisfaction,' said Harwood guardedly.

Summervill looked at him sharply. 'Very percipient of you, Derek. You have no idea how galling it has been to have the Falklands shoved down our throats all these years by the Americans. It would be extremely satisfying to have them in our debt for once, or at least to feel we do not owe them anything.'

'So where do I come in?' interjected Harwood.

But Summervill was not to be rushed. 'As you know, there have been strong rumours in the States, which have been pumped up by avaricious exploiters in Thailand and thereabouts, that hundreds if not thousands of American prisoners-of-war have never been returned by the North Vietnamese, but are still eking out a bare existence in terrible conditions in various slave camps throughout the country.'

'Everyone's heard of that and from what I can gather there is some basis in truth for such rumour,' said Harwood, aching to get to the meat of the matter.

'Some of the more valuable prisoners, those with technical expertise, were moved to safer areas. Areas where the likelihood of a rescue attempt by any American organisations, official or otherwise, would be unlikely.'

'Such as?' asked Harwood.

'Well, it is rumoured some were taken to Russia but I know quite a few were transferred to China.'

'What?' said Harwood disbelievingly. 'The Vietnamese don't get on with China. They've even had a minor war. No way would they pass on potential technology resources to China except for a very high price.'

'How about a couple of million US dollars or more per head for avionics and missile experts who could, with the right persuasion, modernise the ancient MIG 19s possessed by the Chinese up to international fighter standard, so far as the electronics, missile guidance and search-and-warning radar were concerned.' Summervill paused and pointed his finger at Harwood. 'You must appreciate the Chinese have put satellites into orbit, built ballistic missiles, surface-to-air missiles, atomic power stations and other highly technical items. Most of these were utilising the designs of others, I admit, but the actual ability to manufacture to a blue-print or design is all there. These prisoners could provide them with the know-how and that would be the catalyst to bring them more or less into line with their potential enemies.'

'A sight cheaper, I suppose, than buying from the Russians,' agreed Harwood.

'The Russians wouldn't co-operate with the Chinese after the big bust-up they had way back in the sixties,' said Summervill.

'True,' said Harwood, 'and you got to know all this by listening in on your miniature GCHQ here.'

'I did indeed. I monitor traffic on various sweeps every day. I can speak Mandarin, Cantonese and Shanghainese, and understand Hokien, Hakar and some Tezchu, which covers most of the requirements.'

'How the hell did you manage all that?'

'My father was a missionary who spent years in various parts of the country. Everywhere he went my mother and I followed, until she died when I was eight. I never had any European associates until I was an adult, when he sent me to the London School of Oriental Languages on a special missionary scholarship. I picked up Malay and Thai there, as well,' he concluded modestly. 'Anyway, I digress. About a month ago I was beaming in on some governmental chatter between Kunming, that's in Yunnan province, and the big boss in Beijing and they were talking quite openly about progress being made on various defence projects using co-operative Hong Mo Kwais – red-haired devils.'

He got out of his chair and started to walk about. The recall obviously still excited him as much as anything could. 'Well, after that, I really concentrated on that source and was it worth it. There are about forty of these men, all of whom were captured in Vietnam, some over twenty years ago, and all of whom were exceptional in that they had outstanding qualifications from American Flight Academies, or Pax River and Edwards. One or two even went to MIT. Why the Yanks allowed them to be exposed to such risks I cannot understand. Still, I suppose they were all gung-ho types, and desperate for action so they pulled strings and I reckon they deserved everything that came to them.'

'Twenty years. That's a hell of a long time ago.' Harwood shook his head. 'It's a great tale but do get to the point.'

'It's essential for you to know the whole story, so just be patient,' snapped Summervill.

Harwood sighed resignedly.

'I passed all this information back to our American

friends. I even had some names which were brought up by the Chinese in their conversations. Names of the Americans, that was.' He drummed his fingers on the desk. 'I waited ten days before I got any reaction.' It was obvious by his drumming that the wait had frustrated him. 'Ten days, but I continued to listen in. I located their place of work, some of the projects they were carrying out, even their physical state, during those ten days. Then, when the CIA did react, it was like the end of the world was fast approaching. They wanted almost instant action. That was a week ago.'

'What's the rush? Those poor bastards have been in the bag for so many years now. Won't their ideas be way out-of-date?'

Summervill shook his head.

'These are special men. If they are co-operating, if the Chinese have genuinely been able to turn them, as seems to be the case, then their thinking will certainly not remain static. In fact, they could be as innovative and perhaps more so than the rest of the world. Anyway, it's amazing how much so-called secret technical information is in the public domain. In the Western world at least.'

Harwood came to his feet. 'Look, Summervill, I can't take any more of this. I really cannot.' He put his fists on the desk and glared at the other man. 'You are coming up with some hare-brained scheme that we should go in and get them all out. You know bloody well it's impossible.'

'Not quite and don't get so excited.'

'What do you mean "not quite"?'

'I'm not going in, Harwood. I'm too much of an intelligence risk to try anything like this and anyway, we aren't going to try and get them all out. I'm just not trained for it.'

'You're not?' gasped Harwood.

'The Yanks want one man out of that bunch.'

'But – '

'Listen. I repeat, one man. His name is Levinsky. Stefan Levinsky. In his late fifties now. Brilliant man. MIT graduate, Airforce Colonel when captured, and among other things an absolute top man in laser technology in addition to his expertise in general avionics. American satellites have been routed over south China ever since the Vietnam War and in the last year or so it has been noticed that some unusual structures have appeared in an isolated region to the south west of Kunming.'

'They think this is something to do with laser technology?' asked Harwood.

'Initially they thought it looked like some kind of accelerator and reckoned it was an attempt to build a new type of atom smasher. Then just before I passed them Levinsky's name they received pictures of what looked like giant reflectors. The Americans have been working on the possibility of laser space defences for their Star Wars programme. They realise the potential, and their sighting of the reflectors, virtually coinciding with my passing them Levinsky's name and whereabouts, really made them shit themselves.'

He smiled wryly. 'The CIA are quite clear in their requirements. We must get him out before the project is activated. From the satellite pictures it looks as if it still has some way to go, but they can't risk any delay.'

'For Christ's sake, Brian,' Harwood complained. 'You keep saying "we" and then tell me you are too much of an intelligence risk to go in yourself. That leaves me with the conclusion that I go alone.' He put his head in his hands and groaned. 'Why can't the Americans do it themselves? What expertise in such matters do I have that justifies sending me?'

Summervill looked as if he were positively enjoying himself. 'Don't underestimate yourself, Derek.' He put up his fist. 'One,' he said sticking out his thumb, 'you speak Mandarin, which most Chinese understand. That's the obvious one. Two,' raising his forefinger, 'you can fly and also I am sure we can hone up your old SAS techniques. You were quite a lad in your day, I understand.

'Three, and this is your greatest asset, your lady friend, so we hear, has now got considerable influence within the Chinese democratic underground movement and should be able to smooth your way, particularly if she accompanies you on this venture.'

Harwood found it difficult to believe such effrontery. 'No way do you drag her into this,' he protested firmly.

'I doubt she would have to be dragged,' retorted Summervill. 'For some reason she seems infatuated with you, and of course she is all for the cause as well.' He coughed and winked slyly. 'Now to answer your first question as to why the Americans can't or won't do it. It appears they have lost confidence in themselves. Have you heard of an American operation of this type that has actually been successful? Look at Iran and the other occasions when they tried to extract prisoners of war from North Vietnam. Total disasters. They couldn't even kill Castro for heaven's sake, and Grenada was a pig's arse.'

Harwood found it difficult to argue against the facts as presented. 'But the CIA must have their own local agents in that part of the world to do their dirty work for them?' he suggested more in hope than expectation.

Summervill snorted sardonically. 'The CIA have rather fallen out with their local boys. After the Phoenix affair in Vietnam, a particularly nasty operation which again was unsuccessful, the CIA just exited smartly and left their South Vietnamese operatives to the tender mercies of the communists. Word of that sort of behaviour gets around, and from what I can gather their recruitment in China of agents they consider trustworthy is negligible.'

Summervill rubbed his hands and shook his head. 'No, I'm afraid it's up to us, or rather you. The CIA insist on a white face being in charge. Of course they will provide you with all the logistics, money, weapons and anything else that springs to mind, but for heaven's sake don't let them load you up with all sorts of unnecessary kit like helicopters and so on. Nasty, noisy things anyway, and so unreliable.'

'And if I refuse?'

For a second Summervill went rigid and his eyes narrowed with fury. Then control returned and he said: 'There is another advantage in using your services. You cannot refuse, or it's back to a Chinese pokey you go. And' – he leaned forward, chin thrust out – 'that lady friend of yours goes with you.'

'Bastard,' Harwood muttered under his breath. Summervill ignored him. 'We'll give you some concentrated training and just to help you out Peng Kiong will go with you. That's the Chinese who escorted you here. To his friends he's known as Odd-Job and I can tell you it's no misnomer.'

'What happens to me in the unlikely event of this project succeeding?' asked Harwood.

'You will be given a large sum of money, a new identity and an acceptable set-up anywhere in the world you wish to go, outside of the Orient. With a ticket to get there.' He thought for a second. 'Two tickets if your friend wishes to accompany you.'

'Very generous.'

'I think so,' said Summervill. 'You'd better trot along now and persuade Ching-hua to do the right thing by you. Odd-Job will take you back. It would be a good thing for the two of you to get to know each other. Be ready to depart for Bangkok in, say, ten days. We will launch Operation,' – he thought for a second or two – 'yes, Operation Quits, I like that, from the northern Thailand border. It'll only be about 150 miles to Mengwang, your objective, straight up the Mekong river, so you can't get lost.'

'Piece of cake,' said Harwood, sullenly.

'Exactly,' retorted Summervill. 'I'm so glad you're feeling more sanguine about things now.'

5

Thailand   May 1965

Colonel Stefan Levinsky was not a happy man and his thin saturnine face, with its gloomy deep-set black eyes and fiercely-knit brow, made his feelings very clear.

The colonel was an F4 back seater, and, as such, handled most of the technical gear in the Phantom fighter bomber in which he was presently seated. His pilot, a bouncy extrovert, knew it would be wise to pander to the colonel's mood, and kept conversation to an absolute minimum.

As the pilot, Captain Theodore Crain, whilst of junior rank, was in overall command once they climbed into the aircraft, but Levinsky was something special and Crain had been told to treat him with kid gloves. The colonel shouldn't really be flying anything but a desk, but for this operation, in particular, expertise in laser technology was required and orders had come from Command Centre Saigon to Ubon airbase in Thailand that Levinsky was to be accommodated in any way he wanted.

What Crain didn't know was that the previous day Levinsky had received a letter from his wife, wanting out from their marriage. Levinsky loved his wife, couldn't understand what the hell had happened, and had gone through the whole gamut of shock, tears and rage. He was presently undergoing the last phase and it was imperative that he regain control of himself right now and get to the business at hand. He took a deep breath, sighed heavily and his eyes and hands began to run through the necessary checks required before take-off.

Phantoms attacking with laser-guided bombs operated in pairs. Throughout the fall of both planes' bombs a laser beam had to be kept pointed at the target as the bombs homed in on the laser energy reflected off it.

These smart bombs were a comparatively new idea and had proved accurate within twenty feet in practice runs back in the States. Colonel Stefan Levinsky had the steadiest hands in the business. He also knew better than most how the equipment worked, as he had helped design it.

He himself had suggested the target, which was the Paul Doumer road and rail bridge at Hanoi, which lay astride the Red River to the east of the city, and carried the only rail link and the main highway from the port of Haiphong to the capital.

It was over a mile long and rested on 18 masonry piers. Being built of steel trusses braced throughout with girders, it was a very strong structure and most resilient to air attack, as the open work construction provided a minimal area for blast pressure or fragmentation. Direct hits were necessary to achieve success and the Colonel reckoned that destroying a goddam bridge and as many gooks as possible was a great way to vent his spleen. It would also be dramatic proof of the weapon's efficiency, and a boost to his own prestige which would certainly do him no harm.

Such a significant and damaging air strike as this, as soon as possible after the Tonkin Gulf Declaration by President Johnson in 1964, was what all the top brass had recommended. Also the president was getting nervous over the escalation of Chinese troops on the northern border of North Vietnam, and the last thing he wanted was a second Korea.

To oppose this he had authorised a large-scale transfer of American war planes into South Vietnam and Thailand, America's passive ally. The Navy also added two carriers to the force in the Gulf of Tonkin.

The war could have been finished quickly with the nuclear option, or by bombing the dykes in the north, which would have inundated the country, destroyed its food source and drowned tens of thousands, but the resulting domestic and worldwide clamour would have done immense damage to America's credibility as a peace-loving power.

So the theory was to restrict the enemy's supplies from entering the country by mining the principal harbours such as Haiphong, to cut the flow of men and equipment to the south by destroying the infrastructure, and wipe out stock piles of military stores wherever they could be found. The Paul Doumer bridge was the main choke point, and Stefan Levinsky was to be given the privilege of taking first strike with massive backing.

At Yankee Station, out to sea off the demilitarised zone, US carriers with attendant destroyers were readying themselves to launch diversionary strikes on Haiphong. At dawn a U2 had slipped quietly up to 70,000 feet from U-Tapao, and would act as a communications relay over the heart of enemy territory. After it, a stripped-down weather reconnaissance Phantom had penetrated enemy airspace to check whether the target was in cloud.

Now, after their briefing, Crain and Levinsky had taxied out and sat at the threshhold to the runway in a fully-armed Phantom carrying two 2000-pound laser-guided bombs, and three Sparrow missiles.

Crain was not happy at flying on what was obviously a hot mission with someone he did not know. Particularly someone as sour as this one. His usually cheerful, boyish face was unusually glum, and even Levinsky, full of his own troubles, sensed his significant share of the gloom in the cockpit.

'Everything's okay back here, Theo,' he said reassuringly. 'Sorry to be such a misery, but I'm always like this when I concentrate,' he lied.

Crain instantly perked up. 'Not to worry, colonel. You concentrate as much as you like. I'm all for it.'

'Theo.'

'Yes, sir.'

'Call me Stefan, and remember you're the captain of this heap.'

Crain wasn't sure he appreciated his beloved Phantom being called a heap, but at least the old man was trying to be friendly. 'Thanks, Stefan, and remember you're going to give me the direct hits we need. This one's gotta work.'

Levinsky smiled wryly. He knew when possible blame was being apportioned, knowingly or otherwise. 'Just get me there,' was his laconic comment.

By 8.05 a.m. they were airborne with several other support aircraft scheduled to penetrate North Vietnam.

The crew of every attack plane searched visually, as well as with on-board radar for enemy MiGs or SAM missiles. All of them were fearful, pulses hammering, eyes and heads constantly swivelling, nerves strung taut. To be laid-back in such a situation would be asking for trouble of the worst kind.

The calls were beginning to come in a stream from the navy's offshore electronic surveillance force, which carried such sophisticated equipment it could pick up and identify electro-magnetic radiation from MiG fighters hundreds of miles inland, and, by taking a running bearing, track their immediate position. Similarly it could give warning of any SAM batteries about to set off a launch. In aerial combat the side that first locates its opponent is likely to be victorious.

Surveillance told them four flights of MiGs were airborne. There was one at zero-one-six-forty miles, another at zero-five-zero-fifty, and so on.

Then, with an urgency that made Levinsky jump. 'Look out for more bandits coming on zero-three-five at twenty-five miles.' The MiGs were becoming more aggressive. Without further warning, they began to appear on the Phantoms' radars.

'Parabola One has contact zero-three-five at twelve miles,' sang out Levinsky, naming his flight with the heading, and distance from the enemy. He felt the sweat break out from under his helmet and trickle down his face. No time to wipe it clear. Too much information to be monitored.

Other contact advices were being transmitted as the two forces closed at speeds in excess of 1000 knots.

Levinsky picked up the MiG IFF transmission on his equipment, and informed his pilot accordingly. 'He's squawking MiG. Get ready to shoot, Theo.' There was nervous assent from forward.

The same type of instructions were coming from other flights as the back seaters locked on their radar and switched to attack with missiles.

With the nearest MiG ahead and slightly higher, Crain commenced a shallow climb. Then, with the radar locked on the target, he squeezed the trigger and the Sparrow burst away, trailing smoke. The twelve-foot missile accelerated from its launch speed of 600 knots to 1800 knots in a matter of seconds, and the effect of its exploding warhead was devastating.

'Parabola One's a hit,' yelled Crain excitedly, bouncing up and down against the restriction of his harness, as the enemy fighter tumbled out of the sky, its left wing shot off and trailing fire and smoke.

Out of nowhere, a MiG 19 appeared to their right and banked with remarkable agility to bring its cannon to bear.

'I'm getting the fuck out of it,' snapped Crain, and using full after-burner accelerated away from the fight. His main objective was the bridge. Much more of this and he would have to abort for lack of fuel.

The attack force thrust hard into the western edge of the enemies' defences, flying at close to 600 knots. And then the SAMs began to come at them. Vast numbers, it seemed. The visibility was so good they could be seen for miles going everywhere. Under, over, in front and behind. But the American radar jammers had done their stuff and most had been launched virtually blind by their ground batteries. No one could be sure which of them a SAM was supposed to be tracking, so until they went past the airmen held their breath for what seemed an age, sphincters twitching, bodies jangling, lips moving in silent prayer interspersed with voluble profanities.

Crain and Levinsky saw the Paul Doumer bridge after they turned on to their bomb run. It was dark brown in colour at the north-east of the town. As they began the run-in, the radar warning receiver gave a threatening rattle.

'Got us again. SAM heading straight at us,' shouted Levinsky. 'Is it visual?'

'Negative. Jesus we gotta keep on this approach if we're gonna line up on the target,' gritted Crain.

Levinsky just grunted.

He's a cool bastard, thought Crain. Little did he know.

'Working electronic countermeasure,' muttered Levinsky, as if he'd read Crain's mind.

At that precise moment Crain picked it up. 'Got it,' he yelled. 'Still straight for us.'

'It's lost guidance. Should pass over us,' said Levinsky hopefully.

The SAM shot over their heads, so close Crain ducked involuntarily. It blew up a mile or so down range.

'Shit. Next time that happens, Stefan, you give me an estimate of distance. In inches if necessary.'

An enormous exhalation of breath was Levinsky's only response.

Heading north along the Red River, the raiders flew steadily through ever-increasing enemy defensive fire, with the sun behind them. Fear was tearing at them all the time, but its bite had been numbed somewhat by familiarity. The guns defending the bridge were blasting away. Accelerating tracer, interspersed with stationary smoke-balls from exploding shells, covered the sky in front and around them.

Levinsky took over. His main job was about to begin. 'Release at 12,000.' They dived down with the colonel calling the altitudes. 'Sixteen, fifteen, thirteen.' He'd switched on his laser and held the beam on a point at the near end of the bridge.

Crain shut out everything but the job in hand. There was so much happening it was the only way. Everything about him seemed to go silent as he tracked the bridge under his sighting pipper.

'Twelve thousand.'

Crain released both his 2000-pound bombs and followed them down so the laser could guide them. At three thousand feet he pulled his stick back and watched the horizon disappear below his nose, as the G-force shoved him hard into his seat. Then he was back in the real world again. A world of radio transmissions and the noises of war and the continuance of searing fear, kept under control by massive doses of adrenalin and thousands of hours of rigorous training.

He rolled to the left to see where the bombs had gone and shouted with satisfaction. The first span was definitely sagging and out of operation. The rest of Parabola flight were following him and doing more damage. Levinsky had switched off the laser designator and, pulling into a steep turn, Crain accelerated fast away from the bridge and its attendant dangers.

'Congratulations, Captain Crain, you appear to have done your stuff.'

'With you in the back how could we miss?' Crain could sweet-talk when he wanted. 'Now I've got to get you home.'

'That would be appreciated . . .'

The cosy chat was interrupted by a shouted warning from an accompanying Phantom. 'Hey, there's a bandit at your level, four o'clock, Theo.'

Tearing in from their right were two MiG 21s.

'Turn right, Theo. Turn right at 'em,' came another warning followed by: 'He's firing at you, Theo.'

Crain pulled off desperately to his right, swearing a blue streak, but at this comparatively low altitude, the MiG turned inside him still firing.

The Phantom shuddered as the 30mm shells hit home. The right engine exploded so the plane yawed fiercely, barely under control. There was hydraulic fluid everywhere.

'Hydraulic pressure zero,' said Crain in a resigned voice. 'Jesus help us.'

They both knew what that meant. Without hydraulic pressure the flying controls ceased to function and the plane would crash. One minute triumph, the next tragedy.

Crain shook his head. 'I guess we've had it. Better bang out.' Then as the captain of the ship. 'You go first, Stefan.'

''Fraid so, Theo. We're down through six thousand and it's getting awful hot back here. There's a real blaze behind me and its getting worse.'

'Go for it, Stefan. Hope we meet up.'

'Me too.'

The world seemed strangely quiet for a few seconds as both men looked death in the face. Levinsky reached for the handle between his legs with both hands and pulled hard. The canopy blew off and he was out. As the parachute jerked open, a MiG went past him at maximum speed and very close, virtually sucking all the air out of his 'chute, which for a heart-stopping moment appeared to collapse, then refilled.

'Bastard,' he yelled uselessly after its disappearing tail-pipe. Then he looked down. Beneath was a thickly wooded hill. Seems isolated enough, he thought. Should take some time for them to find me.

As he hit the trees, some thirty feet or so high, he drew up his knees and put his gloved hands between his legs to protect his crutch. 'Don't want to leave the family jewels on some tree in North Vietnam, do we,' he muttered under his breath, tensing for the moment of entry among the branches. The crash, when it came, wasn't as bad as it might have been, though he ended up with a minor crack on the head and swinging ten feet off the ground, his 'chute snagged on a branch.

Slightly dazed, he unthinkingly hit the quick-release buckle and dropped the remaining distance, landing hard enough to twist his ankle painfully. He sat there taking stock, cursing foully, when he realised he couldn't reach his 'chute which would surely give him away to anyone in the near vicinity. With it stayed the majority of his survival pack, strapped to the harness. A double blow.

71

One thing his confused mind latched on to. He had his beeper radio. He switched it on and made a short call. 'This is Parabola One. I'm okay.' Then he switched off quickly to ensure his transmission did not give away his position. Better get away from here before they come after me, he thought, and limped painfully off along a jungle path.

The likelihood of being rescued this far into North Vietnam was slight but at least he was going to give the gooks a run for their money. Then the thought of running with an ankle like a football made him laugh sardonically.

Nevertheless he was quite a distance away from where he had landed before the local search party found his parachute. They made enough noise over the excitement of their find to carry to Levinsky, so, forewarned, he crawled into some deep bush, and resigning himself to his situation he went to sleep. He awoke before dawn feeling extremely hungry and thirsty, with his ankle hurting like hell. How he had slept at all was a minor miracle.

As the sun began to rise, he continued his desperately slow move away from the area and had only gone a few hundred yards when he heard the villagers recommencing their search. There was nothing he could do but dive for cover again and pray that the searchers had brought no dogs with them. As the sun rose higher they seemed to move away from his area. Either it was too hot for them or they had given up.

As an exercise he ran through his possessions. Besides his boots and the clothes he was wearing, he had about his person two beeper radios – he made a mental note to make another call soon – a survival knife, a mosquito net, some medical kit, cigarettes and a lighter, a signal mirror, flares, two pints of water, a couple of high-vitamin-content snack bars, and finally a .38 calibre pistol with ammunition.

He promised himself not to drink the water until he found a source to replenish his bottle, but within minutes his erratic passage caused him practically to stumble into a stream. My lucky day, he thought wryly. Being well up a ridge, the stream was pure and cool. He drank his fill, ate a snack bar, and, taking off his boot and sock, plunged his swollen ankle into the soothing water. The relief was almost instantaneous.

Free from pain he lay back and dozed, leaving his foot dangling. A quarter of an hour later he found himself with a half a dozen leeches on his ankle. Hurriedly he divested himself of his clothes and, sure enough, the revolting blood suckers had crawled inside, almost to the top of his leg. Nervously he burnt them off with a cigarette after assuring himself there was no one in the vicinity. In the jungle, cigarette smoke can be smelt at a thousand yards. To his surprise, he found the swelling of his ankle had reduced significantly. Whether it was due to the leeches or the cold water he could not make out, nor did he care. It was better and that was all that counted. Taking a bandage from his medical kit, he bound the ankle firmly before putting his clothes and boots on.

As there was no apparent effort by the locals to find him, he reckoned the area was safe and decided the only way he could obtain food was to shoot it. There were squirrels about and he had a couple tries, but without success. They never seemed to stay still long enough. He was exhausted from hunger now and considered giving himself up.

With this intent, he worked his way to the edge of the forest and looked down towards the paddy fields by the twisting Red River. There before him was a small, cultivated plot and on the ground, vulnerable and waiting to be eaten, were clusters of pineapples.

With a grunt of delight he broke cover and, drawing his knife, cut a couple of their stems and retreated rapidly back into the surrounding undergrowth, which was just as well. Walking casually along the ridge came an old peasant carrying a couple of baskets on a pole over his shoulder, and in his hand a long knife.

He placed his apparatus on the ground within a couple of feet of where Levinsky crouched, frozen behind some undergrowth. Muttering to himself, the old man picked up a single basket and, taking his knife, walked to the far end of the plot where he commenced harvesting his crop in a most expert fashion.

Levinsky stayed doggo, waiting to see what the old boy was going to do. His nose twitched. Wafting toward him from the other basket was the delicious, unmistakable aroma of cooked rice. He peered to where the Vietnamese was working. The old man was squatting, his back to Levinsky, slicing away at a pineapple stalk.

Levinsky couldn't help himself. He put his arm out from his cover and lowered it into the basket. His fingers touched a still warm pot lid. He lifted it aside, took as big a handful of the contents as he could and commenced cramming it into his mouth. He closed his eyes with the exquisite pleasure of it, savouring the taste and texture as if he had never eaten rice before. When he opened them again the old man was standing over him.

Levinsky quickly pulled out his revolver and pointed it at the Vietnamese. The man's reaction surprised him. He cackled cheerily and lifting his hands said, 'Je suis un ami. Ne tirez pas m'sieur.'

It took Levinsky a moment to gather he was speaking to him in French, and furthermore that his intentions were friendly. This was borne out by the fact that the man could quite easily have taken advantage of him when his eyes were shut and struck him with the razor-sharp blade he was still holding.

Levinsky smiled nervously and desperately tried to recall his schoolboy French. Of course Vietnam had been a French colony and the older Viets probably had to speak French of a sort to communicate with their colonial masters.

'Bonjour. Comment ça va?' he stammered. What a ridiculous exchange this was, Levinsky thought, but what the hell, if pleasantries were called for, why not?

The old man looked at him keenly. 'Moi, je vais très bien merci, mais evidement vous avez faim, n'est-ce pas?' The peasant rubbed his stomach to illustrate his meaning.

Only half-understanding, Levinsky nodded and smiled.

The old man nodded in his turn and, reaching over,

pulled the basket containing what was obviously his midday meal between them. With a gracious movement of his hand he signified his willingness to share the rice and vegetables that were still steaming in the smoke-blackened cooking pot.

They sat in companionable silence for the next ten minutes, Levinsky eating as delicately as he could with his fingers, and his companion shovelling away with chopsticks. When they finished, they simply stared at each other, not knowing how the situation might develop.

Finally Levinsky remembered his manners. 'Merci beaucoup, m'sieur.'

The Vietnamese waved his thanks aside. 'Ce n'est rien, m'sieur. Je n'aime pas les communistes.' And as if that were sufficient explanation for his behaviour, he rose, said: 'Bonne chance, mon ami,' and went back to his work.

Levinsky concluded that that was as far as the strange relationship was to go and tactfully moved away. His hunger temporarily appeased, he refrained from going further down into the valley, but continued to skirt the trees along the ridge.

Suddenly there was a great rushing roar as a SAM battery not far away launched a missile. SAM missiles meant American aircraft in the vicinity. Levinsky activated his beeper.

'This is Levinsky, back-seater Parabola One. If anyone reads me reply on emergency frequency.'

To the south-west of him, one of a Phantom flight returning after an attack on Phuc Yen picked up his transmission and passed the news back to base. A few minutes later, to his delight, Levinsky was called back.

'We've told 'em about you and the support will be on the way.'

Levinsky couldn't believe his luck. 'But,' continued the voice, 'you've got a question to answer first.'

He knew that as a precaution against the Vietnamese luring a rescue force into a trap he had to give a correct answer to at least one of several personal questions. 'Okay, okay, shoot,' he snapped irritably.

'What's your mother's maiden name?'

'Maria Konin.'

'Okay, you seem like our guy.'

'Bet your ass on it.'

Now they knew for sure no one was telling him what to say. The disembodied voice continued. 'Get your signal mirror and flares ready.' Then Levinsky heard quite clearly the first few bars of the American National Anthem being hummed.

'Okay, wise boy, I read you,' he called back, wondering if the enemy would pick up the association too. *Oh say can you see by the dawn's early light.*'

So, replete and hopeful, he moved well back under cover and lay thinking of what sunrise might bring. Understandably, he found it difficult to sleep, but finally his eyes closed and he was woken in a panic by the sound of early morning birdsong.

The sun was coming up and light was flooding into the valley below. Where the hell were they? Then four Phantoms rolled over the hills opposite and streaked straight at him. Desperately he flashed his mirror, almost too late, but the last in the group waggled its wings as they went over the top of him at 500 knots. Clattering up the valley from the south, attended by half a dozen Grumman Intruders, came two Sikorsky helicopters hugging the deck.

Levinsky heard the sound of heavy explosions from behind and to the north as the Phantoms bombed the nearby airfield to interdict any action by MiGs.

He continued to use his signal mirror, and for good measure lit a flare. He found himself jumping up and down at the excitement of it all. Surely they can't miss me now, he told himself.

Then to confirm his thoughts his radio was squawking at him. 'This is Rescue Recovery. We have you, colonel. Keep low profile.' To avoid unwelcome attention they were telling Levinsky to cool it. He complied immediately, dropping on his belly and shielding the mirror.

The monstrous helicopters continued past him then swept

in a wide curve towards his position. They were only a few miles away now, moving in behind the Intruders. Then the first machine clattered over the top, pulled into a tight semi-circle and nosed down towards him in a slow hover with the back-up helicopter waiting nearby. Levinsky broke cover to charge the last hundred yards to his rescuers, leaping and laughing with delight, the pain in his ankle of no consequence.

The ear-blasting passage of the 37mm high-velocity shells from the hidden position in the undergrowth behind must have been within a couple of feet of his head. He was stunned and flattened, his mouth and nose clogged with earth, but his eyes were unaffected. With dreadful clarity he saw the shells impact on the hovering giant, which sagged in the middle and crashed, broken-backed, to the ground, a ball of fire and oily smoke. No one got out.

Levinsky shrieked with rage and horror and struggled to get to his feet, but the shock had deprived him of the use of his legs and he could only remain there a useless witness to the destruction of the second machine as well. The back-up helicopter had turned to escape, but a second burst of accurate fire struck it from behind, destroying the rear rotor so that control of the machine was totally lost, and it cartwheeled helplessly down to the valley floor below, a heap of shattered wreckage.

At the same time four MiG 21s came screaming down the valley from a completely unexpected direction and drove off the slower, supporting Intruders. The Phantoms had left thinking their job was done, but the MiGs had come from another field and had obviously been alerted in advance.

'It was a set up, a goddam set up!' Levinsky pounded the ground with his fists in frustration. Worse still he'd been the bait. The thought of it made him sick to his stomach. But how had they known exactly where he was? How had they anticipated everything so perfectly?

The 37mm gun was easily handled and highly trans-portable. They could have brought it up from below during the night and moved it among the trees while he was asleep.

The Viets were known for their ability to move quietly. But that still begged the question of how they knew. He moved on to his knees. His legs were working again. He felt a hand on his shoulder and looked up.

'Bonjour. On se revoit, M'sieur le colonel.' 'Good day we meet again, colonel.'

Now he knew. It was the old peasant, his expression as benevolent as ever. He too was wearing the uniform of a colonel, but of the People's Army of Vietnam.

He noticed Levinsky's anguished expression and said, almost comfortingly, 'C'est la guerre, mon ami,' and then in heavily accented, but perfectly understandable, English: 'You were a valuable prize alone, but now we have you and...' He left the sentence unfinished, and waved his hand at the carnage before them.

'I suppose,' said Levinsky bitterly, 'you even know the American national anthem.'

The North Vietnamese colonel nodded his head. 'Just the first few lines, but that was enough,' he replied.

6

They stripped Levinsky of his flight suit, various oddments of equipment and, much to his annoyance, his watch.

He'd wanted to complain about his treatment to the colonel but the old man had gone and his angry protestations were met by stony silence and finally a slap across the back of his head. Not hard, but enough to shut him up. There was worse to come.

His hands were tied in front of him and a rope attached round his waist by which he was led, with another round his neck, for constraint from behind, should he get too obstreperous. To compound this, he was blindfolded.

In this undignified manner he was pulled along various embankments among the paddy fields, staggering and slipping without being able to see or know where he was going or what was going to be done with him. He felt very lonely and yes, frightened.

After an hour of this they came to a village, his hands were untied and he was given a drink of tepid tea that tasted like nectar. They also removed his blindfold.

The locals stood around staring and making belligerent noises, but to his relief his guards protected him and one even gave him a cigarette. Finally a truck arrived and he was shoved roughly into the open back with a couple of guards to keep an eye on him.

Levinsky did not know it, but his destination was the infamous Hoa Lo prison in Hanoi, known to the prisoners, somewhat inevitably, as the Hanoi Hilton.

On the way, they passed hundreds of military vehicles parked at the side of the road under cover of trees along the route. Obviously the North Vietnamese were gathering their forces for a big push. As they bumped along, a couple of US Airforce Thunder Chiefs streaked overhead at high speed and very low.

Just my luck to get strafed by my own side, thought Levinsky. Make my day fellahs.

The temptation to wave at them was enormous, but very sensibly he restrained himself. His guards had so far behaved quite reasonably. No point in inciting them to any rough stuff.

He actually managed to sleep, and only woke as they drew up outside the grey, grim prison where he was to be incarcerated. He comforted himself with the thought that at least he would be quartered with his own kind, but he was shoved into a cell by himself where he was left for an hour before being hurried along to an interrogation room, accompanied by much shoving and shouting. It was getting on for midnight.

Waiting for him was his old acquaintance, the colonel in the People's Army, and with him a civilian of similar age. Having once shared a meal with his military equal he felt there might be an empathy there worth cultivating.

'Good to see you, colonel,' he started off cheerfully. 'I always seem to meet you when I'm hungry. Haven't had a thing pass my lips except a cup of tea since I shared your meal.'

The Vietnamese colonel's face was like stone. 'Sit on that chair and be quiet,' he said. He then turned to the civilian and gabbled away in Vietnamese, obviously explaining Levinsky's opening remarks. He then turned back to the American. 'I am Colonel Lim Nguyen Giap and this is your interrogator, Mr Ng Chi Minh. I will translate for him.'

He paused and pointed a finger at the prisoner, jabbing the air as if to emphasise his points. 'We are not barbarians, Colonel Levinsky, but I earnestly recommend that you answer our questions without delay. You will then be given a drink and some food. However, if you refuse, then you must appreciate our patience is not inexhaustible...' He left the rest of the sentence hanging, an unissued threat.

Levinsky tried hard to keep his equilibrium, but the whole experience since he had been shot down was becoming too much for him. He raised his long, lanky frame from the chair and, moving toward the other man, towered over him. 'There are certain conventions in war, colonel, and what you are implying goes against them.' In his turn he shook his right index finger at the other man's face. 'You will not get away with this, you bastard. The United States also has limits to its tolerance. We could bomb your dykes or simply carry out an atomic attack which would totally devastate –'

The old man's hand shot out like a striking snake and grasped the American's finger. There was a violent crack and the broken finger hung uselessly at an impossible angle from Levinsky's raised hand.

For a couple of seconds he was too shocked to react and then, fury overcoming pain, he swung his left fist at the impassive Vietnamese still sitting in his chair. Colonel Lim swayed his head slightly out of the way and Levinsky felt his left forearm gripped as if by a steel claw. The pain that flew up his arm and into the very centre of his head was utterly devastating.

The Vietnamese let him loose and he fell to his knees, head bowed, mouth slack, utterly devoid of any aggressive intent. 'God in heaven what was that?' he moaned.

'A pressure point. There are seventy-eight about your body, each of them extremely painful, and I know them all.'

'I'll bet you do,' gritted Levinsky.

He came round the table and helped the white man to his feet and back to his seat. He was almost gentle in his demeanour. 'Come now, colonel, we must co-operate with each other. I do not wish to resort to brutality. Rather we should discuss the situation and practise self-criticism.'

Levinsky nursed his aching hand and shook his head. 'I don't want to go in for all that communist crap,' he said.

'But you talk about torture as if it were abhorrent to you,

yet you drop napalm and high explosives on helpless civilians, you hold the heads of prisoners in barrels of water until they almost drown to get information out of them.' His voice had become barely audible. 'Yet you consider us less civilised than you.'

'For Christ's sake look what you've done to me,' said Levinsky.

'You were leaning over me poised to attack, were you not? I merely sat in my chair and motioned at you. You lost your self-control and I had no option but to protect myself.'

'Yes but...' All of a sudden Levinsky cut himself off. I'm indulging in exactly the sort of discussion the bastard wants, he thought. Next thing, I'm going to approve of what he has done to me. He's going to make me feel guilty of crimes which I have not committed. Goddam it, he'll keep on and on at me until I agree with him.

He smiled secretively to himself. 'Okay, colonel, you've got a point there,' he said, 'but do you reckon you could get a splint on this finger of mine? It sure hurts.'

'You will be treated shortly and we will come back to this most interesting discussion later, but remember only true confession merits absolution, and meantime Mr Ng has a few questions which he wishes you to answer.'

All through the drama of the last few minutes the civilian had said nothing, nor had he even appeared to show any interest in the proceedings. Now at his colleague's cue, he unfolded and placed upon the table a flight map taken from a downed American warplane. Various anti-aircraft and SAM sites had been circled with chinagraph pencil. There were also lines denoting flight tracks to be followed to targets. There was a short conversation between the two Vietnamese, and Colonel Lim started to make, at his colleague's behest, numerous enquiries concerning US military intentions.

At first Levinsky protested he was quite unable to meet their demands, but eventually, after hours of harassment, at 3 a.m. he began to give way.

Again and again he protested that he only knew the

objective of the specific attack in which he had taken part, namely the Paul Doumer bridge, which was something everyone knew anyway. He said the circles on the map were placed round various possible anti-aircraft sites. He stated a thousand times he knew nothing of the Seventh Air Force's future intentions, except to damage airfields and the infrastructure as much as they could, which was already obvious to the meanest intelligence.

Then came the really difficult question. 'Why are you, a colonel of considerable seniority, flying back-seater on a mission like this?'

'My name just came up on the roster,' he said blandly. 'We are all expected to keep our hours up, you know, and I can say with due modesty I'm pretty good, as you'll appreciate when you see your bridge.'

Colonel Lim shook his head and translated for his companion who frowned and growled back.

'Mr Ng says please do not think we are so naive, colonel. We realise that another colonel, who commands the Eighth Tactical Wing, was flying in the attack as well, but he is a pilot. You may be able to fly an aeroplane but that is not your job. You are technical, and usually you are a staff officer.'

Careful boy, thought Levinsky, these guys know a helluva lot more about you than they should. What the hell is going on here?

'Okay, colonel, I'm technical. In fact I'm pretty good on the operational side of what we call smart bombs, which I'm sure you know all about already, as details about them have appeared in the Western press. Headquarters wanted to make sure your goddam bridge was smashed so they put me on to it. It's as simple as that.' I haven't told them anything new, he thought, and I'm damned if I want another broken finger from sheer bravado.

The two Vietnamese conversed for some time, occasionally turning to look at the American as if to catch an expression that might imply deviousness. Levinsky put on a pained look, which was wholly genuine, and groaned. His finger was agony and his hand had swollen up most impressively. They had been at it now for four or five hours and it was close to dawn.

Finally Colonel Lim spoke to him: 'We know that you are telling the truth but there is more to you than you would like us to know.'

The civilian handed Lim a sheet of paper that he extracted from his briefcase.

Colonel Lim began to read from it: 'Colonel Stefan Peter Levinsky. 1930: born, Niagara Falls. Religion, Jewish. High School exam results: good; above average in mathematics and physics. 1948: joined US Air Force. 1950: graduated from officer training school as pilot, but with special expertise in matters technical relating to radar and allied skills; rank of lieutenant. 1954: special posting with USAF sponsorship to Massachusetts Institute of Technology; rank of Captain. 1959: seconded to NASA. 1961: Returned to USAF; various postings; rank of Major; married Joanna Drew. 1964: posted Vietnam as Colonel.'

Levinsky quite forgot the pain in his hand, or how thirsty and hungry he was. This was staggering. These bastards knew everything about him. Well, practically everything. Boy, was there ever a leak in security in Records for that information to get out.

The only satisfaction he garnered from the read-out was that they had not gotten hold of the unabridged version – the version that described in some detail what exactly it was he had been doing at MIT and NASA. Even that comfort was snatched away from him when the next question came.

'Please tell us in detail exactly what work you were carrying out at MIT from 1954 to 1959, then with NASA for two years.'

Colonel Lim's question was very specific and the tone in which it was delivered brooked no extemporising.

Nevertheless, it took another fifteen hours of continuous, hammering interrogation before they got sufficient information to satisfy them.

They did not actually beat him or physically torture him,

although for lengthy periods he was made to squat in the Asian fashion, to show sufficient respect to his captors, which in itself produced grinding pain in his thighs, his muscles being unused to such a position. They gave him water to drink and a small bowl of noodles to eat. Also a medical dresser came to splint his finger during that gruelling period. It was continuous verbal persuasion, until it seemed the worst thing that could happen was not to die but to see his inner self change.

He held back a great deal but was obliged to give part-way and felt that he had at least kept the core of his soul to himself. When they had finished with him, despite his limited provision of information, they realised that they were holding a very special prisoner indeed – a man who was probably among the top in the world in laser and avionics technology.

What could they do with him? If he were to give them all the information in his head, Vietnam still did not have the manufacturing facilities nor the skills to turn his ideas into blueprints and then the end product. The Russians might be interested, but they were in the forefront of such scientific achievements anyway, and their interest would be academic as to how they rated against American technology. Anyway, they were notoriously mean and would probably want Levinsky for virtually nothing, and then set his value off against the enormous amount of military hardware they were already supplying to North Vietnam for the common war against American imperialism.

The two elderly Vietnamese looked at each other and simultaneously the same thought came to them. China, in its pride, had not had dealings with Russia for many years. But they had built many MiG 19 equivalents that they called the Shenyang F6, using the jigs and plans they had purchased from the Russians at inflated prices during the days of so-called social fraternalism.

This aircraft had an excellent dog-fighting capability, but its avionics were more than ten years out-of-date. When they sold the machines to the North Vietnamese, the new owners stripped out the technical gear and replaced it with Soviet equipment, and it performed very well against the Americans. Because of this, China who could not, or rather would not, buy Russian equipment, was desperate for a means to update her airforce to the same standards of the surrounding powers, upon whom she looked with xenophobic eyes.

Mr Ng said: 'It's just as well that loyal cadres such as ourselves thought of this idea first, or otherwise someone of lesser moral standards might be tempted to exploit the situation to their own advantage.'

Colonel Lim nodded in grave agreement and stroked the wispy, white hairs on the point of his chin. 'Very true, comrade, very true.'

Levinsky, dazed with lack of sleep and pain, looked at the two of them deciding on his future and felt that if he had not known better he would have thought of them as an amusing couple of old dodderers. But he did know better and he was genuinely frightened.

Thus it came about that Colonel Lim and Mr Ng disposed of Colonel Stefan Peter Levinsky to the Chinese for the sum of five million US dollars in a Swiss Bank account, and emboldened by the success of the first venture despatched quite a few more prisoners of lesser, but wholly acceptable qualifications, for a more modest sum of two or three million dollars apiece, depending on what the market could stand.

The two of them became very wealthy indeed, and finally made it to Hong Kong after the cessation of hostilities in Vietnam. There was never any danger that they would be forcibly repatriated, as happened to thousands of their fellow countrymen in poorer circumstances.

7

Hong Kong   30th September 1989

As Brian Summervill had guessed, Ching-hua had needed no persuasion. Anything calculated to frustrate the ambitions of the dangerous old men in Beijing was good enough reason to stick out her beautiful neck.

When Harwood passed this on, Summervill smugly commented: 'I told you so. Now get her to line up her contacts in Yunnan so that you have a satisfactorily large, well-armed bunch to greet you on arrival. About twenty would probably do.' He paused, thinking. 'Don't tell her – or them – too much yet, and we'll have to get a drop to them with radio equipment so you can contact them from Thailand at the shortest possible notice. We want them to make sure Levinsky's around when we go in, but we don't warn the treacherous bastard, or he could screw up the operation.'

It seemed a bit unfair to Harwood that Summervill had taken Levinsky's guilt for granted. If someone stuck a gun at my head I'd probably co-operate, he thought.

Summervill smiled. Organising missions obviously gave him pleasure. 'The Yanks can drop in the radio and some weapons. They're good at that sort of thing.'

Harwood nodded in a numb sort of fashion. It was all going a bit fast for him. He realised he'd have to get with it, and bloody quick too, but was finding it difficult to move into gear, mainly because he couldn't believe it was happening to him.

'Take a look at this,' said Summervill, gleefully rubbing his hands. He pushed a couple of buttons and a screen emerged from the far wall. There was a quiet hum and a projector threw a picture on to it. It didn't look like much to Harwood but Summervill was obviously delighted.

'Taken by satellite. Clear as can be.' He took a light cursor from his drawer and aimed it at the screen, talking all the time. Harwood became almost hypnotised by the little circle of light moving across the picture, as Summervill made his presentation.

'This photograph is, of course, greatly enlarged and is focused down to a hundredth of the original, which reproduced about 500 square miles of territory from Kunming in the north to the Thai border in the south.'

'So we are looking at about five square miles here, right?' interjected Harwood trying to sound intelligent.

'Exactly,' said the other, apparently pleased that his pupil was beginning to show some interest. 'Down in the southwest corner of this enlargement, you can see a huddle of primitive buildings which constitutes Mengwang – population about two and a half thousand – and here just to the east of it,' – the ball of light jumped obediently – 'is the Mekong River. Clear?'

It was beginning to make some sense to him now. 'Yes, and I suppose that long pipe with the dish objects, to the north-east, is the thing that has caused all the excitement.'

'That is the beam accelerator and those are the reflectors, about five miles away from any habitation. The device produces a powerful highly coherent and very narrow beam of light and can be originated by the utilisation of natural crystals such as rubies which, of course, you appreciate, are quite common in Burma.'

'Right next door,' murmured Harwood, but he might as well not have existed.

Summervill was in full flow now. 'The narrow beam can then be increased in power many times over by the reflector mirrors, like a sort of magnifying glass, and directed into space at any angle, depending on how those mirrors are set.

The theory is that anything in the way gets frazzled: satellites, planes, rockets, the lot. But no one has quite mastered the art yet, and everyone's worried to death that perhaps Levinsky has.'

'Fascinating,' said Harwood.

'Yes isn't it.' The light ball bobbed about a bit and settled in the south-east area. 'Here we see a considerable plateau, within a mile or two of the quarters where the American prisoners are housed, which is several miles away from the actual project, for safety purposes.'

'I think I've got the general picture,' said Harwood, 'but getting from any strip our collaborators clear to the residential area could be a problem. It's very hilly country and there may be unseen undulations in the ground that could bugger up the timing completely. What's your problem with using a helicopter and landing next door to the bloke?'

Summervill gesticulated irritably. 'I repeat, the bloody things are too noisy, they're always breaking down at the crucial moment and in that part of China there are plenty of piston-engined small planes buzzing about, but hardly a single helicopter.' He looked earnestly at Harwood. 'If you are really keen on a helicopter I suppose it could be arranged, but the minute you leave Thailand and head through the eastern tip of Burma you'll be like the proverbial spare prick at a wedding, and they'll be waiting for you.' He moved the cursor again toward the laser site. 'This is the only really sensitive place in that part of China, and it wouldn't take a genius to guess your destination.'

'Okay. I accept your advice. Presumably all I'll need is a four-seater for myself, Ching-hua, Odd Job and Levinsky.'

The intelligence man nodded agreement.

'I reckon a Cessna 182 will be about right. A three hundred-mile round trip, say three fifty or almost four hundred to be safe, is well within its capabilities.'

'I'll see you get that,' said Summervill, 'and anything else within reason that your heart desires.' He paused and added in an off-hand fashion: 'You'll be expected to go in at night, of course. And out as well. Presumably you have a night rating? We don't want any bureaucratic idiot of a Thai official to block your flight at the last moment.'

'I wouldn't have attempted it in daylight anyway,' replied Harwood wearily, more to put the smart bastard in his place than anything else.

As he left, Summervill tossed a slim package across his desk.

'This is your passport.'

'But I already – '

Summervill interrupted him. 'When you travel on business for me, you don't use your own name.' He tapped the side of his nose. 'Your alias for immigration purposes is Peter Arthur Mayo. Got that? "Pam" for short.'

Harwood looked at him, surprised, but Summervill was deadly serious.

'As you will see the passport is some three years old and somewhat scuffed but completely legitimate. Better warn your girlfriend. Okay.' He paused and frowned. 'Ah yes, one more thing. I want you to memorise this telephone number.' He scribbled rapidly on a piece of paper. 'I have also written down the name which you will use for me when you are in the field. It's "Map", which is your code name "Pam" spelled backwards. Schoolboy stuff, but you might need it some time, so don't bloody well forget.' He glared sternly at Harwood. 'Remember this is only to be used in dire circumstances. Very dire circumstances. Clear?'

'Clear,' replied Harwood, gazing at the scrap of paper which Summervill had given him.

'Good. Destroy it before you leave this room.'

* * *

Peng Kiong had really put Harwood through the hoops and took a certain sadistic pleasure in pushing him to the limit.

The urgency of the situation cut the training down to ten

days, but in that period Harwood's unarmed combat skills and rapid-fire reactions with weapons were considerably sharpened. He'd never get back to the old SAS standards of years ago and it was only a matter of months since he'd been declared totally fit after the horror of being buried alive, but Peng Kiong had given him grudging praise for his progress.

As far as Ching-hua was concerned, she was young, had recovered well, and showed an enthusiasm and quickness that was in keeping with her commitment to the cause. Anything that prepared her for the struggle for democracy in her beloved China was to be assimilated with grim earnestness, and that was precisely what she did. Peng Kiong obviously adored her. When she was around, his square, dead-pan face actually relaxed a trifle, and the suggestion of a smile, or something that looked very like one, appeared.

And now Harwood was here in Chiang Mai, one of the most delightful places in the world, bedded down with his Chinese beauty and restlessly working through what tomorrow might bring. Tomorrow the American CIA chief in Thailand would be giving them an update with the latest satellite pictures and information received from Chinghua's Yunnan contacts. It appeared that the radio drop had gone off without a hitch and the reception party would be there to light up the strip and support the operation by taking out any opposition, which hopefully would be minimal. Ching-hua slept like an innocent babe.

Christ I wish I had her guts, he thought, and turned over restlessly for the hundredth time.

A small, cool hand crept over from the other side of the bed and gently massaged his stomach. 'Peace, my darling. Peace,' she said. 'I am with you and love you. Whatever happens, will happen to both of us.'

He turned and kissed her. She took his face to her breast and stroked his head as if he were a child. He sighed, and within minutes fell asleep.

* * *

91

Stefan Levinsky ran easily, driving his tall, thin, muscled body forward in distance-eating strides. His hair was silver-grey now, but there was still plenty of it. His body was that of a fit forty-year-old, but his real age was nearly 20 years older than that.

Beside him, matching him step for step, ran a young man in his early twenties, of the same athletic build and almost the same height. Only his features showed a distinctive difference. The face was somewhat less aquiline, and the eyes above the high cheek-bones were those of his Chinese mother. They were dressed in running outfits, tee-shirts, shorts and jogging shoes, and could have melded easily into any group of such fitness enthusiasts in the Western world. When they did converse, which was infrequently, it was in English, and it was obvious their relationship was that of friends as well as father and son.

The sun rose over the hills to the east as they crossed the wooden bridge over the swiftly-flowing Mekong River and headed out on to the plain of lush grazing land that led to their living area. Their skins were covered in light droplets of sweat, which prickled with reflected light from the golden orb spreading its brilliant tentacles through the valleys and crags of the superb, unspoiled landscape that lay before them.

Ever since Levinsky had gained the trust of his captors over 20 years ago, he had determined that if he had to eke out his life in this environment he would at least make the best of it. The first months had been hell.

He had not been maltreated, but the boredom of his situation, cooped up in a cell with little or no exercise and no knowledge of even where he was or what was expected of him, drove him to the brink of madness. There had even-tually been two other American airmen who had been brought in to share his loneliness, and his situation had improved thereafter, mentally at least.

His Chinese owners had played their cards very cleverly. Levinsky was valuable property. They had made sure of that through their own information network in the States before paying out for him. They did not want damaged goods, just someone who was malleable. There is a fine line between coercion and co-operation.

True scientists worked because of the fascination that their specialist subjects held for them. Money came into it, but for many it was secondary, as long as their living requirements were met. The Russians had found that out. Their initial rocket programme had depended totally on the German scientists they had captured after the Second World War and taken to the vast reaches of the Siberian plains. They had paid them modestly, by Western standards, but given them status, spared nothing in the supply of their technical requirements, and concentrated heavily on the techniques of applied psychology. They were only allowed to leave after they were no longer required, which was many years later, but apparently bore little or no grudge against their captors.

It had come to the knowledge of the Chinese that Levinsky's marriage was on the point of breaking up, and that he had no children, so there was no real human relationship for him to hanker after at home. He had been orphaned at an early age and been brought up by various foster parents who, whilst caring, had by no means been loving. It was only his obvious genius at high school that had allowed him to break out of the numbingly depressing circumstances of his childhood and be accepted by the United States Air Force.

When he was just old enough to take it in he was made to learn very quickly what being a Jew meant. His parents had had the foresight to leave Poland as soon as fascism began to rear its head in Italy and Germany. As a result, Stefan, with the good Christian name they picked for him, was born a United States citizen.

Nevertheless, his high intelligence at school had excited the jealousy of others less well-endowed, and the terms 'Polak' and 'Yid', or even the combination of both, had been bandied about with sickening frequency until the day had come when he had turned and totally demolished the school bully, who was built like a house, in front of his sycophantic following. They'd had to call in the doctor to set the ruffian's nose and tape his ribs.

Levinsky had been hauled before Mr Griffith, the school principal, for that. Luckily the old man was by no means a bigot, and had an inkling of what had been going on. 'Stefan, you must appreciate that your race has always been persecuted and probably always will be, simply because of their *penchant* to keep to themselves, and in the main their diligence and ability produces a standard of living that is the envy of others. Therefore you could say that racist taunts in respect of Jews are really inverted compliments.'

'Yes, sir, I understand what you are saying, but it is only in the Christian religion that one is told to turn the other cheek. We did, and got the Holocaust for our pains. I have been told many of my family in the old country died in the death camps. Never again,' he ended fiercely.

The principal sighed. 'True, Stefan, but remember it was a Jew that said it, and also remember the true Christians consider a Jew as God's son and worship him accordingly.'

Levinsky shrugged his shoulders. 'To us I am afraid he was a clever charlatan and an iconoclast, but I do not deride you for worshipping him as the Godhead.'

The principal blinked at the quality of the boy's language, and then, beginning to enjoy the discussion, replied, 'The orthodox Jew, as you well know, is the most bigoted person alive, and pray what does the term "Goy" mean if it is not derogatory?'

Stefan had the grace to laugh. '*Touché*, sir. I think it might be wise of me to concede you the winner of this polemic and leave the field to you if you allow it.'

'Let's call it a draw,' replied Griffiths, 'and in future please control your fists. I think the school boxing team might be looking for someone of your ability.'

'I'll think about it, sir, and thank you.'

Levinsky never told anyone that he had been taking lessons from a retired ex-pugilist called Jo Abrams, who in his time had achieved considerable success at the profession. He had been delighted to help a fellow Semite.

94

Levinsky never joined the boxing team, but he never had any more trouble at school either.

His time in the USAF had been without racial strife, except during the early recruit days when once again he had settled the problem with his fists, but in a less contentious way, by challenging his adversary to put on boxing gloves, and showing him quite painfully that Levinsky was not fair game. Nevertheless, the undercurrent was still there and no matter how impressively he performed he doubted he would go any higher than his present rank.

The Chinese had two reasons for keeping Stefan in limbo for several months. The really obvious one was that anyone in Levinsky's situation is invariably grateful to his captors for small mercies, and when, without explanation, he was transferred from a miserable prison cell to what could only be described as comfortable accommodation in a ranch-style three bedroom house in pleasant surroundings, the contrast was such as to produce near euphoria.

He was advised that the house, with surprisingly modern fittings, was for him alone, unless he required some company. This was put to him rather shyly by a lady interpreter who was most certainly not unattractive. He wasn't stupid, and he knew he would have to pay for it in some way but at that moment it might be true to say his cup was running over and to hell with the consequences.

He replied cautiously that he was quite happy to be on his own for the time being, and was somewhat surprised when Mei Ling remained in the house in a small room off the kitchen, and carried out the duties of cook and cleaner for him. She was unobtrusive without being obsequious, and had the ability to anticipate his requirements with surprising alacrity. She also, at his request, began to teach him Mandarin.

Sitting next to each other, heads close together, almost touching, studying from the book she had provided, he felt a sweet excitement in her presence that he had not experienced from other women. He watched with close fascination the graceful movements of her long, slim fingers

95

tracing the Chinese written characters that were in themselves things of beauty. Most of all, he luxuriated in the sensual delight of her lips, teeth and tongue as she enunciated the tonal qualities of the language for him, and then delighted in the joyous giggles his clumsy efforts elicited from her. And that was as far as it went. He had a delightful ten days, and still no explanations for this special treatment which was given him.

Then inevitably came the second reason, or perhaps it should be described as the stick, the carrot having already been provided. He was told what was required of him, and hanging over the interview was the unspoken threat that it would be back to prison if he would not co-operate.

A couple of middle-aged Chinese had come to his house, by appointment. Mei Ling had provided tea, then left the men to their discussions. They introduced themselves as Mr Leung and Professor Chung.

Levinsky's stomach turned a trifle as he met them. They reminded him of the Vietnamese colonel and his colleague, and he wanted no more interrogation of that sort. The main difference, of course, was that the surroundings were pleasant and the two Chinese spoke perfect English. The professor even had an American accent and chatted amiably about the post-graduate degree he had taken in physics at Princeton. They were very soon on the same wavelength, as was exactly the intention.

'Colonel, you are undoubtedly anxious to know what is going to happen to you and I intend to tell you without prevarication.'

'That would be most gratifying, I think,' replied Levinsky cautiously.

'There is nothing sinister about this I assure you,' interjected Mr Leung.

Levinsky nodded without comment.

'You see,' continued the professor, 'a China surrounded by enemies.' He waved his arm vaguely about. 'Russia looms over us from the north. Taiwan to the east. India in the south-west and Vietnam in the south.'

'But I was sent to you from Vietnam,' protested Stefan.

'Certainly, by a couple of old rogues who sold you to us for five million US dollars, and other, less valuable, technical personnel shot down in recent raids, for more modest sums. I wouldn't be surprised if we have to go to war with Vietnam in the not-too-distant future, which shows you what their co-operation is worth.'

'Holy cow,' whistled Levinsky. 'Am I worth that much to you?'

'We think so,' replied Chung, 'provided, of course, that you are prepared to, er, assist us.'

Christ, thought Levinsky, I'm just a bloody package to them. He said: 'You say there's nothing sinister about what you want me to do but what you're doing to me is, to put it simply, high class slavery, and totally unacceptable by any standard of civilised society, as you well know.'

'Please, colonel, let me finish,' interrupted the professor on a slightly sterner note. 'We are in a situation where we have no option but to take drastic steps. If these transcend the bounds of normal, civilised society let me make it clear to you that these are not normal times.' He waited to see if he had Stefan's total attention. 'All these countries I have mentioned are, I assure you, genuine enemies of China and have war planes of superior quality to us, either from the United States or Russia, because of their greater sophistication in ancillary electronic equipment. We can build a basic aircraft and engine that is perfectly satisfactory but ...' and he then laid out in considerable detail how Levinsky could help them with the design of airborne search and defence radar, as well as weapons-guidance, like the laser bombs, that would overcome China's present lag. 'We can manufacture things for which we have the design or blueprint, but we need the kick start from someone like you to overcome our ten-year deficit in knowledge.'

Levinsky shook his head in surprise. 'Even if I were capable of doing this, what makes you consider I could possibly behave in such a traitorous way?' asked Levinsky quietly.

'You have missed the point, colonel. It is not our intention to carry out offensive acts against your country. Far from it.' The professor sat back and opened his arms in the classic gesture of innocence. 'Your president has recently, in fact, been in touch with Beijing through Geneva, in the hopes of engineering a *rapprochement* between our two countries, as you might have heard.'

Levinsky was not, in fact, aware of this but would not have put anything past a politician. 'So why not get what you need from America?' he asked reasonably.

'In the light of your relationship with Taiwan, it would not be politically expedient for your president.'

That was a fair comment, Levinsky had to admit.

'Do you understand that we merely wish to defend ourselves, colonel? Can you imagine us actually wanting to attack the USA? The idea is laughable.'

'I would never be able to go back to my country if I did this thing.'

Good, thought Chung. He is at least considering the possibilities. 'Is there all that much for you to go back to?' he asked gently.

Levinsky, to be honest, didn't really have much to say to that, so he resorted to bluster. 'Well, at least the living there is better than in this crap place,' he exclaimed rudely.

'You've hardly given this place a chance have you?' commented Mr Leung.

Levinsky, almost ritualistically, refused to co-operate. As he was returned to the prison he was struck by the look of real concern that crossed Mei Ling's face as he was taken away.

They held him for seven days in solitary confinement with a powerful light blazing night and day, and when that didn't seem to break him they turned on a speaker system that broadcast cacophonous Cantonese opera without cease. Once a day, he was given a bowl of rice gruel containing a chunk of gristle, and a tin container of so-called drinking water. There was nowhere other than the concrete floor on which to sleep, and in the corner was a bucket for his bodily functions which was only emptied when it was full, which could take several days.

After a while he amazed his captors by being able to snatch a few hours of sleep at night, a sleep of sheer exhaustion, and even when they shook him awake, he would immediately relapse into a semi-stupor that seemed to provide some relief from the misery of hunger and deprivation he was undergoing.

But it was a losing battle. It could not go on. He had terrible nightmares during the minutes of unconsciousness he was allowed: nightmares of the gas chambers and torture his relatives that had stayed behind had endured in the death camps of Poland. He reached the stage of wishing for death himself, and then from somewhere dragged out yet another grain of strength, of desire to live. He would not go meekly to his final agony.

And then Professor Chung arrived on the scene. He was genuinely horrified at the state in which he found the American. 'I so much regret this barbaric behaviour,' he wailed, practically wringing his hands.

'Not half as much as me,' muttered Levinsky. He grinned wryly. 'If you don't do something soon, professor, you're gonna lose your five-million-dollar asset, that's for sure.'

'To hell with the five million dollars,' Chung replied shortly. 'I am very angry that this has happened. They have far exceeded their brief. Admittedly you were to be deprived of your freedom, but there was to be nothing like this.' He threw up his hands.

'What are you going to do about it?' asked Levinsky, genuinely curious.

'I intend to tell them that I have persuaded you to co-operate and take you out of here immediately,' Chung whispered.

'But you have received no such assurance from me, and – '

'Ssh,' the Chinese hissed imperiously. 'Just do as I tell you and agree with everything I say.' He smiled gently. 'Just remember I'm the only person technically capable of ascertaining whether or not you are co-operating, and I have absolutely no intention of seeing a brain like yours destroyed in this useless fashion.'

'I hope it works,' said Levinsky fervently.

'It will,' assured Chung, 'and maybe one day, no matter how long it takes, I can persuade you to see things my way. It will then be well worth it.'

'Fat chance,' grunted Levinsky, secretly delighted by his victory.

But Chung was playing it smart. There was no doubt now that Levinsky owed him. It took Levinsky another six months of frustrated boredom to realise he was desperate to work.

Professor Chung was a frequent visitor and their lengthy discussions, covering all sorts of topics, besides the esoterics of their scientific fields, gradually built between them a bond that was as near to friendship as could be.

More important Levinsky felt he could trust the older man, so when Levinsky finally expressed his need to do something productive, as long as Professor Chung could assure him that the end result would not in any way prove harmful to his country, and Chung gladly gave such an assurance, Levinsky accepted the situation and went to work with a conscience that was almost, if not a hundred percent, clear.

At no time, during the many lengthy discussions he had with Professor Chung and Mr Leung, was the question of laser technology mentioned, other than as an adjunct to the guided bomb. The professor had not, in truth, been to Princeton, but had gone to MIT from Taiwan, and then absconded back to China as a matter of genuine loyalty to the country of his birth. In fact, during his stay at MIT he had known a great deal about the parameters within which Levinsky had worked, and had read several of his strictly confidential papers, copies of which had been clandestinely misappropriated by communist sympathisers.

The professor had stuck out his neck with considerable

confidence when he recommended the payout for Colonel Stefan Levinsky.

* * *

As Stefan and his son ran through the entrance to the compound, where the bungalows stood of the various Americans employed on the project that he controlled, the PLA guard gave them a cheery wave and went back to his perusal of the *Red Star.*

They trotted along between carefully-tended properties and homes which could have been in a suburb of any small American town in the sunshine states, exchanging greetings with those of the occupants up early to water their gardens before the sun grew too hot.

As the plateau was some 3000 feet above sea level, the climate, despite falling within the Tropic of Cancer, was temperate with modest rainfall, and the air from the foothills of the Chamdo Himalayas which could be seen to the north was pure and brilliantly clear. 'Like California without smog,' was the description frequently mentioned by Stefan's compatriots. To Stefan the term 'Shangri-la' was more appropriate.

He looked at his son and smiled affectionately. The youngster, catching his glance, grinned back and said cheekily, 'How's the old man doing?'

'Race you home, Jake, and you'll see,' replied Stefan, accelerating.

The run was virtually a daily ritual, as was the exchange at the end. Jacob Levinsky edged ahead on the last uphill bit to where the Levinsky house was placed, looking over the rest of the small colony in acknowledgement of the occupant's seniority.

His wife, Mei Ling, was, as usual, waiting for her two men on the wide verandah that ran round the front of the house, and with her was the servant girl bearing a tray with glasses of orange juice. The three of them sat in companionable silence on the steps of the verandah getting their breath

101

back and gazing at the beauty spread before them. Levinsky put his arm round his wife's shoulder and gave her a hug.

'Phew, you smell of sweat. Go take a shower,' she replied, wrinkling her pert little nose. I come scrub your back.'

Jacob looked at his parents fondly, and asked slyly, 'Is that all you do, mama?'

'You are a very cheeky boy. You mind own business.' But she was smiling.

The conversation was carried on in a mix of Mandarin and English. It had taken Mei Ling four years of coaching to get Stefan's Chinese to an acceptable standard. He had been guarded in his approach to her but sitting for several months in close proximity to her during his Mandarin lessons had driven him to the stage when he could resist touching her delicate perfection no longer. His first tactic had been to take her fingers in his and press them to his lips.

Her reaction had been a sharp intake of breath, followed by a gentle rebuff. Levinsky was surprised, and his expression obviously showed it. She trembled and, averting her face, moved slightly away.

'But I thought...' he stammered, leaving the sentence unfinished.

'What?' she whispered, turning back to him, eyes downcast.

'When we came here you said, or at least implied, that I might be provided with some company should I require it.' He stopped embarrassed. Her cheeks had flushed.

'You thought I meant that I would provide that sort of company?' It was a straightforward question. She had control of herself now, and was looking at him in a quizzical fashion.

'Okay. Since you ask, yes, I did,' he replied, feeling like an uncouth lout.

'Did I not provide you with company?' she asked. 'I cooked for you, I cleaned, did your laundry. Is that not enough company?' She stressed the last word which irritated him.

'No, it isn't,' he replied sulkily.

'Your bottom lip is sticking out like a small boy who has been told he cannot have what he wants,' Mei Ling said, and putting out her finger touched his mouth.

He felt as if an electric shock had been applied to his face, and instinctively grasped her hand. This time she did not pull away. Emboldened, he put an arm around her. She was firm, yet pliant, and smelled delicious.

'I have longed for you a very long time,' he said simply.

'In English, is that the same as lust?' she asked innocently.

'No. It is a mixture of desire and love.'

'I am so glad. I think lust is a very unpleasant word.' She paused and looked at him brightly. 'It is good that you do not lust after me.'

'Oh God, you are playing games with words. I want you in the worst possible way and you indulge in semantics.'

'What is this semantics?'

'I knew it. I knew it.' He picked her up and, holding her tightly, marched towards the bedroom.

'But...' she protested.

'Later,' he said, and kissed her on the mouth.

When they took time for breath, a small voice said, 'You do not have to force me.'

He stopped and set her down. 'You are not doing this because you have been instructed to do it?' he asked.

'No one instructs me what to do with my body,' she replied indignantly. 'I have known you and watched you for several months. I want you too. It is as simple as that.' She took him by the hand then, and led him into the bedroom. It was cool and quiet, but the heat rose in him.

Without any attempt to play the *femme fatale*, and with quiet deliberation, she stripped herself and stood before him. The sunlight on her body turned it into an ivory statue. She could not yet have been twenty and was perfection in every way, her breasts pert and firm, her belly flat and muscular, her legs unusually long for a Chinese, tapering finely to the ankles and small, beautifully-shaped feet.

'Well?' she asked unsmilingly.

'You are truly beautiful,' he said moving toward her.

'Thank you, and remember no one forces me,' she repeated quietly. He still could not believe her, but when she cried out with painful pleasure as he entered her, it was the greatest surprise of his life.

She had come to him as a virgin, and almost on a whim, but the love and tenderness she had shown him over the years had never ceased to amaze him. Nor had it ever been cloying. She was the love of his life, she had borne him a son and there was no doubt in his mind that his love was wholeheartedly returned. Their sadness was that she could have no more children. Not for physical reasons, but because the autocratic government of China so decreed, in its desperate attempt to keep the population at a sustainable level. Levinsky had railed against this restriction but Mei Ling took it philosophically for, as she exclaimed, it was for the greater good of those to come, and that included her son on whom she doted.

He stood up and stretched. 'I should be very grateful if you would indeed scrub my back,' he said gravely, and took her by the hand.

Colonel Levinsky was a happy man, totally fulfilled by his family and his work. There were times when he had wished for the sophistication and the good life of the States, but as the years went by the desire had receded, submerged by the obvious benefits of his present situation. This was a life without frills but at heart Levinsky, despite his soaring mental ability, was a simple man, and things as they were suited him down to the ground.

To the ever omniscient Professor Chung, Levinsky's satisfaction with his lot had come through clearly many years before. The defence capabilities of the Chinese airforce had benefited enormously as a result of his work and that of his willing accomplices, most of whom had also settled down with Chinese women, and the professor felt it was time to go for the big one.

He had most assiduously fostered his relationship with

Levinsky as time passed, and in truth they had a genuine liking for each other. The professor had the ability to think, behave and even feel like an American or a Chinese, which ever way he wanted. One day Chung asked, 'Tell me, friend, what do you consider the possibility might be of setting up defences against ballistic missiles?' The Levinsky papers Chung had read made it clear that this was, in fact, the main project on which the American had worked in his shuttling between MIT and NASA.

The two exchanged looks. 'Why has it taken you so many years to ask me that?' queried Levinsky, smiling gently to himself.

'You have been expecting the question, Stefan?'

'Of course, and also, to a great extent, the work on upgrading your aircraft electronic technology is complete and you have many well-trained technicians of your own now to carry it on.'

Chung nodded agreement. 'So?'

'So this is the obvious next step. A gigantic step indeed, which requires a great deal of original, yes, even tangential, thought, leap-frogging known conventions.' It was clear Levinsky was becoming enthused, his mind beginning to race ahead of his tongue.

'You ask why I did not mention it before,' interrupted Chung. 'I can tell you it took great self-control on my part.'

Stefan laughed then looked serious. 'You knew I had been working on this at MIT, did you not? This other project to update your aircraft was just a lead-in. Am I right?'

'Perfectly right,' agreed Chung soberly. 'But there was another reason why I delayed.'

'Give it me,' said Stefan.

'I wanted you to trust me. To believe me when I said we had no aggressive intentions against America, or any other country for that matter. We have enough problems of our own without looking for more.'

'I accept that entirely,' said Stefan seriously. 'So now you want to know if it would be possible to create a defence against ballistic missiles for China?'

The other nodded.

'It is possible,' said the American flatly.

'But it would be impossibly expensive,' interrupted Chung.

'If you approach it in the conventional way, yes,' replied Levinsky.

'But your tangential thinking, as you call it, might bring it within the bounds of economic reason?'

'Possibly.'

'Would you be prepared to help us?' asked Chung. 'On the same basis as your previous commitment, of course.'

'I don't see why a purely defensive system like this would be harmful to anyone, except those of evil intent who might wish to attack our country.'

'Stefan, Stefan, do you realise what you said just then?' Chung's voice was almost breaking with emotion. 'You said *our* country, Stefan. *Our* country, meaning China.' The professor flung his arms around the other man.

'So I did, old friend, so I did,' replied Stefan.

And so in the early eighties the great project started. Instead of re-inventing the wheel, Levinsky introduced a number of daring innovations, producing a series of brilliant breakthroughs in laser beam generation and control, rather as if man, instead of inventing the emission valve as a means of controlling and amplifying electrical energy for radio, had leaped straight to the silicon chip, with a million times the efficiency and power, combined with an infinitesimally smaller size and weight.

By 1989, China's prototype equivalent of a Star Wars installation was ready for testing, ahead of the world. A rocket was duly fired from Lop Nor, and at a height of 220 miles over southern China, was destroyed by laser beam. Levinsky's employers, as he thought of them now rather than captors, were delighted, and Levinsky himself was quietly satisfied, but as he said to the professor, this was only the beginning.

What had really disturbed American Intelligence was that

they had picked up the Lop Nor launch, and noticed the south-west trajectory towards the Indian Ocean, but had lost the missile long before re-entry. This was a mystery which had to be solved, and their satellite pictures of Yunnan, with its unusual structure in the area of Mengwang, seemed an excellent place to start their enquiries.

8

Harwood was going through his pre-flight checks.

The Cessna had fired first time after he'd called the 'Clear Prop' warning, and the oil pressure had climbed sweetly and quickly to the required level, which was reassuring. The gauges were all registering normal as he called for taxi clearance from Chiang Mai tower.

'Cessna 182, you are cleared to taxi.'

As he bumped over the grass field toward the threshhold, he turned to look at Ching-hua beside him. She was smiling to herself. Relaxed and happy and completely confident in his ability to get them to their destination. He looked over his shoulder. In the back, grim-faced, clutching his machine pistol, sat Peng Keong, looking more like Odd-Job than ever, with his cropped square head.

The briefing had started at 10 a.m. that morning and had gone on for four hours. It was full of detail and the planning, Harwood had to admit, was meticulous. They had even supplied black jump-suits for the three of them, together with parachutists' boots, all fitting perfectly.

Except for the difference in age, the two CIA men might have been clones. The elder did the talking while the younger worked the projector and fed his superior information in a quiet, nasal New England twang whenever there appeared to be any hesitation, which did not happen very often. The senior introduced them as: 'Call me Al and he's Hank.'

Al started proceedings with a great baring of capped teeth in a totally insincere smile, and a rumbled compliment to 'Ms Ho Ching-hua' for the efficiency of her Yunnan associates, and how important their input had been to the planning of the operation. Nevertheless, Harwood couldn't help but feel the veiled surprise in Al's voice that any orientals could have been so competent. It was also obvious that he rather fancied Ching-hua because he couldn't take his eyes away from her shapely crossed legs under the short skirt she was wearing, until a dry cough from Hank brought him back on track.

They were told official clearance had been obtained for them to take a night flight to Chiengsen, where there was a small landing strip, in the most northern tip of Thailand within a mile of the common border with Laos and Burma. There they would top up with fuel and the Thai officials had been bribed to turn a blind eye to their onward flight in darkness over the border to China.

'There are so many goddam drug smugglers flyin' around at night up there, without lights, it bein' in the Golden Triangle and all, I recommend you keep your eyes real skinned, Mayo.' Al considered the idea somewhat amusing and guffawed chestily to himself, accompanied by a sycophantic snigger from Hank.

'You done this sort of thing yourself?' asked Harwood, seeking to deflate the man.

'Hell no,' he shot back, completely impervious to the comment. 'I leave that sorta thing to young dare-devils like you guys. And, er, excuse me,' – bowing to Ching-hua – 'ladies.'

Again the crocodile smile. 'Now back to business.' He cleared his throat and growled on. 'MET tell me the forecast is for three-quarter moon, high cirrus cloud and light winds, which will be sustained for at least 48 hours, so,' – a low grunting chuckle this time – 'if the bastards get it right for once, there should be no trouble there.'

There was a pause as the slide projector whirred quietly to life and a picture, similar to that Harwood had been shown by Summervill, appeared on the screen. It was far better defined, to the extent that the laser installation and the compound some five miles away from it, where the Americans were housed, clearly showed individual buildings. They could also see two bridges over the Mekong, one to the south of Mengwang and another to the north.

Al allowed them a few seconds to take it in, then, lifting the pointer, drew attention to the salient points, which Harwood was already aware of. Again a pause, as Hank did his stuff, and an overlay appeared that showed a series of eight markers in a straight line, lying approximately south-east to north-west, about two miles south of the compound.

Al used his pointer. 'This here is the landing strip that Ms Ho's friends have cleared for you.' Another bow, another gratuitous leer. 'I reckon it's a thousand feet long.'

'We estimate if you take off from Chiengsen at 1900 hours tomorrow, 1st October, you should, cruising at 110 miles per hour, make it in under two hours. Distance is 150 miles, but following the Mekong in moonlight, for navigational purposes, say 200 miles. Do you agree, Captain Mayo?'

There was a pause. Harwood still found it strange to react immediately to his new name. 'I'm no Captain, Al, but, yes, I agree that's about right.'

'Hell, you're flying the damn thing, that makes you captain. Right?'

'If you say so, Al, but what are the markers on either side?'

'Glad you asked that question. These here' – a couple of touches with his pointer – 'will be lit across the landing strip to show you the wind's angle of variance across the runway, and with the regular winds from the north-east at this time of the year you can reckon on it blowing right to left as you come at it from the southerly end. Okay?'

'I understand.' And wishing to apply some warmth to the proceedings, he added, 'That's very clear, Al.'

'We do our best, captain, and remember, keep the lights

just to your left. I reckoned we didn't want to draw undue attention by delineating both sides of the runway.'

'That'd make it too easy, wouldn't it?' murmured Harwood.

'Oh very good,' snickered Hank, and cut it off quickly as Al glared at him.

'We have been informed some twenty or so armed members of the underground democratic movement will be meeting you, and their leader is a fella called Hung who has expressed his willingness to do anything that this here little lady wishes.' Al shook his head admiringly. 'Now if you folk have any questions, please spit 'em out, as now's the time.'

The radio broke in on Harwood's thoughts. 'Cessna 182 cleared to threshhold and take off.'

'Okay. Here we go. Tighten up your safety belts.' As they lifted off Harwood touched the girl's elbow. She turned and looked at him. 'I love you,' he mouthed.

'Me too,' she answered.

The flight to Chiengsen was uneventful and it was there, while they were being filled up with Avgas, that Harwood made his decision. He clasped Ching-hua's hand and took her round to the side of a hangar, where there was a modicum of privacy. He lowered his face to hers. 'When this is over I want to marry you.'

She touched his cheek with her hand. 'I will not hold you to that,' she said. 'The time is too filled with emotion, but I am greatly honoured and hope you will ask me again when things are more normal.' With that he had to be content.

They took off into the dusk on time, flying as low as was safe above the trees, with the Mekong River beneath them, a moonlit beacon lighting their way. To the left Burma, to their right Laos, ahead the mountains of China, rising out of the jungle toward the towering peaks of the eastern Himalayan massif four hundred miles to the north, and over it all a dark, velvet sky, bright with the tropical constellations. The tranquility of the scene, combined with the monotonous beat of the engine, made his concentration drift.

Suddenly, a black shadow crossed the moon and less than a couple of hundred yards away the silhouette of a twin-engined Beech Baron blasted across his front.

'Jesus,' he yelped.

A sleepy voice beside him said, 'Wassa matter, darling?' She hadn't even noticed, and Odd-Job was obviously dozing complacently behind.

'Okay, you two,' he shouted angrily. 'Wake up and keep awake. We nearly had it that time. I want both of you with heads swivelling all the time, eyes wide open. Do you hear?' There was a hurried chorus of assent around him. 'The next one that goes to sleep walks there.' He tried to make a joke of it to atone for his sharpness, but no one was laughing. Heads were up and turning now.

Within minutes they had another comparatively close call, which justified his previous loss of temper. Ching-hua spotted it coming in from her right and gave him time to take avoiding action as the blacked-out aircraft passed over the top of them. It went by so quickly he could not even identify it. Al certainly had a point, he thought wryly.

They had been flying for over an hour and were well into China, when some miles to their right a searchlight groped blindly across the sky, followed by an irritable burst of tracer. 'Nothing to worry about,' commented Harwood. Then another searchlight blazed on, much closer this time, and more tracer arced towards them. 'Hang on,' Harwood warned. 'This could be a bit dramatic.'

He pushed the nose down towards the Mekong and switched on the plane's powerful landing lights to give him some idea of his height above the water. The aircraft was now well below the tree-tops, banking round the curves in the river and travelling at full power, at close to 140 miles an hour. They shattered the peace of a small village that lay to their left, and continued on their way for another five minutes until Harwood reckoned they were clear and started to climb again.

'That was very exciting,' laughed Ching-hua.

'Just keep alert,' replied Harwood grimly.

There was no question of anyone dozing off now. Another, bigger cluster of lights came up ahead. Harwood checked his watch. 'I reckon that's Cheli to the south of Mengwang. About forty miles to go. Say another twenty minutes.' He looked at his altimeter. Two thousand, five hundred feet above sea level. 'We've got to climb higher now. The plateau's at four and a half thousand.' They ascended steadily for another ten minutes. Height was now nearly five and a half thousand. Harwood said: 'Hope your friends are there, Ching-hua.'

'There's another five minutes to go at least before they're meant to light up. They'll be there,' she replied confidently.

So she had been keeping a check on the time. Good for her.

They'd been flying for an hour and three-quarters. Still blackness, except for the lights of Mengwang to their left. Harwood gritted his teeth and commenced circling. It was important not to overfly the area, but the longer they hung around the more likely it was that authority might take an aggressive interest in their presence. There was a considerable cloud layer coming in, passing over the moon. Again he recalled Al's crack about the MET people. If they had to abort he wouldn't be too confident about getting back by dead-reckoning on a reverse track without the moon's reflection in the Mekong to help him.

'There,' shrieked Ching-hua. A string of lights flickering on to the east. Six, seven, eight he counted them.

'Thank Christ for that.'

He set his altimeter for four and a half, and banked towards the lights, maintaining leeway of five hundred feet. Two lights on each side showed the wind coming from the north. Sixty-five degrees off the line of the runway. No problem; it was a light wind. But then he wasn't so sure. MET could have got it wrong again. Final checks. Temperature and oil pressure OK. Gyro synchronised. Two stages of flap. Make it a longish drag to get the feel of the drift, he was thinking. Crab it in a bit. Down to three hundred over the ground. Speed nicely on eighty, cowl gills open, check the revs. Threshhold, if you can call it that, coming up. Kind fellow beaming a powerful flashlight from the other end, down the centre of the prepared ground, to give some idea of width. Power off, flare, crunch. Heavy, and one bounce, but safe enough. They stopped literally at the last light.

No way was that a thousand feet. More like 800. Still he'd made it. Somebody was waving the torch at him. Showing him where to go. He ended up under some trees, did his after-landing checks, switched off and got out, stretching himself.

The runway lights had already been extinguished with impressive rapidity. They were surrounded by a gang of silent, armed men but there was a discipline in their silence. The one with the flashlight played it over their faces and turned to Ching-hua.

'Ho nu shi ni hao.' 'How do you do, Miss Ho.'

Very formal, thought Harwood, but the warmth of the man's expression as reflected in the light, and the respectful half-bow as he gently took her hand, after she had first offered hers, made it clear that Hung would indeed do anything Ching-hua required.

They were given no time to rest, but marched silently through the darkness for a few miles until they came to the crest of a hill that Hung told them overlooked the compound where the Americans were housed. Waiting for them on the hill-top was a young, slim, bespectacled Chinese. Hung introduced him as Won Wai Lee, a member of the democratic movement who worked as a security guard in the compound.

Won knew the routine. He spoke some English but as soon as he appreciated Harwood spoke Mandarin he reverted to his own language. 'Mr Levinsky and his son go running five days a week for several miles, all around this area but usually across the river over the southern bridge then around the back of Mengwang, returning by the bridge at the other end of the village.'

Harwood nodded for him to continue.

'They start just before daylight about five o'clock in

114

the morning, and it takes them until half past six approximately.'

'So where do you suggest we take him? You know the terrain.' The Chinese seemed somewhat taken aback. His job was to provide information, not give tactical advice.

'It's alright, Won,' encouraged Ching-hua. 'The ying-guo ren, the Englishman, wants you to think of the exercise as if you were carrying it out. Yes?' She turned enquiringly to Harwood, anxious that she might be interfering.

'Ho nu shi is right. Is there a place on their run where we can intercept them without being seen?'

'There is a place where there are some trees and bushes, not far from the bridge by which they return, where you can hide. I sometimes take my girlfriend there.'

'Very good. You will show us tomorrow. Now we must get some rest.'

It was 1 a.m. He lay down beside Ching-hua on the blankets provided, but for the sake of propriety kept his distance, though he longed to put his arms around her.

'Good night, love.'

'Good night, hairy barbarian,' she whispered.

He lay looking at the stars. The cloud cover had drifted away and the MET people would probably be right in their forecast after all.

'Gone pretty well so far,' he said quietly. No reply. She was asleep already. Incredible. On his other side Peng Keong snored like a hog.

* * *

The next thing Harwood knew, his shoulder was being shaken. 'Christ, I've only just gone to sleep,' he complained.

Hung was bending over him. 'You slept well.' In his right hand was a cup of Chinese tea and in his left a bowl of noodles. Harwood took the offerings gratefully. It calmed the nervous sickness in his stomach that had come with consciousness, as reality flooded back.

Ching-hua and Peng Keong were up and at the brow of

the hill, looking out towards the compound through night glasses. The Englishman came up beside them. 'Good morning you two. Why did you let me sleep in so late?'

'You did all the work yesterday. We thought you deserved it,' she replied taking him seriously.

'Look,' Peng Keong hissed, his finger pointing.

A light had come on in one of the houses below. Won appeared on the scene. 'That's his house,' he said shortly.

'Good. Now we have to wait and hope they run round the village. Give me the glasses, please.'

Harwood took Peng Keong's pair and looked at the house. There was virtually no light yet, though dawn was not far away. He picked out a blurred shape moving behind the curtains. He put the glasses down and lay on his stomach waiting. There was nothing more he could do now. It was nearly 5 a.m. There was the faintest blush to the east, and in silhouette he saw the bulk of the 9,000-foot peak of Ningerh. Lucky he hadn't overflown the landing area. It could have been painful.

Peng Keong grunted beside him, which seemed to be his normal mode of communication.

He looked again. The two men had come out on to the verandah. The light had gone off inside. The lady of the house obviously decided another hour of rest was required. Harwood yawned and wiped his eyes, which were watering slightly. He peered through the glasses. The two Levinskys were limbering up prior to starting off.

'Come on,' muttered Harwood, wanting to get it over with.

They had left the house now and were trotting easily down to the security guards' hut. Harwood focused on to it. No one there unless the man was sleeping on the floor. He snorted. Some security. Won came and lay beside him.

'Well?' queried the Englishman.

'Another minute,' said Won. 'If they take the right fork they'll be going on their usual run for sure.'

'If not?'

Won shrugged. 'Then they could be going anywhere.'

116

They waited. The two runners did not take the right fork.

'Shit,' fulminated Harwood. 'That means we've got to go after them.' He began to stand up.

'Wait,' said Won. 'I think we are alright.' He was pointing. The two men had gone out of sight behind a rise, but now they had reappeared and seemed to be coming straight up the hill to where they were waiting.

'One in twenty times maybe,' said Won.

'You mean come up here?'

Won nodded. 'Very lucky,' he said. 'It is some three kilometres so it will take a while.'

Harwood kept his glasses on the two, and out of the corner of his mouth said: 'Ching-hua, please get Hung to move his men back and catch them after they come over the rise. He'd better leave a few on the lip in case they try to bolt back down the hill.' He looked to his left. She'd already gone. She'd been way ahead of him. Smart girl.

He crawled away. Everyone except himself was completely hidden. Where the hell were they? A peremptory hiss to his left, followed by a beckoning female hand from behind a patch of long grass. Hurriedly he joined her.

'Presumably they've left a few . . . ?'

'To cut them off. Yes,' she said, finishing the sentence for him.

'Don't know why I'm needed,' Harwood grumbled.

'To fly the plane, of course,' Ching-hua replied, then giggled to show she was only fooling.

It was a steep hill and they seemed to wait ages. The urge to go to the edge and peep over was almost overwhelming.

'God, I hope they haven't changed their minds,' whispered Harwood. 'I can hear them breathing,' she replied. Then it came to him. The rasping breath as the two runners forced themselves up the last ascent. And then their heads came over the top and, without looking about them, they stopped and turned to look at where they had come from.

'Haven't done this for some time; it was a toughie,' said Levinsky Senior.

'It wasn't easy even for me,' said his son, with unconscious superiority.

His father tousled his hair. 'Come on lazy bones; let's go.' They'd gone half a dozen paces when Hung sprang the trap. Suddenly their way was blocked by four armed men. More appeared to the right and left of them. Levinsky turned. Behind stood Harwood with Peng Keong and Ching-hua, pistols at the ready. Harwood could see from the look, first of shock and then almost immediately of full awareness and acceptance, that Levinsky knew. He turned immediately to Harwood as the only white man there and said, 'Don't harm my son.'

'We have no intention of harming anyone,' he replied.

'But you're British,' Levinsky said, surprised.

'Does it make a difference?'

'I guess not. They employ all sorts.'

'Thanks,' said Harwood sourly.

'If you've no intention of harming anyone why is that thug waving his machine gun in my direction?'

'I'm no thug,' said Peng Keong angrily. 'I've got orders to kill you if you don't come quietly. It's as simple as that.'

'To hell, you say!' sputtered Harwood, shocked.

'Now I am confused. Who's running this show anyway?' asked Levinsky.

'He is,' interjected Ching-hua, indicating Harwood.

Peng Keong nodded sullen agreement.

Harwood felt he was losing control of the situation and intended to stamp his authority without delay. 'You are to come with us. Your son will be held until we are clear away, then released unharmed.'

'I take it that all this has arisen because of the installation here, and that you intend to return me to the States so they can dispose of me in any way they see fit.' Levinsky seemed quite in control of himself. He was even jogging gently on the spot as if anxious to be on his way.

'Something like that, but I'm not at liberty to go into detail,' Harwood replied feeling like a bogus policeman.

'This is, of course, a totally pointless exercise,' continued the American coolly. 'I presume they think my absence will make the project fold.'

'Won't it?' asked Harwood.

'Certainly not. There are at least three Chinese scientists who are more than capable of putting in the finishing touches.' Levinsky laughed dryly. 'You've come too late.' He paused and shrugged his shoulders. 'Now if it were a case of starting from scratch, that's a different ball game.'

'Dad, you don't have to tell them anything.' It was the first time the boy had put in his penny's-worth, and it just emphasised the point he was trying to evade.

Harwood took him up on it immediately. 'So I guess it means the whole lot has to be destroyed. Right?'

'You got it in one, Limey, and how do you propose to destroy a thousand tons of concrete and half a billion dollars-worth of equipment, not to mention me, if you don't want the operation to be repeated?' he concluded triumphantly.

'It's not within my brief,' replied Harwood frowning in concentration.

'You betcha it isn't, unless you happen to be carrying a small nuke with you, and if you aren't I doubt even the States are into starting a nuclear war to try and destroy someone else's defensive system.' Levinsky was grinning triumphantly. 'It's checkmate, friend. I made it. I'm the only one who knows enough to self-destruct it and...' He shut up suddenly and finished lamely. 'Abducting me won't help, will it?'

The son was scuffing his foot in the dirt, shaking his head.

'No it won't,' agreed Harwood coldly. 'You Yanks find it difficult not to shoot your mouths off, don't you.' He saw the younger man staring at him and knew inwardly that he now had the whip hand. 'We take your son. We leave you to destroy your death ray or whatever you call it, or else...' He could feel his old SAS training rolling back the years. Being a hard bastard again came easier than he would have thought possible. Everybody's mouth was hanging open.

'You son of a bitch,' shouted Levinsky and threw himself at Harwood, his hands like claws. Harwood kicked him in the stomach so that he fell, doubled up, gasping for air.

'Oh God,' Levinsky moaned, his mind racing, hate and fear rolling over him, in alternate waves. Can I never get away from them? he was thinking. Always there's someone waiting to hit you or kick you, even kill you if you're a Jew. So the school bully wins in the end, he thought wearily. Got to get up, though, for more punishment. It's the honourable way to go. He forced himself to try and rise.

Harwood noticed Ching-hua was looking at him, her expression unreadable. Then Peng Keong stepped forward toward the American, now on all-fours.

'No way do we let him go,' he said mechanically. 'My orders are to kill him if he doesn't come with us.' Peng Keong was pointing his pistol at the helpless man's head, intently taking aim.

Harwood shot him through the chest so that he was flung backwards, firing harmlessly in the air. The sound of the shots rolled away. Everyone stood motionless, perception of what had happened slow to come. Harwood was still pointing the gun at the motionless body, his arm rock-steady, his lips drawn back from his teeth. Hung stepped forward hesitantly, not knowing what was going on. Harwood swivelled his gaze toward him, tensed, waiting for trouble, the killing mood strong. Ching-hua rattled off at Hung, who backed away, watching the Englishman intently. How the hell do I explain this? thought Harwood.

'He shouldn't have tried to take over,' said Ching-hua, as if reading his thoughts and giving him the way out.

Levinsky was on his feet now, still finding it difficult to breathe. 'You're a right mean sod, Limey.' Harwood glared at him. He raised his hands and backed off. 'I believe you mean what you say. I know what to do now. Thanks for not letting him shoot me. I wasn't quite ready to go yet.' Harwood wasn't sure how sincere the American's gratitude was, but took it at face value.

'It's nothing,' said Harwood, and then, 'your son will not

be harmed if you co-operate.' He stared sternly at the American. To himself he wondered if he could ever execute an innocent in cold blood. The thought of it made him feel sick. Peng Keong's elimination, however, had left him strangely untouched.

'I want a word with my boy please before I go back. In private, if possible.'

Harwood grudgingly gave them a couple of minutes. They talked softly to each other, slightly apart from the rest. Then the father put his arms round his son, who began to weep quietly. Levinsky Senior turned away. 'You should hear either from your collaborators here, or perhaps even pick up something on your spy satellite within a week. Will that be alright, because I doubt the New China News agency will be quick to report anything?'

Harwood nodded. 'That sounds reasonable,' he said, then changed the subject. 'How do you explain your son's absence to the security guard?'

'I'll tell them he's staying with friends at Mengwang. Something he does often.' He paused, bit his lip.

'I will, of course, have to come clean with my wife. Jacob would never spend time away without telling her.' He frowned and shook his head. 'That's going to be a difficult one,' he said.

'Your problem, I'm afraid,' replied Harwood, the tough guy.

'I'll go now.' Levinsky gazed lingeringly at his son, turned abruptly away, and jogged off.

They buried Peng Keong hastily in a shallow grave covered with some brushwood, well away from the path, and proceeded at a trot back to where they had left the plane. Hung tied a rope lightly around the boy's waist to ensure he did not try to make a break for it but he was too shocked to make any trouble. They all waited, under cover, on the plateau near to the Cessna, until dusk began to fall.

'What do I tell Hung to do with Jacob?' asked Ching-hua softly. 'You really want him killed?'

'I can't see any profit in it. I reckon we'll give Levinsky two weeks to call my bluff. If he does we've lost and Hung sends the youngster back home unharmed. Do you agree?'

Ching-hua nodded and said, 'You realise this means you are sacrificing yourself and could get deported to China?'

'I couldn't be responsible for the kid's murder, so there's no other way is there?' he replied simply.

Ching-hua hugged him. Kid? she thought. He's probably my age. Where did my childhood go?

To Harwood she said: 'I'm glad you're not the beast you made yourself out to be back there.'

'Don't be so sure. I have my moments.' He touched her cheek affectionately. 'I'm also not a complete simpleton, and now I've disposed of my guard dog there's no way I'm going back to Hong Kong until I know the way the land lies. I've transferred all my cash, which is a considerable amount, out of there to a Swiss account and I've a few thousand US dollars with me now.' He grinned at her cheerfully. 'I reckon you and I deserve a couple of weeks' holiday on a pleasant beach somewhere while we wait to see what happens.' He stood up and pulled her with him. 'Let's go and tell Hung what we've decided and bring young Levinsky in on the picture. It should ease his mind.'

As they came towards Levinsky's son he ignored Harwood completely, looking straight at Ching-hua, who returned his gaze, an unexpected pulse of excitement in her throat. As if by tacit agreement Harwood stood to one side while she told Jacob of his reprieve. A bright flash of emotion appeared in the young man's expression. He moved up to her, took her hand and kissed it fervently, much to Harwood's surprise. He then let go of her hand, and turned to the Englishman. 'This is her idea, isn't it.' It was a statement not a question. He looked at Ching-hua then back to Harwood. 'The day will come when you may regret your woman's benevolence.'

Ching-hua and Harwood were both too taken aback by Jacob's temerity to contradict him. Harwood simply shrugged. 'Don't push your luck, Levinsky,' he growled.

9

Mengwang   2nd October 1989 – 6.30 p.m.

The take-off from the plateau needed a stage of flap and all the power he could coax out of the engine. He chickened out half-way first time, and aborted. Next time round he ran her up to full power and held her on the brakes so that the Cessna roared and rattled as if it were going to break up.

When he did let her go she did her stuff and they were away into the night sky just before the runway's end. At 200 feet, Harwood lifted the flap and calmed down a trifle as they climbed away at 80 miles an hour. He wiped the sweat off his forehead and turned to his companion. 'That was the shortest damn 1,000 feet I've ever seen.'

She reached over and kissed his right ear. He laughed with the delight of her, then banked sharply on to his heading so that Ching-hua squealed and moved rapidly away from him.

The return trip was downhill all the way. The cloud cover was virtually nil and the moonlit Mekong showed them the way back like a well-lit highway. Over Cheli they left Chinese airspace, entered Laos and prepared to turn right for the Thai border at Chiengsen.

Unfortunately the moon, besides reflecting off the Mekong, also silhouetted their slow-moving Cessna perfectly against the glittering river, so that the patrolling Chinese MiG 19 at five thousand feet saw them as clearly as if they had been caught in a search light. The MiG pilot received considerable sums in bribes, as did his colleagues, to let pass approved carriers of contraband. To identify them there was a particular codeword used on a particular frequency, neither of which were known to Harwood.

On the other hand such pilots were expected by the higher authorities to find occasionally a sacrificial lamb in the shape of someone behaving in a subversive manner, such as gun running to dissidents, or simply trying to operate drugs outside the system. Harwood was just what was called for.

The fact that they were already over Laotian territory was beside the point. They had become fair game for hot pursuit tactics. As the MiG prepared to attack, Harwood had tuned in to the Chiengsen frequency and was in touch with the airport controller. Preparatory to a direct approach on finals, he did his down-wind checks, reduced power and put down two stages of flap. The Cessna slowed considerably to about 80 knots and also lifted somewhat prior to settling down for the run-in.

At that crucial moment the MiG was coming up behind them at 400 knots and preparing to open fire. When his target reduced speed by some 50 knots, and instantaneously rose vertically out of his sights, the MiG, whose pilot was not exactly experienced anyway, flashed underneath the Cessna so close that its high tail-fin ripped a ten-foot gash in the light aeroplane's underside, and at the same time destroyed a major part of its own rudder.

The MiG pilot didn't have a chance. Flying at less than tree-top height, with virtually no lateral control, the next bend in the river a mere second away, which was long before he could bring his elevators into play, he ploughed straight into the jungle, cannons blazing furiously at nothing.

In the Cessna, moving along at a far slower speed, things did not appear to be happening at such a furious pace. But the shock of the totally unexpected jarring collision which flung the Cessna's nose up into a near-stall situation just as all seemed well, was too much to take in, particularly when it was followed by the blazing tail pipe of the MiG shooting ahead of them, and exploding among the trees with a sensational display of pyrotechnics.

Anyone who learns to fly has instilled in them a healthy fear of a low, slow-speed-stall, until their reactions are instant and automatic. Harwood instinctively shoved the wheel forward, to bring the nose down, and slammed on power swearing at the top of his voice and shaking like a leaf. Ching-hua screamed and went into shock. The Cessna was now under control, of a sorts, but diving hard for the river. Again his trained reflexes came into action and with little room to spare, he flared out and struggled for height. But it was not to be.

Not only had the Cessna been ripped open, but the gash proceeded far enough forward to destroy the engine mounting, so that the engine was shaking the plane to pieces. Just at that moment a cloud chose to pass over the moon so that they were in virtual darkness.

'Oh, God, please let the landing lights work.' They did. At least he had a point of reference now. 'You okay, darling?' he shouted. No reply. Ching-hua was motionless staring straight ahead, eyes hooded.

He had no option but to ditch, and he didn't really know what the hell the river below them had to offer, but at least it was better than landing in tropical jungle. If his engine cut, the generator would stop and that meant no more landing lights.

'Got to go for it now,' he muttered, sweating heavily. He turned to Ching-hua. 'For Christ's sake, girl, get with it, you're going to need all you've got to get the hell out of this.' No reply. He twisted towards her and, keeping an eye on his progress, slapped her hard across her face with the back of his hand. She jerked her head away, her eyes wide open. At least she was out of the fog now. 'Sorry, darling, had to do it. Need you awake,' he shouted, wrestling with the soggy, yawing aircraft.

'What happened?'

'No time to explain now, we're going in.'

'Into the river?' she said in disbelief.

'Got it in one. It's safer than the trees.'

Ching-hua shook her head in resignation. 'I feel sick,' she exclaimed piteously.

'That makes two of us,' replied Harwood, feeling the fear rising in his own throat.

'Get your door open and jam a shoe in it,' ordered Harwood, awkwardly complying with his own instructions as the plane rattled and roared only a few feet above the surface.

Desperately he tried to recall ditching instructions. He glanced at the instrument panel. Speed seventy-five. Barely acceptable. Frantically he checked Ching-hua's harness. Tight. Good. Fuel off. Engine off. Touchdown with full flap, at stalled attitude. With the nose up he dragged the tail as far as he could. Zero flying speed. Bang. The belly came down hard. Water immediately rushed in.

He scrabbled for his harness release and, leaning over, undid Ching-hua's. With the plane's underside split open there was no question of slow immersion. In seconds the water was up to their necks and they were in darkness.

'Kick the door open and get the hell out. I can't help from here!' he shouted frantically.

Obediently Ching-hua turned and, placing both feet on the right-hand door, shoved it open with her feet. Harwood stayed in long enough to give her behind a helpful push, then, taking a deep breath just before the water covered him, he exited from his side and, struggling upwards, banged his head painfully on the high wing. Goddamn bitch of a plane, he thought, she's trying to take me with her.

Fear was replaced by anger and kicking hard he pulled himself round the leading edge. His lungs were practically exploding. Can't hold it any longer. Got to breathe. Sweet Jesus help me now, and then his face was in blessed air and he could see the moon above him. Frantically he twisted his head.

'Darling, darling,' he shouted. 'Where are you?'

Not a sign. Big gulp of air. Back down. Oh shit, I can't do this for long. Where the bloody hell is she? Back up to the top.

Then he saw her, a faint dark shape in the water, feet away, a feeble flailing of an arm. He came to her as fast as his exhausted body allowed.

He turned her on her back, putting his hand under her arms and over her breasts, and towed her backwards with her face above water. He headed out for what he thought was the nearest bank of the slow-moving river. It seemed an age before his feet touched a bottom of sorts. He staggered upright, and wearily dragged her inert body on to a stretch of soil or sand that seemed clear of the river.

Her eyes were closed. She was totally lifeless. 'Come on, my love, don't you die on me.' He turned her roughly on to her stomach, checked to see her tongue was clear, and pressed strongly and evenly on her back.

'Dear God, let her live.' He was almost sobbing now, breath rasping with effort. He redoubled his efforts groaning with the strain. There was a sudden coughing grunt and a rush of water from her mouth. He pushed again and was rewarded with another stream of water, then turned her on her side.

'Wake up,' he shouted, giving her cheek a resounding slap. Oh, Christ, he thought, that's twice I've had to hit her in the last few minutes.

She opened her eyes and turned to him, a puzzled expression on her face, then as if answering her own query said, 'I drowned and you saved me.' She put her hand to his cheek. 'I died and you brought me back.'

He bent over her, tears of relief now falling without check. They lay down exhausted and fell asleep in each other's arms.

* * *

Ching-hua woke first. Her eyes opened to bright sunlight. She turned and saw Harwood. A great wave of love filled

127

her breast. She turned over and put her lips on his. He blinked sleepily and, rising on one elbow, pulled her body against himself. Then without warning, in one violent movement, he flung her away and leaped to his feet. She was so shattered she lay there incredulous. And then she saw.

At the water's edge was the long, grinning snout of a crocodile. Harwood pulled her up and held her tightly, his eyes intent upon the hideous creature. The crocodile returned his gaze and slowly stirred its tail.

They were on a small sand bar, in the middle of the river, about 100 feet from the nearest river bank. Harwood took his revolver from its holster at his belt. He opened it up and spun the chamber. He'd only used one shot on Peng Keong. The question was whether or not it would fire after the soaking it had undergone. He aimed at the crocodile's eye and pulled the trigger. Nothing.

'Shit. It could take hours to dry out,' he exclaimed.

'So we wait,' said Ching-hua philosophically.

'What do we do if that bugger comes after us before it's dry?'

'It would do that?' asked Ching-hua tremulously.

'It certainly would, and it moves a sight quicker than you might imagine.'

She held his arm tightly. 'Let's move away from it,' she suggested.

They walked the length of the sand. The crocodile swam alongside them in a companionable fashion. Harwood bent over, picked up a stone and flung it, striking the crocodile on its back. To their relief, it swung away and submerged.

They reached the end of the sand bar and turned round, preparatory to walking back. The crocodile had crawled up on to the other end and was sauntering towards them in a contemplative manner.

'You son of a bitch,' shouted Harwood. He picked up another pebble, let fly and missed.

The reptile never hesitated, continuing to waddle forward. Only a bullet could stop it now and that would have to be well-placed. Harwood shut the chamber of his pistol, aimed, and pulled the trigger. A useless click. His bowels turned to water.

'There's no option now but to swim for it,' he said. She was trembling. 'You go first,' he commanded. 'I'll keep the bastard occupied as best I can.'

'No we'll go together.'

'Just do as I say, okay? He pushed her gently to the water. 'When I run at him you go without any hesitation.' Somehow he raised a smile. 'Now,' he shouted, giving her a firm shove, then, scooping up a handful of sand, he ran straight at his enemy, yelling at the top of his voice. He did not look back.

For a moment the brute seemed to hesitate, then continued implacably toward him. At the last second Harwood flung his handful of grit and jumped for his life, clear over its gaping upturned jaws. The crocodile instinctively turned to face the other direction. Its tail, thrashing violently, nearly struck his leg, missing by inches. At least there seemed to be no question of it going after Ching-hua now. He risked a quick look to check her progress. She was well over half-way.

'Come on, you son of a bitch,' he shouted, shuffling backwards from the thoroughly enraged reptile. It needed no invitation and moved after him in a shambling trot. 'Bloody hell.'

He turned to sprint away and its mate was standing in his path. It didn't need to do anything: just had to wait for its dinner to be driven into its jaws. Harwood looked at the river. He'd never make it. They would catch him in the first few feet. He stood there feeling bloody hopeless, but at least Ching-hua had made it. She was on the bank now. Waving and pointing. At what? In the only direction he hadn't looked. In the direction where there were neither crocodiles nor Ching-hua.

He glanced over his shoulder. It was only a small dugout, but it was the most luxurious thing in the world as far as he was concerned, and the Meo tribesman paddling it was a very brave man, as one sweep of a croc's tale could have smashed it to pieces. The little tribesman was waving Harwood urgently towards his rescue craft. Harwood needed no urging at all. In his mad scramble to board, he nearly turned it over but just got away with it and collapsed in the bottom, retching with relief.

By the time he reached Ching-hua she had been joined by a Thai border patrol who had heard the MiG doing its noisy stuff, and had come as quickly as possible to find out what the hell was going on. Harwood's protestations that he had simply lost his way were met with well-merited cynicism. Finally he saw no option but to bring the CIA into the act.

* * *

Al, as he put it himself, was really 'pissed' with developments. He wasn't worried about Peng Keong's demise but he was infuriated when it finally dawned that Levinsky had neither been brought back nor disposed of. The veneer of camaraderie and gallantry completely disappeared.

'Goddammit! All you have achieved is to kill one of your own, destroy a fuckin' CIA aircraft, create an international incident by bringing down a fuckin' Chinese MiG, thus drawing a great deal of unwanted attention to our operation, and to cap it all you have completely ignored the whole reason of the exercise.' The false grin had changed into a very genuine snarl, and even Hank was wincing at some of the language being used.

'I think,' commented Harwood to Ching-hua, 'if this foul-mouthed coolie is going to continue in this way it might be best if you left.'

Ching-hua laughed. 'I can assure you that a real coolie's language makes him sound like a schoolgirl.'

Al became almost apoplectic with rage and stuttered to a halt, mouth open, literally gasping for air.

Harwood turned to the other American. 'We are going to our room now because we are extremely tired. I suggest you call us in about seven hours when we will consider discussing the matter further, provided you are in a more receptive

130

state and allow me to tell you exactly what happened and how I arrived at the decision I did.'

Taking Ching-hua by the elbow he exited with some dignity. Al said nothing. Hank merely nodded dumbly.

The second meeting passed more successfully. Harwood explained how he either had to believe Levinsky's claim that there were other Chinese scientists who could complete the project, in which case abducting him would be useless, or persuade him to destroy the site by threatening to kill his son if he did not co-operate.

'So,' concluded Harwood, 'we wait and see, and if in ten to fourteen days nothing happens, we send him his son's hand in a box and ask him to think again.'

'You arranged that?' asked Al incredulously.

'Sure, why not?' replied Harwood straight-faced. Ching-hua nodded her head in silent affirmation.

'Son of a bitch,' said Al, impressed.

'Well then we'll be back in touch in a couple of weeks,' said Harwood briskly, 'and if I guessed wrong you can tear all sorts of strips off me, but if I'm right you kiss ass. Okay?'

'Hold it, hold it,' roared Al wrathfully. 'You're not goin' anywhere without me knowin' where!'

'Go to hell, Al. You'll undoubtedly put a tail on us, which is alright by me if he doesn't annoy us. If he does I'll probably break his leg, and remember I've plenty of motivation for keeping in touch. Summervill tells me there are five million of them.'

He started towards the door and stopped on an after-thought. 'By the way, I leave you to put Summervill in the picture, and for your and his information I have sent a letter to my tame advocate in Switzerland, in which I have outlined the details of this little operation, including the likely destruction of the Laser installation. Should you or Summervill try to screw us in any way then the truth gets disseminated world-wide. Should make some great headlines!' He turned away. 'Goodbye for now, and to make matters easier for you, we're off to Phuket first thing tomorrow.'

On the internal flight from Chiang Mai they got slightly tipsy on champagne, held hands and tried to unwind from the tension they had gone through the previous two days.

'Now,' said Harwood, 'I suppose we've got to wait in dreadful anticipation as to whether or not I'm going to be able to retire on my ill-gotten gains or run like hell from the long arm of Chinese extradition.'

Ching-hua put her head on his shoulder. 'Please, for a few days, let's think only of each other,' she pleaded.

2nd October 1989 – 6.30 a.m.

As Levinsky took one last look at his son and turned away, he railed bitterly against the fates that had placed him in such a situation. By triumphing in the thought that he had the murdering Limey bastard in checkmate, he had crowed too much at his cleverness and been hoisted on his own petard. All that was left now was the comfort that if things went right he'd be able to save his son's life and that of his wife, though the whole scene would be tricky, to put it mildly.

Explaining matters to his son – at least they'd allowed him that – had been hell. 'I'm afraid I'm in deep, irreversible trouble, with no way out. With a whole skin that is.'

The boy had looked at his father with eyes so full of sadness that the older man had to turn away for a second before going on.

'If I were to go with them,' he'd continued, looking sideways at Harwood, 'they'd probably put me in jail for the rest of my natural life, which I couldn't stand. If I destroy the project so the incident can be traced to me, the Chinese will put me up against a wall and shoot me, and probably your mother as well.'

Jacob's eyes had begun to spill over at that. Poor kid, thought Levinsky, hugging him, and none of it's his fault either.

'So listen, Jake, I have only one aim left and that's to

132

ensure you and your mother are okay, and get taken good care of by the authorities. I'm going to self-destruct the whole damn thing, which would only be accepted as a genuine accident by the big boys in Beijing if all the workers and scientists on the site go in one dramatic burst of light energy. That includes Professor Chung, and also me, together with all the other scientists, so no one is left to split on me. Okay?'

'I will have to tell your mother what has happened. She will, I am sure, be brave, and when I have done this terrible thing you will be returned safely to her and you must never mention this to anyone. You must wipe it from your mind and give your mother strength to carry on. Do you understand all I am telling you?'

Jacob had nodded his head, swallowing convulsively, and given him one last embrace. Levinsky's eyes were so full of tears as he stumbled down the hill that he could hardly see. They'd taken his son away with a rope around his waist. His own son, and how in God's name would he tell his wife?

* * *

She didn't weep. She looked at him wide-eyed, mouth trembling, the pulse at her temple beating furiously.

He tried to explain it to her just as he had to their son but she was uncomprehending, totally shocked, or was it that she had shut out reality, was unwilling to accept? He explained again. How if she and the boy were to be alright, he could only do it by killing himself, along with everyone else on the project.

She did not react. Merely stared at nothing.

He told her he loved her. He told her of his gratitude for the happy years she had given him and how he wished they could go on for ever. But such earthly happiness cannot be eternal and must be paid for. There's the Jewishness in me coming out again, he thought.

She put out a slim finger to touch his lips and hush the babble, shaking her head as if to admonish a recalcitrant

133

child. 'This cannot be happening,' she said, and demanded he confirm it to be a nightmare.

He shook his head from side to side and a great, tearing sob rasped from her distorted, open mouth as if her face were the mask of tragedy itself. Then the dreadful anguish burst over them both and they rocked in mutual pain in each other's arms. Comfort from closeness was the only balm, shutting out the world.

Today is all I have left, he told himself. Tomorrow I cannot afford to grieve for myself. I must plan. Plan to kill my colleagues. All of them. At least all those with scientific responsibilities. It will be done so quickly that they will undergo no conscious pain. Nevertheless it is a terrible thing.

* * *

'Yes, Professor Chung, I insist we call for another full-scale dress rehearsal with everyone, I repeat, everyone on site before we do another test shoot.'

The Professor blinked at Levinsky's insistence, which, uncharacteristically, was close to the point of rudeness.

Why is the old dodderer prevaricating, Levinsky thought. Is he looking at me like that seeking to identify some sinister intention on my part? Stop it, man, he told himself. You've just got so much guilt over this thing you're becoming paranoid. Better ease up a bit.

'Do you really require yet another full-scale test? Why should you think it is necessary?'

'Because I'm a perfectionist, old friend, as you well know.'

Levinsky put out his hand, laid it gently on the smaller man's shoulder. 'I want you to run right through the whole works. Test the power generation, the energy take-off from the electron bombardment of the magnetic field, the precise frequency of the beam, the variation of the reflector mirrors. I don't need to give you all the details, you know them as well as me.'

The Professor sucked through his teeth. 'When do you

wish this? I have to go to Beijing for ten days from tomorrow.'

Levinsky frowned. The Chinese saw his dissatisfaction and looked hard him again.

'Oh alright,' sighed Chung. 'I'll see what I can do to delay the Beijing trip till after the test-run. It'll give me something to talk about when I do go.'

It'll also hasten his death, poor old bugger, thought Levinsky. Aloud he said, 'Very good, professor. I do appreciate your co-operation. I'll take it you can delay the Beijing visit and I'll set up the test-run for three days from now.'

Again the quizzical expression from the old man, the searching question cloaked by a gentle smile.

Levinsky began to sweat. Surreptitiously he wiped away the perspiration with a finger but his colleague noticed it.

He looked concerned. 'You have fever?'

'No, professor, I don't think so. It's just a bit hot in here.'

Chung looked around as if seeking for the source of the heat but let it pass. 'And your boy. He is well?'

'Oh, he's fine, very fit. Staying with friends in Mengwang at the moment. There's a girl.'

They both chuckled at this perfectly normal statement as if it was very funny that a young man should have a girl. The American wondered why the sudden switch in conversation. Nothing further was said, however, and as Chung moved away he began to relax a trifle, then felt sick thinking of what was to happen.

* * *

Everything had been arranged for tomorrow. Today was to be his last day on earth. Tonight was the last night he would hold his beloved in his arms. Trying to act normally was an almost insurmountable task for him. Everyone commented on how drawn and preoccupied he looked. Chung, full of smiles, thought he was pandering to the American's idiosyncrasies, when he told him that the bosses would allow him to put back his visit to carry out the tests.

He genuinely likes me, thought Levinsky sadly, and I him. Committing premeditated murder on a grand scale like this, especially of one's friends and colleagues, is soul-searing but one's own must come first, surely? If they do not, such an act could not be justified.

If it meant simply killing himself to escape this dilemma he would have done it, but he knew it would not help his family. It would merely emphasise his guilt and ensure their persecution.

I know what I am, Levinsky reasoned, I'm just a bloody gene machine. I'd destroy everyone and anything to ensure the continuance of my line. It is human nature and I cannot escape it or rise above it. I could sacrifice Jacob. That would be the simplest way – one life only and not my own, but I'm no Abraham nor is my son Isaac.

Last night he had mentioned it casually, as an alternative, to Mei Ling. He covered up the suggestion with a half-groan as if he truly realised it was impossible, but the coward in him was begging her to jump at it, begging her to say: 'I need you more than life itself. I love Jacob but I love you more and I am still young enough to have another son.' He was looking at her from the corner of his eye as he half-whispered the idea, and saw the look of amazed shock on her face. There was absolutely no question of who held priority in her mind, and it wasn't her husband. Understandable but hurtful nevertheless.

He'd followed up by making it abundantly clear that it was out of the question. Something rejected before it was really considered, but since then he'd caught the glimpse of suspicion in her eyes: the expression, albeit fleeting, of someone who mistrusts one. Now he felt he did not even have the total love of his woman. It really was too bad that she would not completely believe in him until he was dead.

To retain a semblance of sanity throughout his misery, he continued to run in the mornings. But without company his strides shortened, the spring had left his feet and he felt as if he were dragging a lead weight behind him.

Half-way round one morning he was stopped by a Chinese

who was almost obsequiously polite. He said he had been instructed to ask when it was going to happen. He professed a total lack of knowledge about 'it', so Levinsky simply told him tersely that tomorrow was the day and asked him how his son was. The Chinese looked blank and could not help. How very cruel. Just a word that Jacob was alright would have brought him happiness of a sort. Then, as he entered the compound, the security guard, Mr Won, asked him to enter his hut. There he handed over a note, heavily sealed, which had Levinsky's name on it in Chinese. Won said a friend of Jacob's, the one in Mengwang where Jacob was supposed to be staying, had handed it in. He'd looked at Levinsky in a knowing way that had a touch of sympathy about it, as if he were obviously aware of more than he let on.

The American thanked him, took it with a trembling hand and raced home before opening it. The note was dated that day, the ninth. It was in Jacob's handwriting. 'Dearest parents, I am fine. I hope to be back before the deadline allowed which is the twelfth, as I have to do some studying in preparation for the next term. Love you both. Jake.'

So the message, obviously dictated to him, was clear. The deed had to be done by the twelfth. He was aiming for the tenth so there were two days' grace. At least he knew his boy was safe and could not blame him for the apparent triviality of the message.

He called for Mei Ling. She read the note without comment, then begged forgiveness for letting her husband go to his death in their son's place. He supposed it was her way of saying that she no longer doubted him, which was a relief, but there was no question of any suggested last-minute reprieve on her part.

* * *

He thought his impending death would have killed any sexual desire on his part and only went to bed at the usual hour on the last night as he needed some sleep, if such a thing were possible, so as to be on the ball for the final act. But Mei Ling was obviously determined to make his last night a memorable one, for as long as his memory was to exist, that is.

She insisted he close his eyes and relax as best he could and abandon himself to her caresses so as to feel the rising fever of lust pulsing within him for the last time. Determined in her wish to please, she bent over him, her hair asweep, her lips and tongue playing about him until he trembled with uncontrollable excitement, desperate for fulfilment, everything but the immediate need for her swept from his mind.

'For this I should die every day,' he said afterwards, trying to inject some black humour into the scenario, but it only made her cry. So he started to weep as well, and they fell asleep sobbing in each other's arms.

Professor Chung came into the air-conditioned complex a few minutes after Levinsky had arrived at dawn. He looked around and rubbed his hands briskly. 'You know I love all this, Stefan.' His gestures took in all the intricate equipment of the power generators and beam-convergence systems surrounding him, and at the centre of the technological marvel the master-control-panel at which Stefan sat, already tuning in various circuitry. 'And,' continued the professor cheerfully, 'the wonderful thing is it's all designed by you and crafted by Chinese engineers. I am proud, and you, Stefan, must be very proud of what you have brought about.'

Levinsky gave him what he hoped was a smile but it obviously didn't impress the old gentleman.

'By the Gods, Stefan, you look as if you were at death's door. What's the matter with you? Family problems? Do you want to talk about them? Your well-being is most important to us and if there is anything I can do to help I most certainly will.' He bent over and touched his friend's shoulder.' Is it something to do with your son, Stefan? I know he's staying with friends, but have you received bad news about him?'

The American began to sweat. What does the old devil know? he wondered. But the old man just sighed. 'Children are such a worry and he's reached that stage where he thinks, quite without foundation, that he can be independent. I know what it's like. My children were headstrong in just the same way. The scrapes I had to get them out of.'

Levinsky felt the tears pressing at his eyes.

'Why, my dear Stefan, without you around that family of yours would just collapse. I know Mei Ling is very good about the house but ... Oh dear, Stefan, my friend, are you so upset? You eyes are quite red.'

Levinsky turned away embarrassed looking for something to occupy himself.

'Please ignore the babblings of an old man. I do go on too much.'

'No, no,' Stefan replied, struggling for control. 'It's just, I really think I have a fever coming on after all. Haven't felt very well for days. Runny nose, eyes watering. You know.'

'Ah that would explain it,' beamed Chung. Delight in the fact that he had at least been given a reason for his friend's appearance overcame the sympathy he would have normally offered to a sick colleague. He moved away to his appointed place at the control-board and was soon immersed in initial calculations, checking the mobility of the reflector mirrors, which was his particular sphere of expertise.

By 7 a.m. the entire team was there. Levinsky did a hurried check. No one was missing. He didn't have to give instructions, merely set the procedure going; then the checks and countdown progressed by rote. Everyone was fully conversant with what they had to do.

Within minutes the beam was activated. One moment the convergence system was a lifeless piece of case-hardened steel and perspex. Then, as the unit went critical, the beam pulsed into life down the two-mile-long guidance conduit, its diameter decreasing to less than a millimetre as molecular concentration was applied, and instantaneously the destructive power increased by a shattering factor, in the millions, as the huge magnifying reflector mirrors caught it and hurled it out into space, at the required deflection to strike the target.

It was now that he had to do it. If he waited too long Chung would reduce output, considering the test complete, and the operation would cease. Levinsky had to get behind him and carry out the act while he was still holding the power at maximum destruction value.

The Chinese was completely immersed in his work, even humming gently to himself, with his right leg twitching involuntarily as was a habit of his. Levinsky got nearer to him as his right hand started to move toward the reduction switch and commence closure.

He said quite normally, 'Just a second, professor, I would like to check the reflector temperature before we run down, if you don't mind.'

Chung started. He had not realised his colleague was so close to him. Then he turned and made a gesture with his hand which told Stefan to help himself. So completely trusting, and why not? They were comrades after all.

Levinsky put the palm of his left hand upon Chung's shoulder, and in one smooth movement reached past him with the other hand and diametrically reversed the deflection control on the reflector mirrors.

'Goodbye, old friend.'

10

The CIA satellite passing 300 miles overhead faithfully recorded the deep gash in the earth's crust that denoted the almost surgical-like extinction of Levinsky's brilliant project. Within minutes the director at Langley was told.

He rubbed his hands. 'So for once the Limeys haven't fucked up,' he commented to his aide. 'Get Washington for me, and you tell Head of Station Thailand. Al somebody-or-other.'

The president was delighted and rang London. He was fulsome in his gratitude. The prime minister accepted his comments with cool grace.

'I hope,' she said, 'this will go some way to balancing our account.' A pause, then, just in case it wasn't clear: 'The Falklands, you recall.'

'Oh, ah yes, of course, ma'am.'

'Our special relationship is alive and well and is most precious to me,' she continued, knowing full well that she would obtain the most benefit from it by far.

'Me too,' the president hurriedly replied.

'Fine. Well, goodnight, George.' The phone went dead.

'Dammit, she's always doing that to me,' grumbled the president and went back to tying his black tie. He was off to a formal dinner, which would undoubtedly bore him to tears but the good news would buoy him up through the lengthy evening. After all it was OK for the good old USA to

141

have such things, but not a bunch of nut-cases in other countries.

The prime minister looked at her watch. It was after midnight. In Hong Kong it was 7.15 a.m. Within half an hour of the happening, the news had travelled round the world, and Summervill had been informed.

His initial reaction had been rage when Al had told him what Harwood had done immediately after his return from Mengwang. But Summervill was very methodical in his thought processes, and it didn't take him more than a few seconds, while Al was still on the phone in fact, to realise that Harwood had taken the only course open to him.

'I can see Mayo's problem,' he commented, 'so let's wait and find out how it goes before we condemn him.'

Al had chuckled. He knew how to set up a scapegoat as well as anyone.

Now, thought Summervill contentedly, he had been justified in sending in an amateur, and had accepted the Governor's congratulations for himself without even a mention of Harwood. Anyway, he hadn't particularly liked what Al had told him about Harwood's threat to tell the media if he didn't get his five million dollars. Cocky bastard. Pity that, he thought, but what the hell, he'd arranged for Langley to fork out ten million if the operation was a success. By God, it would make his budget look pretty good this year. Probably worth a CBE at least with all the kudos flying around for his department.

* * *

Harwood felt his shoulder being shaken in a tentative sort of way, and opened his eyes to peer sleepily at the black silhouette between himself and the sun.

'Sorry to disturb you, sir,' came the respectful American voice.

'I should think so too,' exclaimed Harwood irritably. 'You're supposed to be shadowing me, Columbo, not interfering with my sunbathing.'

'My name is Hislop, sir. Hiram Hislop.'

'Look, H.H., I don't give –'

Ching-hua put a restraining hand on his arm. 'Take it easy, darling. It's not his fault, and I think he's got a message for you.'

'Thank you ma'am,' and, turning to Harwood: 'This is for you, sir. Came by special messenger and I'm to wait for any reply you may wish to send.'

'Make or break time,' murmured Harwood, as he opened the envelope.

'Satellite pictures and radio confirmation from Hung advise installation totally erased. My personal congratulations and I take it all back. Summervill delighted and anxious you contact him. Warmest regards. Al.'

He turned to Ching-hua and, oblivious of his audience, gave her a long and passionate kiss. 'We've made it sweetheart,' he whispered in her ear. Reluctantly he let her go and got up from the sand. 'Please tell your masters, the message is received and understood. And tell Al I will present my posterior to him for osculation purposes in due course.'

The American looked at him and smirked. 'I'll be glad to do that, sir, and may I say I appreciate your quaint turn of phrase.'

'By God, Hiram, you're human after all.'

'Very much so, sir,' he grinned, gazing appreciatively at Ching-hua who looked particularly fetching in a minuscule bikini.

'Okay, Columbo, enough of that. On your way.'

'Yes, sir,' replied the CIA man, instantly serious. 'May I have the message back, please. For security reasons I intend to destroy it.'

'So what do we do now, Derek?' asked Ching-hua, as they watched Hislop walk away.

'We don't hurry back, that's for sure. We can really relax for a few days and, as for right now, I don't know about you but I'm feeling incredibly in love with you, and have an overwhelming urge to take you to bed for a very long time.'

'Funny you should say that.'

He had his face very close to hers. She smiled at him but her eyes were contemplative.

'I love you, dear hong mo kwai. I have already killed for you and I would die for you if needs be. Never forget that.'

Harwood put his arm about her and, as they walked back along the beach to their chalet in the bright glittering sunlight, the sea lapping and retreating about their feet, he suddenly shivered as if a clammy hand had grasped him by the back of the neck.

'What's the trouble, darling?' she asked worriedly, looking up at him.

'Nothing, my little poppet,' he grinned. 'It's just anticipation.'

Nevertheless, that evening he cleaned and checked his pistol with utmost care.

* * *

This is the life, thought Harwood, stretching out in his first-class seat on the Cathay Pacific Tristar. Being served by attractive stewardesses, eating great food with a glass of chilled champagne before you, and a gorgeous female companion beside you, is something to be commended.

Al's greeting at the American Embassy in Bangkok had been positively effusive. He had almost gambolled about them like a spring lamb in his anxiety to please. They had been wined and dined and transported wherever they wished to go by a chauffeur-driven, air-conditioned, Cadillac, and at Harwood's particular request Al had used his influence with the Thai authorities to turn a blind eye in respect of his handgun during the boarding procedure.

On the secure line from the embassy he had spoken to Summervill, who appeared as pleased as Summervill ever could be and required both their presences at the earliest opportunity so that a debriefing could be carried out. Also, there was much to discuss in relation to Harwood and Ching-hua's taking up new identities elsewhere.

144

'As quickly as possible,' concluded Summervill. 'Beijing are beginning to ask awkward questions as to your whereabouts and they won't be satisfied with our professing ignorance.'

'I understand.'

'Good, good. I'll arrange for you both to be met off the plane and brought here in one of our darkened cars. You know what I mean.'

'Yes I do. I've had the experience before.'

Summervill laughed shortly. 'Of course you have. Under somewhat less pleasant circumstances as I recall. You'll both be secure in our compound which is the main object of the exercise.'

'Anything else?' hinted Harwood.

'Ah yes, I nearly forgot,' said Summervill. 'There's the small question of money. Where you want it remitted and all that sort of thing.'

'Five million of it,' pressed Harwood.

'I'm fully aware of the amount promised,' Summervill snapped, 'and did you really write that letter to your Swiss lawyer?'

'You betcha,' said Harwood, 'but he'll never open it so long as he hears from me regularly that all's well.' The phone slammed down at the other end.

Ching-hua was gazing out of the plane's window at the Chinese coast, some fifty miles away. Harwood squeezed her hand and she turned to look at him. Her eyes were full of unshed tears.

'What is it, my darling?' he asked solicitously.

'I'm looking at my homeland for perhaps the last time and it upsets me, that's all.'

'I'll make it up to you, wherever we go. Anyway, in time things may change. The old men in Beijing can't last for ever.'

'Mr Mayo is there anything I can get either of you. More champagne? Coffee?' The Philippina stewardess was a pretty little thing and anxious to please.

'Why not, indeed,' said Harwood. 'Another glass of champagne would be very nice, thank you.'

145

'This is Captain Brady speaking. We have a minor problem.' The disembodied Australian voice suddenly demanded attention. 'We have to carry out a small diversion as the runway at Hong Kong is temporarily closed, due to a plane collapsing its undercarriage. Taipei is also closed in by weather and we are past the point of no return, which leaves –'

'Oh no. Dear God, no. Sweet Jesus, no. Please not that!' He was shouting. He knew it was coming. He rose to his feet to protest, to tell them no way. He saw Ching-hua's shocked face staring up at him. The stewardess approached him hands raised to calm him.

' – us with no option but to land temporarily at White Cloud International Airport at Canton.' The voice went on remorselessly. 'We will probably be there for less than an hour, if that, and it is unlikely, but possible, that Chinese customs and immigration will require to see your identification documents, so please hand them to the stewardess who will be coming round to collect them. We should be landing in about half an hour.' The voice ceased.

Harwood calmed himself but still stood towering over the stewardess. 'Please tell the captain I must speak to him. It is desperately important.'

The chief steward, a Chinese, came hurrying up to find out what the commotion was about. All the passengers in first-class were staring and whispering among themselves. Ching-hua sat hunched in a corner of her seat, which suddenly seemed far too big for her, looking like a school-girl who was lost.

The chief steward glanced at her then back at Harwood. Another few minutes of precious time had gone by. 'Would you please tell me why you wish to see the captain? Perhaps I can help. You see Captain Brady is in the middle of preparations for landing and cannot be disturbed.'

Harwood clenched his fists and struggled to control himself. The man was only doing his job. You can't have passengers bursting in on the captain at crucial moments. Harwood switched to Mandarin which in itself was sufficient to grab attention. Foreign devils don't speak Chinese, particularly perfect, fluent Chinese.

'The Captain must not land this plane at Canton, otherwise she,' – he nodded over his shoulder – 'will die. It's as simple as that and I really haven't got time to explain further.'

He saw the steward take a long look at Ching-hua. He raised his arms in exasperation and saw the shutters come down over the Chief Steward's face. Don't lose your temper with Chinese, he reminded himself; it gets you nowhere. 'There's a thousand dollars in it for you,' he muttered quietly.

The man's expression didn't change, but he moved to the flight-deck door. Over his shoulder he said, 'Wait there, sir.' He knocked.

The door was opened from the inside, and he entered, closing it carefully behind him. Within a minute he opened it and gestured Harwood toward him. 'Alright, you may go in, sir.'

The flight engineer shut the door behind him and went back to his dials. The co-pilot in the right-hand seat concentrated firmly on the job in hand. Captain Brady, a weathered-looking man of some fifty years, with a drawn, heavily lined face and bright blue eyes, was half-turned in his seat.

On the few occasions that Harwood had been up to the flight deck of a big passenger aircraft, it had always fascinated him. They were so incredibly complicated, compared with what he had ever experienced in light planes, that it induced in him a feeling of inferiority mixed with admiration for the men who could handle such equipment with apparent ease. Because of this it took him a second or two to collect his thoughts.

'How can I help?' the captain asked. 'My chief steward says he recognises the lady you're with. That she's a kind of heroine in some Chinese underground movement for democracy. Is that what this is all about?' He peered quizzically at Harwood.

147

Harwood allowed himself a slight sigh of relief. At least lengthy explanations were not called for. He nodded. 'If you land at White Cloud and there's an identity check, she's a goner. It's a simple as that.' He paused and shrugged. 'And me too, probably.'

The captain nodded. 'My chief steward was not so complimentary about you. Said you offered him a thousand bucks to see me.'

'I was desperate and I'm sure you can understand why.'

The captain took it all in and nodded again. 'So that's the bottom line, is it?' he asked.

'You could say that.'

Brady looked up at Harwood. 'I reckon I believe you, Mr Mayo.'

Harwood's heart leaped with hope.

'But I'll now give you my bottom line.'

Harwood lowered himself on to the jump seat without being asked. He knew bad news was coming and he felt sick with apprehension.

Brady looked pretty down in the mouth too. 'It's like this, Mr Mayo. Hong Kong's out for at least three hours or maybe more. I told a little white lie to the passengers back there. The runway's in a hell of a mess. Taiwan's out till maybe tomorrow. Manila's too far, and as I told you we are way past the point of no return, so Bangkok's out as well. There's nowhere else to go except China, Mr Mayo and I'm not taking any risks trying to make it to some other place with less than two hour's fuel left, and three hundred and fifty passengers on board.'

'Okay. Thanks for at least believing me, captain. Better leave you to get back to work.'

'I'm really sorry. You'll have to hope that the Chinese officials don't ask for any documents. They usually don't bother in circumstances like this.'

Harwood made to leave, then turned back. 'I've just had an idea. Is there anywhere on board where we could hide her?' he pleaded.

Brady shook his head. 'I can't play games like that, Mr

Mayo. You don't know the politics of everyone on this plane.' He splayed his hands. 'It only needs one informant to pass the word, then the whole crew end up in jail for harbouring an enemy of the state and the plane gets confiscated into the bargain. You were lucky that Mr Wong the steward is a sympathiser.'

'Yeah. I guess it's too much of a risk,' agreed Harwood unhappily.

'Well, it's certainly a risk I'm not prepared to take. I'm sure you understand.'

He turned back to his controls. 'Right, Mr Mayo, I really have to get on with it now.' To his co-pilot he said: 'I have control,' and reached for the control column. As the door closed behind him Harwood heard the second officer sing out: 'You have control, sir.'

Well at least I bloody well tried, he thought. He sat down beside Ching-hua and put his arm about her. From the look on his face she knew he hadn't got anywhere. 'I'm sorry, darling. The captain says there's no option. He explained it all to me and I'm afraid from his viewpoint he's right. He can't go anywhere else without putting everyone's life at risk.' He gave her a squeeze, desperate to try and comfort her. 'He says it's most unlikely they'll even bother to board us, let alone check our documents.'

'I understand,' she replied tonelessly.

'If they take you, darling, I'll insist on going with you,' he said.

'You'll do nothing of the sort,' she said, sitting up determinedly, as if she had come to a decision. 'In fact I will sit elsewhere. You know how these dedicated cadres hate Chinese girls mixing with foreign devils. It might provoke them to ask questions unnecessarily.'

'If they try anything with you I'll raise hell, I promise you,' he said angrily.

She pressed against his arm and took his hand firmly in hers. 'Darling man, I love you so very much, but if you try to do anything silly it will not help. It will make matters worse.' She looked at him determinedly. 'We will act as if we do not

149

know each other,' she declared firmly. 'If they take me you will say nothing. You will not even look upset. I will do the same if they want you to leave with them. One of us outside can do more to help the other than both of us inside. Promise me you will be sensible.'

The brightness of her courage made him come close to tears. Come on Harwood get a grip on yourself, he told himself. If she can behave like this so can you. 'What a wonderful woman you are,' he said. 'Whatever happens we'll get together. My life on it.'

She kissed him, and repeated, 'You'll be sensible then?'

'Yes,' he promised.

She got up to go to a vacant seat further up the cabin. 'I love you,' she whispered as she left. Harwood couldn't trust himself to speak.

The plane rumbled gently to its allocated parking area, past a row of workman-like MiG 19s. From the window he saw a set of steps being brought to the rear door. So someone was going to board after all.

As the door opened, a rush of warmth came up the length of the plane, and with it the stink of burnt aviation fuel and hot metal common to all airports. He forced himself to refrain from turning to look. Any sign of curiosity inevitably draws attention to oneself. But on the other hand to disregard completely the presence of officialdom could be akin to an insult. He decided to merely raise his head, as whoever it was, passed on their way to the flight deck. Perhaps a nod might be in order.

Ching-hua was sitting two seats up in front of him. He was confident of her ability to maintain a calm demeanour, more so than himself in fact. An unpleasant thought struck him. All this time he'd been worrying about her, believing in the protection of his false passport, as far as he was concerned. What about me? he suddenly thought. I've been in and out of China tens of times, and come up against literally scores of customs and immigration officers. What if one of them recognises me? Feeling doubly vulnerable now, he scrunched down into his seat and held his newspaper before him. The fellow will probably walk past without even glancing around him, he told himself. Stop worrying.

The stewardess was coming out of the flight-deck door, walking down the plane, looking past where he was sitting. She stopped right by him, in her hand the documents and passports of the first-class passengers. Harwood looked up. The Chinese customs man was standing beside his seat. The stewardess offered the passports.

Silly bitch, he thought. He hadn't even asked for them yet. Why, why? Harwood held his breath.

The official shook his head and brushed past her to go to the flight deck, so that the stewardess almost backed on to Harwood and then turned and followed him.

For Christ's sake don't press the damned documents on the bloody man, thought Harwood angrily. He craned into the aisle and watched anxiously.

A voice above and behind him said: 'Excuse plis.' He had stuck his head and shoulder out so far into the aisle he was impeding a second customs officer. He looked up at the man's face and his mouth dropped open. It was the senior official who had saved him at the Luohu customs point before his ill-fated Beijing trip. On that occasion he had asked Harwood for the password and treated him as an old acquaintance, even though they had never met. This time the only recognition was the slightest frown of warning.

If he wants to play it that way, it's OK by me, thought Harwood, moving hurriedly back into his seat. Surely it would be alright now. At least one of them was an ally, but they seem to be taking a long time. What the hell are they all doing in there?

He looked at his watch. They'd been nearly 15 minutes already. The flight deck door opened and the captain came out. With him were the two Chinese, and behind them was the stewardess with the passports.

The captain gave Harwood a quick wink as he passed. Everything must be OK, he thought. He shrivelled with

151

relief like a deflated balloon. The stewardess started to hand back people's documents.

The two Chinese had stopped further down the cabin and were talking to each other in Mandarin. Harwood gathered that there had been a difference of opinion between them. The first on board had wanted to take away the documents to scrutinise them more carefully in the airport office. The second and more senior had over-ruled him, had said it was unnecessary. Harwood could still hear them in sharp dispute as they trailed off to the exit and left the plane. Ching-hua looked at him over the back of her seat. She was smiling, but she stayed in the same place, obviously not prepared to move back until they were in the air. The two Chinese left. The door closed and the steps were taken away.

Captain Brady walked back toward the flight deck. As he passed Harwood he put his thumb and forefinger together, as if to say: 'Everything's okay.' The stewardess bustled about producing drinks and food in the age-old custom of airlines throughout the world. If you have bored, upset, irritated, angry passengers, shove some food and drink down their throats.

They waited another hour and then the captain came back on the intercom. 'I'm pleased to tell you that Hong Kong will be ready to accept us in half an hour, and we should be taking off in ten minutes or so.'

Harwood rose and moved forward to where Ching-hua was sitting. He leaned over her. 'Seems alright now, darling, but boy was I worried for a moment or two. That second customs man was one of your lot. He got me out of trouble at Luohu, last time I crossed the border. He seems to have helped again. Do you know him?'

She frowned, then shook her head. 'He smiled at me, but I don't remember his face.'

'He was probably just trying to get off with you,' grinned Harwood. 'Anyway it doesn't matter now, does it?' He touched her arm. 'Would you join me, miss?'

At that moment the stewardess came up to him. 'Captain

Brady has invited you to sit in the jump-seat for the short flight to Hong Kong. Will you join him?'

He turned to Ching-hua. 'Okay?'

'Of course, darling. Off you go.'

He moved quickly on to the flight deck, enthusiastic at the prospect of seeing professionals in action.

'Come on in,' said Brady in welcoming fashion. 'Get behind me and buckle up.'

'Thanks,' said Harwood. 'This is great.'

The Tristar started to trundle down the taxi-way. A few minutes later she was ready at the holding point, waiting to proceed on to the runway proper. Brady twisted round in his seat and gave Harwood the thumbs up sign. 'Looking good,' he said, and smiled.

With a short burst of power from the starboard engine, they moved in an arc on to the runway proper and ended up at the threshhold, waiting for final take-off clearance. Brady's hand went to the throttles, and then he seemed to change his mind. Harwood saw him reduce power instead of applying it. There were a few seconds' voluble interchange on the radio, which Harwood was not a party to.

Brady turned to him, pulled a face, then switched over to the cabin tannoy system. 'I regret to inform you,' he intoned, 'that there appears to be some problem with the authorities. I have been instructed to return up the taxi-way and hold take off until the situation is clarified.'

'Just take off now,' said Harwood. It was said in such a controlled tone of voice that Captain Brady was inclined to ignore him. 'Now!' demanded Harwood, taking out his gun and jabbing it hard into the captain's ribs.

'You're a nut-case, Mayo,' protested Brady. 'For Christ's sake, I can't possibly take off without official permission.'

'Tell 'em you've been hijacked. I'm sure they'll understand,' said Harwood, cynically. 'But make sure you're off the ground before you do. I don't want some fool driving a truck in front of us.'

Brady hesitated.

153

'Goddamn it, now!' yelled Harwood. 'Or I'll shoot your co-pilot.'

'Oh shit,' breathed Brady.

'Exactly,' said Harwood, 'and tell that idiot flight engineer of yours not to try and be a hero or he'll get badly hurt.'

The worthy in question relaxed back in his seat, where he'd been half-poised for a go at Harwood. Brady argued no more. With his first officer in attendance, they pushed on full power and went straight into their take-off run.

As the wheels came up, Harwood said: 'Give me a pen and paper.' The first officer complied. Harwood wrote on it and handed it to Brady. 'Get the tower in Hong Kong to patch me through to that number and give me a head set. Chop-chop.' It only took seconds to comply. He heard Summervill's furious voice.

'What the hell's going on?'

'This is Pam.'

'I know it's bloody Pam, for fuck's sake.'

'Shut up, Map, for once in your life, and listen.'

There was silence.

'Good. You said dire straits. Well they couldn't be direr, I assure you. Can I talk?'

'Yes, we have a scrambler on to your transmission.'

Harwood told him the tale.

'Okay, Pam, I read you. You'll be met on the runway.' Summervill seemed calmer now. 'If you're not shot down *en route*, of course.'

They landed in one piece at Kaitak airport. The Chinese were nowhere near scrambling anything in the few minutes it took them to get to Kaitak, but they certainly raised political Cain with London, who in turn requested Hong Kong to give an immediate explanation and demanded to know what was to be done. Harwood couldn't be allowed to get away with this, not demonstrably, anyway, because in point of fact there was no doubt that Harwood had the whole boiling lot of them by the short hairs. Oh no, the matter must most certainly not enter the public domain.

The dovecotes in Washington, Whitehall and Hong Kong were all dramatically aflutter.

The problem was how to satisfy the Chinese that the perpetrator of this hijacking, a crime which the West abhorred, be punished to the full extremity of the law. But how to do it without dropping officialdom right in it?

Harwood, from being a hero, on the quiet that is, became an instant public pariah. Again.

11

At Harwood's first interview with Summervill the latter was at his gloomiest.

'It's a bloody mess. We can't use Ching-hua again now. If this hadn't happened we could undoubtedly have got some more mileage out of her.' Then as an afterthought. 'And you too.' He groaned and put his head in his hands.

'Beijing are raising all sorts of hell. Relations with them have deteriorated significantly. They want your head on a platter and if they don't get it London will be held up to the world as supporters of terrorism.' He gesticulated in a helpless fashion. 'And the whole damn baby's been dropped in my lap.' He looked slyly at Harwood. 'You know, Harwood, in a worst-case-scenario it could almost be said that the operation was not a success after all.'

Harwood seethed. His self control had even amazed himself, but this was too much. 'Don't try and pull that one, you perfidious bastard. I did what you sent me to do with complete success and you know it.' A pause. 'After all, you cheerfully took all the credit, I'll be bound.'

Summervill, touched on the raw, interrupted angrily. 'Now listen here, you.'

'No, you listen to me. If you try to renege on paying what I am owed, or if anything unpleasant happens to Ching-hua or me, then the whole bloody world is going to hear about Mengwang from the horse's mouth and this little hijack episode will be as nothing compared with what would happen then.'

156

'My dear chap, I wouldn't dream...'

'Oh yes you would, you shit. If you thought you could get away with it.' Harwood drew breath and then started up again before Summervill could get his oar in. 'I can tell you, Summervill, I didn't spend my whole time in Phuket revelling in the joys of sun and fornication. I did some thinking too and a great deal of it was in my own interests, so stop prevaricating and get down to business. My business.' He handed over a piece of paper. 'On this is the address and my account number to which you are to send my five million US dollars. It's a Swiss account, naturally, and if they don't confirm receipt to me within ten days, the balloon goes up. Understood?'

Summervill looked at Harwood and decided to play it carefully. The bloody man could be a real stirrer. 'I read you loud and clear, Harwood, and fully appreciate your viewpoint. Thy will be done, dear fellow.'

Harwood sat back. 'Now what do you intend to do about getting Ching-hua and me away from here?'

'Ching-hua is no problem,' said Summervill quickly. 'We can't hold her for any reason. In fact I intend to see that she gets some protection until you both decide where she is to go.' He shook his head. 'She's okay. It's you we have to think about.'

Summervill cleared his throat. It was clear he was thinking in overdrive. 'Obviously we can't just let you go, can we?' His voice took on an almost entreating tone.

Harwood kept quiet, deliberately not helping.

'We'll have to trot you into court for effect – '

'No way!' said Harwood firmly.

Summervill took no notice of him but continued with his voice raised somewhat: ' – and arrange for you to get ten years or so.' He gabbled off the last bit in a rush to get the message home.

'Go to hell!' exclaimed Harwood, rising from his chair. 'And you certainly will when the shit hits the fan as a result of my attorney giving all the details to the newspapers and TV.'

157

Summervill could take no more. 'If you don't belt up and listen, Harwood, I will see to it that you get life with hard labour and to hell with the consequences, no matter how bloody they might be for me.'

It was said with such cold menace that Harwood sat down again. Summervill definitely seemed to mean what he said. A few seconds went by.

'Okay,' said Harwood. 'I'm listening.'

'About bloody time,' growled the other man.

'Now, as I said, we'll get you sentenced for ten years. You'll be transported back to England, ostensibly to do your time.'

'Ostensibly?'

'Quite.'

'And?'

'Then the foreign office and MI5 will co-operate to create a behind-the-scenes situation that will satisfy our Chinese friends, so you can be released without a stain upon your character, in a very short time.'

'And with my five million dollars in a Swiss account?'

Summervill nodded.

'Sounds very easy.' Harwood bit his lip. 'Too bloody easy, in fact. What's a very short time and what's the catch?'

Summervill leaned forward persuasively. 'My dear fellow, a very short time means just that. Perhaps weeks, and these sorts of things are done all the time between powers of different persuasions. Let me explain a possible scenario in more detail, and for God's sake allow me to continue without interruption. Yes?'

Harwood nodded in acquiescence.

London, December 1989

Abdullah bin Faisal el Saud sat in his high-security prison cell in Wandsworth, where he had been for the last two years, and cursed the bad luck and the treachery that had put him there, as he had every day since he'd been put away.

158

The airport security guard uniform his organisation had supplied him, together with an identity label showing him as Jawal Pillai – some Indians are not unlike Arabs in appearance – had got him through all the problem areas, until he was standing, apparently alone, under the wings of the El Al 747 in the huge service hangar.

In his standard mobile telephone was a timer and enough Semtex to blow a hole in the comparatively thin skin of the machine. At 40,000 feet, rapid decompression would do the rest in a split second.

He had peered round him, and to emphasise his official capacity, should someone see him, moved a flashlight about, inspecting the area beneath the plane. Strangely, there were no Israeli guards around. They, of all people, were fanatical about security. Still, there was no point in looking a gift horse in the mouth.

He had to find his way into the plane where he would remove a panel inside a baggage locker with a minimum of fuss, and place his portable phone behind it. He had practised the exercise many times. Then it would be away to await the resulting explosion, which would be broadcast worldwide, and to receive the plaudits of his fellow conspirators and perhaps to be received by the colonel himself.

He had been able to see that the portable steps were in place and the cabin door was invitingly open. He had moved tentatively towards it, then stopped. He was sweating mildly; an acrid sweat, that betokened a mixture of fear and suspicion. He had expected to come across Israeli security personnel, and was well prepared. Attached to his flashlight was a twin-barrel cyanide gun. When fired in the faces of unsuspecting men, who would, by virtue of his uniform, look upon him as a colleague, the gas would incapacitate them in seconds.

He had moved forward. There was no option but to carry on. He would never get a chance like this again. Abdullah had placed a foot upon the bottom of the portable steps. Very carefully he moved up one step at a time as if each were a potential minefield.

Half-way up, all hell was let lose. Three brilliant spotlights blazed on, concentrating upon him, and at the same time the steps moved backwards away from the plane, so that he was poised helplessly in mid-air, blinded and immobile as a rabbit caught in car headlights.

An impossibly powerful loud hailer assailed his ears in Arabic. 'Abdullah bin Faisal,' it boomed. 'Put your flashlight and mobile phone on the step where you are standing, and come down with your hands raised. Three marksmen have you in their sights.'

How the hell had they known his name? he'd asked himself, and at the same time he knew the answer. He had been betrayed by one of his own for money. Probably a very large sum of money indeed.

Despite protestations from his government he had been found guilty of terrorism and sentenced to ten years. After all he couldn't really expect to get away with it. When one is caught with a time-bomb and a cyanide gun, as well as a totally false identity tag, in a sensitive area, there isn't much of a defence. He was lucky it was the British authorities who had taken matters into their hands. The Israelis would have shot him without hesitation.

There was a rattle of keys and his cell door swung open. He looked up without interest, used to such intrusions after so long in this soul-destroying environment.

This visitor was different. He was an Arab, dressed in Western clothing and of extremely haughty mien, but Abdullah was not impressed until the man opened his mouth.

'Our great leader who values your services to the mother-land has seen fit to arrange for your release. You will come with me and be placed upon a flight for Tripoli.' No more had to be said.

Abdullah went, expressing undying loyalty to the colonel who had taken him from the claws of the infidel, and vowed not to rest until he had tracked down and taken vengeance on the man who had committed the act of treachery that had caused him to go to prison.

The colonel was not deserving of such homage, for it was really the Chinese government that had engineered the process, or, one might even say, it had been initiated by the British, in the usual devious way that such things are done. Whitehall had, without expressing their wishes directly, intimated that they would appreciate being able to release Harwood from his prison in England without the Chinese government raising an embarrassing clamour. Might there be some means of negotiating such a matter?

As there were no actual Chinese citizens incarcerated in British prisons who were of any immediate value to their homeland, there could be no question of an exchange as per the usual Check Point Charlie routine.

Beijing pondered the possibilities. They had a very significant weapons manufacturing potential and were always on the look-out for overseas customers to provide them with the orders and the foreign currency their resurgent economy required.

For some years now they had been trying to get the Libyan colonel to purchase Chinese-made air-to-ground missiles without success. Their product was good and the price was right, but the colonel's purchasing authority was a relative, and, being firmly in the pocket of the French, either by corruption or blackmail or both, the gentleman in question had 'Exocet' indelibly stamped on all his order forms. Only the colonel could over-rule him, and the colonel didn't like being pressured in any way. Tempted maybe, but not pushed.

Then some ingenious cadre in Beijing, who had been informed of the problem with regard to Harwood, made a suggestion: a very good suggestion, which found favour in all quarters.

It was well known that various Arab terrorists were held in the United Kingdom on indisputable charges, and foremost among these was Abdullah bin Faisal el Saud. A man of considerable courage, if not cunning. If the British could be persuaded to release Abdullah in a low-profile way, and the colonel was made aware of the Chinese part in the affair,

161

then perhaps he might show his gratitude by over-riding his cousin and insisting on the purchase of, say, one hundred missiles made in China? At four million dollars apiece that would be a tidy sum in the republic's coffers. And so it was arranged.

The colonel was happy. He'd obtained satisfactory weaponry at a competitive price, and he'd also obtained the release of a valuable henchman, who would, in accordance with the tripartite gentlemen's agreement, spend the next three years, much to his annoyance, out in the desert, training other hopeful murderers in all his disgusting skills. What tickled the colonel was that he'd already come to a decision to buy Chinese next time around, anyway.

The Chinese were pleased because they had managed to effect a satisfactory sale, which would undoubtedly lead to more purchases, and in any case, Harwood would probably have turned out to be a ninety-day-wonder.

Whitehall and Summervill – especially Summervill – heaved enormous sighs of relief, particularly as Harwood had, understandably, been mighty impatient about wasting his time in prison, even an open prison with luxury accommodation, when he had five million dollars and Ching-hua outside. He was released at night and helicoptered to a safe location in the West Country where she was waiting for him.

Summervill kept tabs on him and insisted for the sake of security that his name be changed yet again, as the Peter Arthur Mayo alias had Asian connections which could draw attention.

He was now known as Christopher John Rothnie and it was with that identity that he and Ching-hua got married. Summervill arranged the amended birth certificate to be placed on the records at Somerset House, and Harwood's original to be erased from the records. Very thorough was Summervill.

Harwood protested that the precautions were over-done. The Chinese were no longer officially interested. What the hell was Summervill on about?

162

'Pander to my idiosyncrasies, Derek, there's a good fellow. I have your best interests at heart.' And that was all he could get out of the man.

Harwood, now Rothnie, was left with a vague feeling of unease. Maybe Summervill knew something he didn't, which was exactly what Summervill wanted him to think, so that he would be alert at all times and also be sensitive to anything that might not quite fit.

12

As Jacob Levinsky watched the plane climb away into the night sky, his mind was such a whirl of different emotions it literally made his head ache.

The Englishman was driving his father to an act of unforgivable treachery and mass murder for love of his son, yet at the same time he had allowed his woman to show compassion by letting on that Jacob would not in fact be sacrificed whatever happened.

If his father were to call Mayo's bluff and do nothing, how would he feel towards his father on returning to his family unharmed, knowing that he had been prepared to let him die?

What would I do in the same circumstances? he thought. To be honest, I'd probably chicken out.

From where they were encamped he could see, some miles away, the lights of his own home. Escape would be the answer to all the problems. As long as he could make it before his father committed himself and all his colleagues to eternity. He couldn't just lie here and not even try.

Carefully he tested the rope tied round his waist. The other end had been secured round a branch of the tree under which he sat, and was way out of his reach. He had sufficient slack to move about but the only way for him to get clear away would be to cut the rope.

He scrabbled feverishly at the ground about him, for a

164

stone, or some such, to use as a cutting tool. It seemed impossibly compacted but with determined effort, by first light, he had made some impression, and had moved away the tough, fibrous roots of the grasses where he sat and picked out some of the top soil. As the sun appeared he had to stop, and covered up his work by replacing some of the grass.

He was brought a bowl of mee, and a tin mug of tea by one of his guards. As he reached out to take it, the man frowned and, putting down the implements he was carrying, took his hands and examined them. Jacob saw they were covered in dirt and blood. Obviously he'd damaged himself by his overnight exertions without noticing it.

'How did this happen?' his captor enquired.

'I fell and scraped them yesterday. It is nothing, Jacob insisted, praying he would probe no further.

The man grunted and moved away, his suspicions apparently allayed.

It took him many nights of painful scraping until he finally found something with an edge to it. Each morning he examined his hands and cleaned his fingers as best he could on his shorts and T-shirt, and each morning their condition was such that he felt he could not go on. The dirt was ingrained, and they were bleeding, the nails broken, and desperately sore, but as darkness fell he forced them back to work, gritting his teeth against the pain, racing against time which he realised, from the letter he had been forced to write his father, was desperately short.

At midnight on the eighth night he found what he wanted. A sizable sharp-edged piece of flint, fashioned that way either by nature or neolithic man. Three hours later he had severed his bond and had slipped away unnoticed.

He had thought that, once away, it would be easy, but he had not reckoned on his condition. Days without exercise, and a minimum of food, quickly took its toll and after the first mile he staggered to a halt, the sweat pouring from him. He waited a minute to give his lungs a chance, then started off again. More slowly this time.

Carried downhill, he discerned a faint commotion behind him. He stopped again, turned his ear to the wind. They were definitely after him. Maybe five miles to go.

He carried on, endeavouring to move down the gulleys so as not to show himself against the skyline. At night, the moon or even starlight was sufficient to pick out a moving object on a ridge or hill crest.

The hunters were obviously fit and determined. Without his handicap of having to move quietly and by a selective route they were taking short cuts, realising the direction in which he was heading towards his home. They were closing on him now and would soon catch him. There was only one thing to do – run off in another direction and go to ground, let them pass him, let them cut him off, and use scouting craft and the rough ground to crawl through any cordon they might place between him and his destination. It was the only way.

He moved off in an arc to his left and lay down under a rock overhang, well hidden and perhaps three miles from home. In a few minutes he heard them to his right. Not far away. They had stopped for a hurried conference, then fanned out, and some had moved on.

Jacob started to go forward again. Slowly and quietly. He wanted to get as close as possible before daylight but without stumbling over any of his pursuers. There were two just ahead of him now. One of them had night glasses and was focusing on the entrance by the security hut. It was Hung.

'The boy's not gone through,' he whispered.

There was a grunt of affirmation from his companion.

'He must have gone to ground. We've passed him. No doubt about it.'

There was some shuffling about as they changed their position.

'Keep quiet. If he's behind us we want to get him as he comes through. The others should be within metres of the gate now. He can't get away.'

Jacob crept further forward. Now he knew where they

were he could move around them, with a bit of care. Another ten minutes went by. He'd made some progress. They were over to his right and behind him. The only trouble with crawling was that it hurt his sore hands abominably.

Light was beginning to tinge the valley. He could just make out the outline of the gate, the security hut, and some of the buildings behind it. Still a couple of miles away. Too far to be heard or even seen in this light. No use yelling for help.

He saw his father's car leaving the house in the dawn gloom. Oh, God, he thought, I wish I could reach you, touch you. Save your life. I am so wrong to think you might even consider saving yourself. You'll go ahead, a zealot to the last, spilling out your guts to protect your brood. Even if you had doubts you would overcome them.

Two hours later the sun was well up and Jacob lay staring at the unreachable. He started to cry silently at the hopelessness of his situation. A shadow fell across him.

'It was a good try, lad,' Hung said, not unkindly. 'Come along, let's go back.'

As he bent and lifted Jacob, the earth surged beneath them hurling them, to the ground. Away to the north, from the area of the project site, came a great hissing roar, followed by a rising curtain of flame that sucked up a vast cloud of dust many miles into the air, incinerating it in a blaze of white radiant heat so that it was completely atomised in a split second.

They lay on their faces in the dirt, hands over their heads, helpless in the searing wind that overwhelmed them, wondering if it was the end for all of them. And then, in seconds, it had ceased, as if it had never been, except for the occasional dust-devil whirling about on its own.

Hung got to his feet, and heaved Jacob up on to his legs. Then he looked at him, concerned. There was a four inch gash on his right cheek-bone that dripped a bloody path through the dirt ingrained on his face.

'It is done. We do not need to hold you any longer.'

He pointed towards the cluster of houses that seemed still intact, and now showed a faint stirring of nervous humanity, all, except for the odd security guard, womenfolk and children.

'Go home and see to that cut quickly before it gets infected.'

Jacob stood motionless, the sorrow welling up inside him until he could contain it no longer, and throwing his arms to the sky, the tears flowing, he shouted his rage and grief at the deity, in the ancient language his father had taught him. Taking dust from the ground he poured it over his head and shoulders as a man demented, which in truth at that moment he was.

Hung obviously thought he was crazed and grasping him firmly by both shoulders shook him so that his head snapped back and forth like a lifeless doll. At that, the boy suddenly recovered, and brushing off Hung's grip with unexpected strength, he glared at him with a look so full of implacable hatred that the older man shrank back in genuine fear.

'I will not forget that you and your scum drove my father to do this terrible thing. Hide yourselves well.' With that he shambled off towards the compound.

Despite the threat implicit in his words, a more disconsolate figure would have been hard to imagine. Hung watched him for a minute, then shrugged and retraced his steps back up the hillside. He had carried out the task asked of him.

The women and children were all outside their houses as if in fear of an earthquake, all staring fearfully in the direction from whence the burning wind had come. They were so shaken as to hardly notice Jacob moving dazedly among them, despite his ghastly appearance. As he entered the house he heard the sound of sorrow from his parents' bedroom.

His first selfish instinct on coming home had been to give way totally and seek comfort from his mother, but for the first time in his life he made the conscious decision that his mother should take precedence and that he, as the only man in the household, must bear the brunt of the burden they would both have to suffer.

To his surprise the sudden decision came as a relief to him. It gave him something to strive for. He was facing the reality of having to stand on his own two feet, and quickly at that. He opened the door.

His mother sat naked and sobbing on the floor in a corner of the room, her head bowed, her arms round her knees, rocking gently in abject grief. He stared at her for a few seconds, appalled that his mother, who had always been a figure of strength and authority in his life, should be reduced to this. His hatred of those whose fault it was took hold of him so that he ground his teeth with sheer rage.

Nevertheless, his fury did not swamp the pity he was experiencing for her. His chest hurt with his compassion and the desire to comfort her.

'Mother,' he said softly.

She did not hear him, continuing to rock and sob, in total isolation from everything except her grief. He moved closer to her, arms extended.

'Mother,' he repeated more loudly, endeavouring to break through the shield she had thrown around herself. Nothing. He put a blanket about her and left to call the unit doctor.

The doctor came half an hour later. He had visited the project site in the vain hope that there might have been something constructive for him to do there. A quick inspection of the still smouldering crevasse convinced him his time would be better spent dealing with the traumas of the living.

As befitted the Levinsky family's position, they were granted priority attention. The doctor was unable to bring Mei Ling to her senses and, after the administration of a sedative, he shook his head and taking Jacob aside said there was no option but that she be treated in the psychiatric hospital in Kunming.

It was the first opportunity he had had to look at the young man and he was so shocked by Jacob's appearance and distressed condition that immediately, and without further ado, he packed him off to the local hospital, where they sewed him up, injected antibiotics and gave him a strong sleeping draught. When he awoke there was an elderly gentleman patiently sitting by his bed.

'Ah, Jacob, you are awake. Are you feeling better?'

Suddenly everything that had happened came flooding back, a nightmare turned into reality. He opened his mouth to speak but his throat choked up and he could say nothing.

'Take your time,' said his visitor. 'It is terrible about your mother. I wish to express my very sincere regret.' He paused and made as if to get up. 'I'll come and talk to you later if you prefer.'

'Who are you?' whispered Jacob.

'My name is Leung. I am a friend of Professor Chung, and I knew your father before you were even born.'

'You mean you brought him here after he was shot down in Vietnam?' He turned and stared at Leung. 'My father has told me about you. You were with the professor when he asked my father to help China by supplying advanced technology design. Am I right?'

'Yes, you could say that. Did your father ever complain about the way he was treated?' Leung smiled gently.

'No, he was not unhappy.' Jacob hesitated, smiled back in dour fashion. 'In fact, I think he was very happy. Until he got killed working for you, that is.'

'You have been told of his death?'

The question sounded innocuous enough. He knew because his father had told him what was going to happen. He knew because he had watched his father drive to his death, and no one could possibly have survived such a terrible calamity. But he did not know officially that his father had perished and he certainly couldn't tell Leung what his father had said at their last parting. He had to be careful. This sympathetic old man was dangerous. The doctor could have told him but in fact he had not and that

170

could easily be checked. No use saying his mother was his source. She couldn't, or rather shouldn't, have known for sure and anyway she was in no condition to tell anybody anything. How to explain her prostration? Intuition? More important now: how did he know?

'No, but I saw it,' he said. 'The explosion, I mean.'

'Really?' Leung suddenly sounded interested.

'I was out for an early morning run. Something I do most days.' Yes that was it. A part truth flows easily and is difficult to fault. 'I was still some miles from home, when I felt something like an earthquake that flung me to the ground.' He pointed to the dressing on his face. 'I did this when I fell.'

Leung nodded, sympathetically. 'And?' he prompted.

'I heard this terrible sound. It came from the project site.'

'But what was it you saw?'

'Flames and dust together with white shimmering heat rising to the sky.' He shuddered at the recall. 'I closed my eyes because it blinded me. Then the heat came over the ground with a rush of wind so that I was frightened I would be burnt, but very quickly it stopped and everything seemed normal again, except for little whirlpools of dust about the place and then even they ceased.'

Leung nodded again but said nothing.

'It must have happened at the installation and anyone there must have surely died,' Jacob persisted. He changed tactics and decided to ask questions himself. 'Why do you ask me if I have been told? Is there any doubt after such a happening. Are you going to tell me he may have survived? That anyone may have survived?' Jacob was working up a genuine rage now mixed with his grief, and started to sob.

'And your mother?' asked Leung calmly.

'What about my mother?'

'She knew too?'

'I told her as soon as I got back.' Steady now. Don't embroider it too much. 'I told her what I had seen. She had felt the ground shake and the terrible heat and was already in a state of terror. When I described the rest of it, the fire

171

and everything, she became like a baby and sobbed and rocked and I could not communicate with her. I called the doctor.'

'Do you realise, Jacob, that you are the only person I have found who actually witnessed the occurrence.'

Except a bunch of bandits, he thought. Aloud he said: 'My father? I am right?'

'Yes, I'm afraid so.' He leaned forward, and took Jacob's arm. 'You must be very brave. There is worse.'

'Not my mother,' he pleaded. 'What's happened to her?'

Leung bowed his head. 'She killed herself while in a state of derangement,' he whispered.

'But she's in the hospital at Kunming.

Leung wrung his hands with the emotion of his feeling. 'I am instigating enquiries. I am very angry about this.'

'But how did it happen?' pressed Jacob.

'She jumped off the hospital verandah. Eight storeys up.'

'Oh, God. But surely they were watching her?' he protested.

'Yes, yes, but she evaded the nurse who was with her, so I am told and well . . .' he tailed off and then muttered: 'I will investigate the matter very closely.'

Jacob simply could not take it all in. This could not be happening to him. Happy, secure, surrounded by love and then suddenly ... nothing. At this moment of greatest sorrow he sought desperately for some comfort and then thought the unthinkable. He tried to push it away but it still kept piercing through the veil of misery about him. In her mental state might his mother have given anything away? Might she unknowingly have blurted out the story of what had really happened? If she had done so might this be the reason for Leung coming to see him?

'Did she say anything? Leave any message for me?' Jacob asked, tentatively, his voice shaking. 'Anything at all?'

Leung shook his head firmly.

'Nothing. The poor lady was out of her mind. She said nothing. Only gabbled unintelligible nonsense.' He took Jacob's arm again and squeezed it to give comfort. 'You

172

know there may have been little chance of her recovering. It might be better this way.'

'But what is going to happen to me?' asked Jacob.

'You?' said Leung, raising his eyebrows as if he considered the answer obvious. 'Why you receive everything a young man needs to get on in the world. He smiled gently. The Chung family wish to take you in and treat you as one of them. Mrs Chung has asked that you become her adopted son.' He looked enquiringly at the youngster gauging his reaction. 'I advise you to accept. Chung's family has much influence.'

'I have always wished to follow in my father's footsteps,' exclaimed Jacob. 'He has already schooled me in basic physics and says I have aptitude.' He frowned, and looked at Leung, 'Do you consider the Chung family could assist my advancement in the sciences?'

There's pragmatism for you, thought Leung. 'Professor Chung's name carried great weight in China's scientific circles. There is no doubt that if you have the ability they will support you to the utmost.'

'Then I accept with gratitude, and thank you for coming to see me.' The boy's lower lip quivered. 'I am sorry about the professor. I liked him very much.'

Leung had been very fond of Professor Chung as well, and felt a bit like weeping himself. Young Levinsky certainly had a way of ingratiating himself without showing subservience, and despite his grief had a toughness of character that would stand him in good stead Leung thought.

'Right that's settled then.' He stood up. 'I'll go now but we will certainly keep in touch.' He leaned over the bed. 'Anything I can do to help, within reason, let me know.'

'There *is* one thing, sir.'

Already, thought Leung, wryly. 'What's that?' he asked patiently.

'I feel it would be sensible to assume a Chinese name now that I am all alone.' The boy shook his head. 'I am different enough as it is without accentuating it. What do you think?'

173

'It makes sense. What name were you considering?'

'How about making my name Lee Win Sie, so that it sounds Chinese?' He looked at his visitor enquiringly. 'Obviously contrived, but it has no unpleasant connotations and Mr Lee sounds fine, do you not agree, sir?'

'I most certainly do, Jacob, and I will see that it is arranged if you are sure that is what you want.'

The youngster closed his eyes. 'It is what I want Mr Leung.' He sighed and mumbled, 'Thank you, and now if you will forgive me I wish to sleep. I am very tired.'

Leung stood and looked at the sleeping youth for some time, then slipped quietly away.

After the door closed behind him a complacent smile played about Jacob's lips. He was dreadfully sorry for what had happened and the shock and pain of it would haunt him for ever, but at least his own future seemed to be assured. Now he had to be patient, for he was determined to avenge himself upon those who, in his eyes, had caused the deaths of his parents. Hung, and also the initiators and the organisers. Particularly that Englishman, and those placed over him if he could identify them. He would find them one by one, and when he had finished they would be glad to tell him what they knew about the others. Before he killed them that is. He would spare the woman. He rather liked her.

He slept and dreamed, calling upon Diem Vuong, the Chinese Lord of Hell and Vengeance. 'An eye for an eye! Blood for blood!' Jacob turned and gritted his teeth, tossing about in his sleep until the female orderly worried by the noise he was making, came to him and placed her palm soothingly upon his forehead. His hand clamped suddenly upon her wrist, with inhuman strength, so that she was frightened and squealed with the pain of it.

'You are hurting me,' she whimpered tearfully.

His eyes opened but they looked through her, not at her, and their expression was so bleak she shuddered. He released her and, closing his eyes, returned to sleep as if he had never woken.

174

* * *

The nurse, a handsome, strongly built figure, with thick black hair cut severely close to her head, stepped out smartly toward the Park of Revolutionary Martyrs, a few hundred yards from the hospital, the over-long white gown of her trade flapping against her ample haunches.

It was her lunch period and she intended to spend it away from the overpowering trauma of the Kunming psychiatric hospital. She chose a bench under a shady tree where she could see the children playing with their toy boats in a wading pool. She opened the small packet of dim sum she had purchased from the vendor outside the hospital, and delicately picked at its contents with the small wooden chopsticks provided.

Out of the corner of her eye she saw the tired-looking old coolie dressed in near-rags shambling awkwardly along the path round the pond. He stopped every now and then to watch the children at play and used the opportunity to ease his hunched and obviously aching back. He was about to pass in front of her when, with an apparent last-second change of mind, he turned and lowered his sore old body beside her.

The nurse appeared to find his presence distasteful and her wrinkled nostrils provided due cause. Without being too obvious about it she moved carefully away from him as far as the bench would allow and continued to pick at her food, anxious now to move on. To her intense surprise the ancient beside her spoke quietly in a deep, pleasant voice.

'Sui nu shi ni hao?' 'How are you, Miss Sui?'

A quick sidelong glance, and beneath the shade of the conical hat she perceived the features and eyes of a much younger man than she expected, and furthermore a face that she instantly recognised as the head of her cell in the Kunming democratic movement.

'Mr Hung,' she breathed nervously, glancing about her for any potentially suspicious characters who might be security agents.

'The news of the woman, please,' Hung demanded quietly.

Sui continued eating, talking through her mastication, and looking at the children. 'Mrs Levinsky came to us two days ago by special helicopter from Mengwang. She was accompanied by a Guojia Anquanbu agent, and, as senior psychiatric nurse, she was transferred into my care.' Sui took a moment to compose her thoughts before she continued. 'She was in a state of immense agitation and the doctors prescribed very strong sedation. Yet despite this, she very quickly began muttering quite audibly about the tragedy at Mengwang.' Sui peered into the box to pick out another delicacy. 'She began to mention her husband's name and talked about an airplane landing and her son being held hostage.'

Miss Sui sighed and for a moment a blur of tears filled her eyes which she quickly wiped away. 'There was no doubt that her husband had confided in her more than was wise and in any case she was so very distressed that she had no wish to live.' The nurse shook her head sadly. 'She kept agonising that she was guilty of her husband's death and also her son's situation.'

There was such a long pause after this that Hung had to prompt her. 'And?' he asked.

'It all happened so quickly and I had no instructions from you as to what should be done,' she complained.

The man nodded his head imperceptibly, in agreement.

'I thought she might be in a position to give away information that could lead to our democratic party cell. After all, there were doctors coming in and out all the time to see her, and the Anquanbu man kept asking when she might be fit for interrogation.'

'So?'

'So I took action on my own initiative, and when the opportunity arose I toppled her over the balcony's edge.'

'You will not come under suspicion?' The nurse shuddered. 'I hope not. I tore my own uniform and made out that I had struggled in vain to stop her.' The young woman shook her head. 'It was very quick and she didn't want to live anyway,' she repeated. 'I hope I did right.'

176

'You did, Miss Sui. You certainly did and you may go now.' The woman rose and walked away.

Hung noticed she had left her food box on the bench. He picked it up and peered inside, then extracted the last piece of dumpling and chewed it with relish. He was very hungry.

13

January 1990

Harwood thought it was pleasant enough, at least for the time being, just living quietly in England with Ching-hua.

Summervill and his associates seemed to consider it necessary that the couple continue to keep their heads down for quite a time to come. They even supplied a couple of minders who lived in a gatehouse and constantly patrolled the area. One of them, a Chinese, was probably picked by Summervill.

Why such extreme caution? queried Harwood. Might Chinese sensibilities be offended by too high a profile. Could someone still wish to harm them? It really seemed rather overdone. Like something out of a John Buchan novel. Did Summervill know something he did not? His questions went unanswered.

He had only been held in confinement for two months, after the court case, before being released with extreme secrecy. Being without Ching-hua had made it seem a lifetime. She had been waiting for him when the helicopter dropped him off in a nearby field, and they were driven to the safe-house that sat in grounds surrounded by a high wall heavily topped with razor wire.

Eventually when they were left alone in the privacy of their bedroom he reached out and touched her gently as if to make sure this was really happening. Her eyes widened and, moving forward, she put her arms about him. 'It'll be alright won't it?' she asked seeking reassurance.

'Most certainly,' he said, and kissed her. And so it was. Afterwards Harwood had said simply, 'I have never known such happiness.'

She put her hands to his face. 'Nor I,' she replied, with complete sincerity.

However, after a while, despite the delight of each other's company, they began to chafe at the tight security. Harwood was keen to show Ching-hua the beauties and excitement of the outside world but they were not even allowed off the property. Once as they walked towards the gatehouse, one of their minders suddenly rushed down the drive as if demented. He had seen someone with a telescopic camera taking a picture. The photographer jumped into a car and was off. After that they were told in no uncertain terms that they should refrain from walking where photographs could be taken from outside the grounds.

Summervill kept them informed as to how matters were proceeding over the Mengwang incident, not that Harwood was particularly interested, but he listened with sulky compliance. It transpired that, after the Chinese Star Wars installation was destroyed, Levinsky's wife went quite round the bend. Luckily she was put in the charge of a psychiatric nurse in Kunming who was a member of the democratic movement. The nurse had an idea of what was going on but had not been able to contact Hung immediately when Mrs Levinsky started babbling what, to others, seemed, initially, to be nonsense. On her own initiative she terminated the wretched woman by shoving her over a hospital verandah rail eight storeys up.

Summervill seemed quite amused as he told the tale. Harwood, who felt sick about it, changed the subject by saying he'd be far more interested to hear when they would be allowed to leave the safe-house, as the restrictions were most irksome. Summervill was not forthcoming, and when asked if they were in any danger and was there something being held back, he just put the phone down, after saying

179

that Harwood should be grateful for small mercies and remain patient.

There really was not much option.

Beijing   January 1990

Professor Wu Chai Chuen held the Chair of Cosmology and Astrophysics at the ancient university of Beijing. His papers on quantum mechanics and the unpredictability element in science were given earnest attention by his scientific peers worldwide.

It was the professor's dream to find the unified theory that combined general relativity, or the study of the universe in terms of the curvature of a four-dimensional space time, with his beloved quantum mechanics. Such a theory is the Holy Grail of physics, although it is doubtful that the professor would have thought of it in those terms.

Professor Wu was a very busy man. Besides his work at the University he was also responsible for the main co-ordination of China's rocket programme and the weaponry related thereto. At times his 60 years weighed heavily upon him. Although by the standards of the Chinese hierarchy it was still a comparatively young age, he nevertheless appre-ciated that if he were to achieve his goal he could not wait for too long. What he required was the quicksilver original thought of brilliant younger people who were not afraid to consider the outrageous, in order to attain the apparently impossible. The brains of such persons, fostered and guided by his own admitted genius, would, he was confident, achieve the glittering prize that would place him at the forefront of those straining for the outer reaches of time and the universe. If only he could locate such material.

He stirred his rotund figure in his comfortable chair and, picking up the first page of the somewhat lengthy com-munication on his desk, held it at arms' length in the brilliant sunlight coming through the window, studying the

180

letterhead with casual interest. Wu did not believe in using reading glasses unless it was absolutely necessary. Anything to postpone the advent of age.

'Most Honourable Comrade, Professor Wu,' the letter commenced, 'I have been appraised of your wish to take into your research team young and outstanding physics students capable of highly original thought, which is a faculty seldom to be found in the young these days, after the ravages of the so called Cultural Revolution.'

The man bravely speaks his mind anyway, thought Wu.

'I have been searching diligently, but without success, among our most recent intakes at this seat of learning, to locate such elite students who might assist you in your great endeavours.'

Professor Wu snorted disdainfully. Kunming University came low down the scale of his concept of seats of learning. Nevertheless he had to admit that the author of the letter, Professor Kwok Tan Lock, was a physicist of solid ability. He would never shine, but his opinions were reliable and he was not the type to indulge in correspondence simply for the sake of it. Wu peered at the letter again and irritably pulled his glasses down from his forehead.

'However,' the letter continued, 'I have recently come across a most remarkable young man. He visited the university on the recommendation of the family of one of your old friends, Professor Chung Yip Boon, who so unhappily met his end in the Mengwang incident, of which you are, of course, aware.'

Of course, of course, I am. Get on with it, man.

'This youth is called Lee Win Sie. He is the son of Colonel Stefan Levinsky, who is also undoubtedly known to you, and a Chinese mother, but insists on being called by the Chinese version of his name, which he chose for himself. His western given name is Jacob.'

So he has a mongrel, but acceptable, pedigree and good connections. What about his qualifications? thought Wu.

'He is only twenty-one years of age, without formal education and has led a most cloistered existence...'

181

Why are you wasting my time with uneducated boys. Are you getting senile, Kwok?

'... and I agreed to see him purely as a gesture of friendship to Madame Chung but with the obvious anticipation of rejecting, with kindness of course, his application to become a student in the faculty of science here.'

Professor Wu sighed. I hope there's a point to all this, he thought.

'He is a strikingly tall, athletic youngster of strong features which only vaguely imply Caucasian blood, and is conversant, as I later took the trouble to ascertain, in Mandarin, Cantonese, Hokla and English of the American type.'

So?

'When I asked what he wished to study and how he expected to get into university with such minimum schooling, the educational facilities at Mengwang being virtually non-existent, he modestly told me his father had taught him privately the basics of physics and applied mathematics and he wished to follow in his footsteps.'

Why modestly? mused the professor.

'Belief in my lofty superiority led me to play a game with this serious-looking and self-composed lad. Not that his attitude in anyway implied arrogance, but I thought it might smooth an awkward rebuttal if I let young Lee realise that he had not yet approached anywhere near the level required for entry here, so that I would not appear unreasonable when I turned him down.'

This is beginning to become interesting.

'I started to ask him a few questions. To begin with I made it simple and requested him to draw on the wall blackboard in my work room the basic unit of ordinary matter and to expand upon it. Of course he started by illustrating the simplest atom, hydrogen, and solemnly produced the one electron orbiting around the nucleus. He then launched into vastly more sophisticated structures and commenced to discuss the phenomenon of interference between particles, and the obsolete laws of mechanics and electricity, which

182

dictated incorrectly that electrons would lose energy and spiral inward to collide with the nucleus. He took me through the partial solution by Niels Bohr's theories, then progressed to the resolution of the difficulty by quantum mechanics, taking into account wavelength velocities, bringing in the visualisation of wave particle duality. Utilising concrete mathematical form, he then calculated allowed orbits in more complicated atoms and even in molecules!'

Professor Wu was now totally immersed, his eyes rapidly scanning the pages.

'Thereafter the discussion ranged widely as between equals, covering white dwarfs, spatial dimensions, cosmological constants, black holes, Plank's quantum principle and so on, all illustrated by him with completely acceptable mathematical formulae, until I suddenly realised some six hours and three lecture periods had passed.'

Wu's hand was shaking slightly with controlled excitement.

'In conclusion, my dear professor, and I trust you have found the patience to read this lengthy epistle, I must accept that the discussion I have detailed above was not actually carried on between equals. I must also confess, unashamedly, that this twenty-one-year-old Eurasian's knowledge and potential ability in our field is far in excess of my humble attainment. I must assume his father was an even more exceptional man than we realised, and his offspring is undoubtedly a genius, to the extent that I can certainly not teach him anything here.'

The professor nodded solemnly to himself. His colleague in Kunming was definitely on to something.

'When I informed Lee of my belief, he accepted it without any particular surprise or smugness as might have been the case with a lesser person. He merely asked what he considered might be done to utilise his gifts on his country's behalf, meaning China.'

There's no doubt about that, purred Wu to himself contentedly. That is, of course, if he's half as good as Kwok thinks he is.

'I told him I would explore other avenues for him and come back to him in due course. With this he appeared quite content and thanked me most gracefully for my kindness. A very pleasing young man whom I would recommend strongly for your consideration. Please be so kind as to advise me your thoughts on this matter at your earliest convenience. Your most admiring and sincere colleague. Kwok Tan Lok, Professor of Physics, Kunming University.'

Professor Wu picked up his telephone.

'Call Professor Kwok at Kunming for me, immediately,' he said to his secretary, and thus it was that Jacob Lee soared like one of the stars in the firmament whose secrets he was so anxious to unlock.

14

Beijing   September 1990

Jacob was doing his reading. Professor Wu had insisted that members of his team be provided with all the foreign periodicals and newspapers they required, no matter what their political colour, as careful scrutiny of these frequently produced gems of information to further his own needs. It truly amazed him how much scientific information, let alone anything else, was provided gratis through the Western press to those keen enough to recognise its worth.

Jacob Lee Win Sie had proved to be quite outstanding, and within a few months after being taken on to work in Professor Wu's team he had become a valuable and trusted employee. His work on microwave radiation relating to the expansion of the universe, among other specifics, had been brilliant and there was no doubt that, given free rein, he would certainly help the professor to reach his longed for objective, to the greater glory of China and particularly himself.

It was still very hot and Jacob, despite himself, was finding it difficult to concentrate on the mass of mostly irrelevant data which he was skimming through. Then suddenly he jerked wide awake. In the arts section of an old London *Sunday Times* issue he saw a small photo of a woman's face that he definitely recognised. It was blurred and taken from some distance but was the Englishman's woman, without a doubt. The column was the work of a ballet critic bemoaning the lack of new talent in the world of British dance and he was writing a 'where are they now?' article.

'It has come to my attention,' he opened, 'that Miss Ho Ching-hua, once prima ballerina of the Peking Ballet, and a leading light in the democratic movement in China, who defected from her native land for Hong Kong some time ago, is now residing in the United Kingdom under an assumed name. By the greatest good fortune a friend of mine and lover of the ballet happened to recognise her in a remote West Country village, and it would seem that her presence here is shrouded in mystery. Miss Ho was strolling in the grounds of a large country house and my friend managed to take the photo above through the railings of the entry gate to the estate. One of her companions caught sight of him and hastened over to remonstrate about this 'invasion of privacy' but our alert photographer hurried off in his car before he could be apprehended.'

The journalist continued at some length praising Ching-hua's beauty and ability and earnestly recommended that the Royal Ballet endeavour to employ her without delay, before someone else grabbed her.

Jacob found it difficult to breathe, so intense was his excitement. It was his first lead and opened up enormous opportunities. There was not much he could do on his own but his mentor was a man of power who could help. But would he, once he knew why Jacob wanted his assistance?

The first question the professor would ask was why he had kept the secret of his father's death for so long. The simple answer was because Jacob would have been finished if the truth came out. Would he be finished anyway, if he told Wu now? That was a chance he would have to take if he wished to avenge his parents' deaths, and that he most certainly did. Without undue arrogance, he calculated Professor Wu's need to achieve success was sufficiently dependent upon his protégé that he would probably keep the matter confidential. After all, what benefit would come to him by resurrecting the past? All that would happen is that he would undoubtedly lose a key member of his research team.

The professor was in jovial mood. He had just received congratulations from the ministry on the progress in his work. They did not really understand its significance other than from a propaganda angle, which showed China to be a leading light in a field that the other great powers had thought to be their private domain. Now when China spoke, the great powers listened. Professor Wu had taken the opportunity to press for a sizable increase in his research budget and had been gratified by the immediate favourable reaction. To him, therefore, the world was looking good and he was prepared to spread some cheer around.

'Well, Jacob, what is this important personal matter you wish to discuss?'

He leaned forward. 'Are we not treating you well enough my boy?' he asked, knowing full well that the young man sitting before him was looked after on the same level as the élite in the party, and could have no real complaint.

'It is certainly nothing like that, sir. You have been most kind.'

'Well, then, tell me all about it,' insisted the older man expansively.

Jacob frowned and looked his mentor in the eye. 'I have a confession to make. I was recommended to Professor Kwok in Kunming as the son of a hero.' Wu came upright, all attention now. 'This unfortunately was a misrepresentation,' he continued. 'The fault was not mine, but I was fully aware of the circumstances.' He sighed. 'I am telling you this not to appease my conscience, but because I wish to enlist your influence to aid my plans for vengeance.' As he spoke the last few words the young man's voice rose in volume and the expression of pure ferocity on his face caused Wu to sit back and blink. 'My father was driven to commit suicide, mass murder, sabotage on an immense scale, and also treason against his adopted country...'

And so he told his story, even including his belief that his mother had not jumped but had been pushed from her hospital room balcony by a member of the democratic movement, of which he now knew Ho Ching-hua to be a member, in order to keep her quiet. When Jacob had finished the tale, and reiterated his request for Professor Wu's help to track down those whom he intended to punish, there was a long silence as the old man assimilated the details. Then came the expected question.

'Why did you wait till now to tell me of this?'

'Would I have had the chance to serve you, professor, had you known before I took up my appointment?'

'Probably not,' the professor conceded. 'The point is what do I do now?' Jacob kept silent. 'You want me to utilise the authority of my position to track down certain people both here and abroad and eliminate them?'

'In a couple of cases I would merely require the parties to be located and identified. I would dispose of them personally,' replied Jacob coolly.

'This would not interfere with your work?'

With that question Jacob knew he had won. This powerful old man was going to help him, and once he had done that Jacob reckoned he would be in no position to give his protégé away, without making himself vulnerable to charges of criminal conspiracy. The only problem, as Jacob saw it, was how the professor would justify his demands for the state to back clandestine, terrorist operations of this nature.

'I would make sure, professor, that any interference with my work would be minimal. The more co-operation I am given, the less time I will, of course, require.'

Wu knew perfectly well that he was being used but it seemed he really had very little option, that is if he wanted to retain Jacob Lee's enthusiastic services, which he most certainly did. Forced labour in this case would be totally unproductive.

'May I ask a question, Professor Wu?'

Wu gave a barely perceptible nod.

'How do you intend to explain my needs to the parties whose assistance you will, hopefully, call upon.'

Professor Wu Chai Chuen, the chief of China's space

programme, and controller of the most populous nation's ballistic strike-force, picked up the phone, punched out a number and spoke sharply into the instrument for half a minute. When he put it down he said without emotion: 'That was Marshall Chau Sheung Poon, head of the Guojia Anquanbu – the Chinese Ministry of State Security. He is coming to see me to discuss your little problem at nine o'clock tonight. He owes me and I am calling in the debt.' The professor raised his eyebrow. 'Now, young man, you will owe me.'

Jacob felt a cold shiver run down his spine. He had just witnessed a demonstration of naked power and realised how very close he might have come to being terminated himself.

Wu stood up, all business now. 'I will expect you to come to the meeting. You will say only what is necessary to clarify objectives. No more. Is that understood?'

'Absolutely, sir.'

'And you will present me with a briefing paper on the project, one page please. One hour before the marshall arrives.'

15

The marshall was a cadaverous, beetle-browed, sinister-looking man, whose appearance was completely in keeping with the enormous power he held. Jacob was surprised to see that he was extremely nervous, so it was obvious the professor did have something on him.

Marshall Chau had taken a minute to read Jacob's briefing paper. At the end his hand was visibly shaking with shock. He said nothing but turned back to the beginning to read it again as if he could not believe his own senses. When he finished the second perusal he laid the paper down very carefully, closed his eyes, sucked the air into his mouth through clenched teeth with a hissing sound that made Jacob jump, and said 'Shit' very loudly indeed. He glared balefully at Jacob then turned towards the professor.

'What do you want?' he asked sharply.

'Two things,' said Professor Wu cooly.

'And those are?'

'One. You provide assistance where required in tracking down the evil bastards who originated this operation and those who carried it out.'

'And the second?'

'We keep this whole Mengwang episode, and what we are doing, strictly on a private basis. It must not leak out.' The professor smiled gently. 'After all,' he continued, 'we all have skeletons in our closets, have we not? Some more than others.' He looked pointedly at the security chief, who had once, in his cups, tried to persuade Professor Wu to join him in a coup for power against the illustrious leader Deng Xiaopeng. The professor, as was his habit, had privately taped the exchange and played it back to the shocked marshall afterwards.

Chau nodded bleakly. 'There is no question of this leaking out, I can assure you. After all it hardly puts my ministry in a good light. In effect it is a total failure of security, with appalling consequences. Those prisoners had far too much freedom.' He pointed a thumb at the silent Jacob. 'I take it, Wu, that you stand surety for this young man. We cannot allow this sort of thing to happen again.'

Jacob paled with anger and was about to protest strongly when his mentor interrupted.

'He would hardly have brought the matter to my attention had it been in his mind to carry out a deviationist act. Yes, I stand guarantor for him, without hesitation.'

Marshall Chau nodded. 'When we have found the perpetrators, what then?'

'I will kill them.' It was the first comment that Jacob had made and came out with such venom that the marshall's bushy eyebrows raised dramatically.

'Assuming this to be mainly an operation of British origin,' asked the professor, 'would you have any idea as to who the controller might be, and where might he be based?'

The marshall thought for a minute. 'As it appears to have been carried out with a British operative in charge and with a minimum of logistics I agree with your assumption that it was a British exercise.' He paused and chuckled in a croaky sort of way. 'I could not imagine the Americans doing such a thing with so little equipment. No, it is definitely British, trusting to luck as usual and for once it went their way.' He paused peered at the other two for a few seconds. 'That, of course, does not mean that the Americans are not involved. They are probably aware of the facts by now and it could have been that they used the British as their surrogates.' He nodded to himself as if confirming his own viewpoint. 'The

British have a radio monitoring site in Hong Kong that covers most of China. I am told it is very efficient too. It is like having an eye peeping through one's bedroom curtains at all hours of the day and night.'

'Could be most embarrassing I expect,' chuckled Wu.

The security chief was known for his colourful sex life and was not amused by the implied comment. He grunted impatiently.

'Can you identify the person who is in charge of this installation?' asked Wu.

'Of course,' replied Chau. 'We have pictures of him too, and have long suspected him of encouraging and aiding the so-called democratic movement in their iniquitous activities.'

'Good. Please let me have a copy and all details. He might be number one on young Jacob Lee's hit list.'

'I'll do that, but it wouldn't be politic for it to become known that we're disposing of other nationals in our own backyard, so to speak.'

'Don't worry, marshall. We just point Jacob in the right direction and leave it to him, with perhaps a bit of logistic backing from you.'

'What about Ho Ching-hua in England?' asked Jacob. 'Can you try to find out where she is? And Mayo, too.'

Professor Wu put up his hand. 'Let's try to nail the Hong Kong agent first. Perhaps with persuasion he'll be able to identify the rest of the guilty parties and tell you of their whereabouts. Then we shall consider the next step. Alright?'

'Of course, professor,' said Jacob deferentially, 'but might it not be an interesting exercise for the marshall's organisation to ascertain the whereabouts of that vicious criminal Mayo and put the fear of death into him. It would be a salutary lesson to those enemies of our country who will realise that they are not safe from retribution even if they flee to the other end of the earth.' He looked enquiringly at his seniors.

The marshall nodded slowly. 'It would be a good psychological ploy,' he commented.

'You are a vindictive fellow, my young friend,' said Professor Wu, 'but if the Marshall agrees...' he splayed his hands in acceptance of the idea.

Jacob leaned forward and interjected hurriedly: 'Please do not have him killed. I will enjoy doing that eventually, provided of course you are in agreement.'

* * *

The two men crouched, facing each other on the matting-covered platform in the vast gymnasium. One was short, stocky and in his forties. The other, who towered over his opponent, was Jacob Lee. He had always been tall but now he had filled out in early manhood. He was finely-muscled, powerful and light as a cat in his movements.

Strangely, to the uninitiated, they were practising judo, a Japanese skill, not the Chinese Kung Fu. The instructor was an expatriate Japanese brought in by the government, at great cost, to train their security operatives, and recognised as superior in ability to his Chinese counterparts.

'Hajime.' 'Begin,' the Japanese instructed.

They moved into Kumikata, the initial holding position. Jacob turned and attempted a Taiotoshi, a side body drop. Watanabe slipped round Jacob's hip and, with amazing dexterity, grabbed the youngster's shoulder and, using his own lower centre of gravity, heaved Jacob over into a one-arm shoulder-throw, bringing his feet off the ground and throwing him solidly onto his back. But Jacob maintained his grip and brought Watanabe after him so that they ended in a tangle of arms and legs, straining for advantage.

Jacob knew that the Japanese, as a red belt, ninth Dan, was vastly superior to him and was wrestling down to his standard but he persisted nevertheless, using every particle of his extra weight, which was to his advantage on the ground, until the other, without any apparent effort brought the struggle to a conclusion with an unexpected arm-coil-lock.

They stood up and bowed to each other. 'That was nearly

193

Hiki Wake,' Watanabe grinned, implying that Jacob had practically forced a draw on him.

'Master you were playing with me, but each time I learn a little more and I am grateful,' replied Jacob.

The other looked at him keenly. 'You have reached your third Dan which is very good for one so young. One day,' he intoned prophetically, 'you will reach at least sixth Dan and be entitled to a red and white belt, but do not be in too much of a hurry.' He looked at the wall clock. 'It has been an hour.' They bowed again, the lesson at an end.

As Jacob walked away, Watanabe gazed at his retreating back. If the truth be told, he thought, one day that young man will surpass my own skills and probably do some killing on the way.

* * *

Ching-hua and Harwood were now fed up with their situation. Apparently the stalker who took their picture through the gate had sold it to the *Times*, whose arts critic wrote a column on Ching-hua's talents. As a result, the two of them were moved forthwith as undoubtedly Chinese intelligence would pick it up. Next time Summervill made his regular call, Harwood protested that he was going over the top.

'Look, Harwood, it's your privilege to be a bloody fool but try thinking of Ching-hua. I know you're itching to spend that five million.' He spoke with a snarl of pure jealousy in his voice. 'But it may interest you to know I have received information that Beijing are cracking down on known pro-democratic dissidents, and that's not just in China either. It's worldwide, where ever they can get at them.'

That was certainly food for thought.

'I can tell you,' he continued, 'this makes the Bulgarian poisoned umbrella stunt look like kid stuff. Three or four of the better known pro-democrats here in Hong Kong have died in suspicious circumstances, and the same thing has happened in California recently.'

Harwood found it difficult to believe that Summervill was that genuinely worried about them but was prepared to listen as he went on.

'The pro-democratic organisation in China happens to be extremely helpful to me in my intelligence gathering – incidentally that includes your old friend Kwan – and it has been made crystal clear to me that should anything happen to that girl, who's virtually their patron saint, or the Chinese equivalent, whilst she is under our protection, then ties will be cut and that, Harwood, I do not want. About you I am personally not too fussed. Clear? Furthermore,' he added insincerely, 'I rather like her.' So that was it.

'Alright, alright,' Harwood said, 'I go along with that for a time.'

Summervill took that up very quickly. 'You'll go along with it as long as I deem it necessary.'

The end result was that they moved to yet another safe-house. Summer came and went, and autumn arrived with the first winter nip. Ching-hua had been remarkably patient but her past record showed her to be a free spirit, and as a result of this confinement she was showing very definite signs of strain. She understood why it was happening but the reason of an argument does not always make one feel better. It certainly did not appease Harwood. And, dammit, he did indeed want to start spending some of that five million. They had almost got to the stage where they were planning a breakout. In truth it was doubtful they could have been held by force anyway but they thought if they could sneak out of the place, confrontation could be avoided and all the unpleasantness that goes with it.

The house they were presently in had a small gazebo set on a grassy mound in a corner of the property, up to which a set of some half-dozen steps led. They went there frequently when the weather allowed it, to sit and talk in what they believed to be comparative privacy, where no one could sneak up on them unawares, as was sometimes the case in the house itself. One afternoon they were there in the bright sunlight of an Indian summer, spending a couple

195

of hours in desultory chat until the sun went down and the autumn cool drove them back to the house.

At the bottom of the steps was a very dead Chinese. Their minder. Summervill's man. How the hell he'd got there without their noticing was difficult to comprehend. It was also very frightening. They'd both seen plenty of death in their time, but this sort of thing happening in the quiet of an English country garden was like a killer shark appearing in a village pond. Both were quite unable to speak for a full minute and Harwood's stomach went into the most unpleasant spasms with the shock of it. Ching-hua sat down on the grass and went as pale as death. They didn't touch him but knew he was dead, as his head was lying at a quite impossible angle in relation to his squat, massively-muscled body. They called the police, and a detective from the local constabulary came to examine the body while a doctor stood by, waiting to give his pronouncement.

The detective, a grizzled veteran of such affairs, searched through the dead man's pockets and, among other possessions, extracted, very daintily, a folded piece of paper which he opened up. It contained a crude picture of a striking cobra.

'Strange they should operate here,' he said.

Harwood didn't understand what he was on about, but obviously Ching-hua did. She was trembling. Harwood put his arm around her and asked: 'Who's they?'

'I did a stint with the Met once,' the detective replied. 'Worked Soho fairly regularly.' He nodded at Ching-hua. 'Your young lady'll tell you the Striking Cobra Society is about the most powerful triad in Hong Kong, and in London too. Runs the mafia a close second.' He shook his head and stood up. 'It's all yours, doc,' he said, then turning to Harwood, 'let's take the young lady inside. It's cool out here.'

The other minder, the English one, was hovering around, obviously upset that the police had been brought in without telling him. He flashed some form of identity card in the detective's face which seemed to make an impression. The older man shrugged in a dispassionate way, then as he made to leave he said, 'It seems your friend here will take care of all the details but,' and there was a long pause while he looked searchingly at Ching-hua, 'but to my way of thinking your Chinese friend was remarkably uncoordinated, miss.'

'How's that?'

'It appears,' and he stressed the 'appears' so that it could not be missed, 'that he tripped and fell down the steps breaking his neck. Easily done. Happens every day in homes throughout the country. But that begs the question of the striking cobra sketch. Was it his or was it planted?' He slapped his thigh in a resigned sort of gesture and put on his hat. 'Funny though,' he concluded, 'that he didn't have any scrapes or bruises on his face or hands after a fall like that.'

Harwood thought it was funny too. He checked round the premises extra carefully that night and kept his Browning under his pillow. Before retiring to bed he asked the remaining guard what was going to be done about this.

'Plenty more where he came from,' he replied callously. 'There'll be another colleague of mine along tomorrow and, one thing for sure, we'll have to move.'

When they finally went to sleep that night, wondering how a man of such fitness and physical ability could be so easily disposed of, Harwood dreamed of Mengwang and young Levinsky's final threat. 'The day may come when you will regret your woman's benevolence.'

The next day they moved again, and when Summervill rang to check them out Harwood's only comment was that the killers certainly seemed to find them easily enough no matter where they moved.

'Grow a beard,' Summervill said at the end of the conversation. He didn't know whether or not Summervill was serious but on the premise that every little helps he did just that. Ching-hua took to wearing a wig that did indeed seem to change her appearance radically, at least from a distance.

16

'Do you recognise this man?' Professor Wu slid two six by six photos across his desk.

Jacob picked them up, and slanted the first one so that the light fell across it. It was a picture of a man standing beside a car at the end of a fairly long driveway. He was talking to a woman who had her back to the camera. The picture was taken three-quarter face, with good definition. He knew, but to make sure he looked at the second, snapped full face. 'That's him,' he said, his voice shaking. 'That's Mayo, the murdering bastard. I recognise him even though he's wearing a beard now.'

Wu noticed Jacob's left hand had curled about the arm of the upright chair in which he was sitting with such force that the wood creaked as if about to split. 'His latest pseudonym is Christopher J. Rothnie. Ho Ching-hua is living with him at the address on the back of the pictures, but of course they could move at any time if they suspect anything.'

Jacob turned the photograph over and closed his eyes as if remembering the details, then handed the pictures back. 'Thank you, professor. I am most grateful to you and Marshall Chau.'

'I must admit,' replied the professor, 'that the marshall's men are certainly showing initiative. This is the third house these people have moved into this year and this last time it took our intelligence only a month to trace their latest hide out. By the way, your suggestion has been followed up.

Chau arranged for a triad killer from London to kill a guard. That should make them sweat.'

Jacob was delighted. 'That's good news, professor. I hope he will be so kind as to continue keeping an eye on this Mayo or Rothnie, to ascertain if he should move yet again.'

Wu nodded. 'That should not be too difficult. He has many agents in England, inside and outside of the embassy.'

The younger man stared at the carpet, deep in thought. I have him now, he was thinking. What shall I do. How shall I go about it. Do I kill all of them. Slowly. Quickly?

'What do you intend to do?' The professor's question brought him out of his reverie.

'Do?' Jacob snorted 'Why kill them, of course.' He paused, made up his mind. 'The lot of them.'

'The woman too?'

Jacob shook his head. 'No. She persuaded Mayo not to kill me. I owe her, and also,' he smiled lightly, 'I intend to have her for myself.'

Wu laughed. 'Why not? You have good taste, my boy.' He was pleased to learn his protégé had other things on his mind than science and revenge. 'There is more,' said Wu taking another photograph from the drawer and handing it over.

'Brian Summervill is his name. He runs the MI5 Unit at Little Sai Wan in Hong Kong.' Wu chuckled quietly. 'Apparently he's a thorn in Marshall Chau's side and is undoubtedly the man who controlled Mayo, and of course engineered the Mengwang episode. Furthermore, where you find MI5 you invariably meet up with the CIA. I am convinced they are the real instigators of this evil act.'

'You are exceedingly kind to me, professor. Your influence, assistance and understanding will, I am sure, help me achieve my objectives, but sometimes I wonder if you approve of my private aims?'

There was a long silence while the other contemplated his answer. 'I understand them,' he finally replied. 'And as you need to purge yourself of your hate, I cannot see how I can

199

refuse you, provided your work does not suffer. Is it your intention to cope on your own with the physical aspect of these disposals, whilst accepting logistic support from the Guojia Anquanbu clandestine department?'

Jacob opened his mouth to reply affirmatively but his superior had not finished.

'What I am getting at is that there are other forces that might be prepared to come to your aid.' Wu shrugged his shoulders. 'That is, of course, if you have the courage to consider them.' He paused to collect his thoughts. 'Forces that are beyond your comprehension.'

Jacob had lost the thread and his expression made that quite clear.

Wu smiled gently. 'Unworldly forces that are extant beyond our universe. The Western, so called Christian civilization, makes great play upon such things. They call it the black arts or Devil worship and tell much-embroidered tales of banished angels. But long before Christianity or, for that matter, Judaism there were, worldwide, men of knowledge who used supernatural powers to call upon certain of those that had gone before.'

Jacob was fascinated but felt his skin begin to crawl at the professor's words.

'Such organisations, even then, before modern communications were dreamed of, kept in close touch with each other.'

'How could they?'

'By mental processes. If one's mind is correctly tuned to another's, understanding flows between them no matter what their distance or their mode of speech.' Wu opened his hand in an encompassing gesture. 'Naturally China, the oldest civilization, was the fount of such matters, but on the great Mongol steppes, in the mountains of Tibet, the sands of ancient Egypt, and in the deep primeval forests of present-day Europe, to as far as what is now known as Britain, the brotherhood flourished. Yes, it was even taken by our ancestors across the northern bridge to the Americas.'

Jacob was finding it difficult to take this in but saw no reason why someone like the professor would wish to feed him such tales without reason. 'Where did these seers develop their arts?' he asked curiously.

'There were many centres of learning in China and great numbers still exist underground but it might be said that Hsiao T'un near Anyang in Honan province was and still is the greatest.'

'And elsewhere? I mean outside of China?'

'A considerable number, but a few that stand out are the Lydians of Asia Minor, the Hittites of Anatolia and of course the Druidic centres throughout what we now call Europe and Scandinavia. The greatest of these, and also the most impressive to look upon, is Stonehenge, whose priests had close relations with the Mycenaean world and through them our own Chinese originators of Chè Gów or Devil Religion, as the uninitiated might call it.'

Jacob frowned in apparent disappointment. 'But the Druids are surely a bunch of play actors in white sheets and long beards who like to pretend they can commune with nature? I've read about them in some of the English papers.'

The professor leaned back in his chair and looked at the ceiling thoughtfully.

Then very quietly so Jacob had to strain his ears to hear, he said, 'Am I wearing a white sheet and a long beard?'

Jacob gaped in amazement. 'You cannot be –' he stuttered to a halt.

Wu got up from his chair, came round the desk and leaned over his protégé. 'Should you disclose what I say to anyone else – anyone at all – you will be struck down by all the powers at my command.' He stopped, moved back a pace. 'And they are considerable, I can assure you.'

Jacob nodded dumbly.

'I was initiated into Chè Gów as a child by my father, and he by his father, before him for countless generations. Never at any time have we disclosed our following of the old faith to any outsider.' He grinned wryly. 'To have done so during the Cultural Revolution would have meant incarceration and worse.'

'Then why me?'

'Jacob, I have no son of my own, only daughters who are not to be initiated in such matters. I look upon you as a son. It is as simple as that.'

'I am deeply honoured, sir.'

'Good, and in the light of what I have told you you are already committed.' The old man was all business now. 'We must waste no more time and I will arrange for your instruction forthwith as there is much to learn. Firstly, you must appreciate that our order transcends all questions of race, so that worldwide those who have the power are as one, and once initiated you may call on any of them who make themselves known to you for assistance, but only in respect of matters of serious consequence.'

'But finding time for such instructions?' protested Jacob.

'Time is nothing. It is a tool to be used.' The professor dismissed the problem with a wave of his hand.

'Maybe but...'

'Listen my son, listen,' said Wu imperiously. 'To begin with you are exceedingly clever. That is not flattery, it is fact. Up till now you have by no means utilised your full mental capacity. That you will be taught to do without delay, and very importantly you will no longer waste your life by spending seven or eight hours a day in sleep.'

Jacob was desperate to intervene here but felt it wise to constrain himself.

'You will be trained to make do with far, far less and at times to go for extended periods without any sleep at all.' He pointed a finger at himself. 'I can now do with an hour or less in twenty-four. It is quite sufficient for me, and think of the extra time available that generates.' Wu rubbed his hands together and smiled. 'Within a comparatively short time, with your ability, you will be ready for initiation, and of course thereafter you are always learning.' The professor looked grave. 'You will undergo some experiences that may well make you fear for your sanity, but courage, an iron will

202

and total commitment, all of which qualities I am convinced you have, will see you through, so that you become one of the truly superior beings on the planet.'

Jacob sat awed and excited by the prospect. 'When might I start, professor?'

'Soon, very soon, Jacob, and remember we are exceedingly hard taskmasters. Any disclosures of our doings to outsiders will result in instant immolation. A most terrible demise.'

Hong Kong   1990

Summervill had enjoyed the Christmas festivities at the Hong Kong club and now he was about to enjoy the after-dinner entertainment even more.

He was a confirmed bachelor but the delicacy of his job placed considerable constraints upon his moral behaviour. He very seldom indulged himself, and then only after the most cautious research of the party in question. But recently he had come across a Chinese girl of such stunning beauty that he had been courting her in a most respectable manner for several months. She was highly educated, with apparently impeccable connections, and very charming but with an inner quietness that caused him patiently to restrain himself, despite the fact that her very presence made him almost squirm with desire.

She hadn't actually promised anything but she had given him the address of an apartment in Repulse Bay, where he was to meet her as soon as he could decently leave the club. The kiss she had given him and the way she had pressed herself against him at their last meeting held a promise that made him feel quite giddy. He smiled in a self-satisfied manner, his thoughts painting a picture of delight.

Expertly he took the road up to Magazine Gap and then wound down toward the other side of the island. It was late and there were few lights in the block of luxury flats at which he parked. He locked his car, put the keys in his pocket and jauntily trotted up the steps to the entrance. He pressed the security phone button for her flat. Her voice was warm and promising, even over the tinny instrument.

'Is that you, Brian?'

'Certainly is, darling.'

The opening buzzer sounded and in he went to the waiting lift that moved him smoothly up to the eighth floor. He peered along the corridor. Empty. The door of flat 8B was ajar.

He went in, shut the door behind him, then exhaled slowly. He could see into the bedroom: a pair of obviously female stocking-clad legs that went on for ever, on a bed. Summervill literally tiptoed across the room so as not to destroy the ambience. He pushed the door further back before entering. What he saw took the breath from him. He'd never in his wildest dreams imagined anything quite so voluptuous. The sheer black stockings were all she wore. The rest was what God had given her. She had something both satin and velvet about her. Slender, yet with provocative ripeness, her skin translucent in the bedside light. She was sitting back against the padded headboard, a glass of champagne in her hand, a magnum in an ice bucket beside her.

She smiled at him. 'I thought I would celebrate Christmas too, even though I am not a believer, and that I would give you myself as a present.' She frowned, leaned forward a trifle. Even this slight movement of her body was a delight to him. 'Why are you standing there?' she asked innocently.

'I am overcome,' he replied simply. 'I never imagined you would be so beautiful.'

'Well I hope you aren't completely overcome,' she grumbled. She sounded as if she'd had a few glasses already.

He leaned over and kissed her mouth and breasts.

'Take off your clothes,' she demanded huskily.

He complied and continued to gaze at her, obviously aroused, then bent and inhaled the faint and marvellous odour that came from her body. His slowness seemed to have excited her too; her eyes were shining, her lips parted. She reached out and touched him.

Summervill thought this was the best damned Christmas present he had ever had or was likely to have, and was anxious not to spoil things by exploding all over the place. He moved slowly on to the bed, and just at that crucial moment, with nerve shattering suddenness, a hand of iron grabbed his hair from behind, jerking his head hard back and a large sticking plaster was slammed across his mouth. This was a nightmare he could not believe. He tried to turn and see who was committing this outrage but his arms were wrenched behind him; he heard the handcuffs snap and he was dragged ruthlessly on to the floor where he lay kicking madly until a slip knot was expertly pulled tight about his ankles. He lay naked and totally helpless, mad with himself at falling for the oldest con trick in the book. The girl had put on a gown and was looking down at him with a sneer on her face.

Bitch, he thought. Beautiful bloody bitch.

Her male partner knelt beside him. The lower half of his face was covered by a piece of cloth. In his hand he held a cut throat razor. 'I will take off your gag and you will answer some questions. If you make any noise other than talking in a normal voice I will immediately cut your throat. Is that clear?'

Summervill nodded anxious assent. The plaster was ripped cruelly from his mouth.

'You are going to provide some information about the Mengwang episode.'

'Who the hell are you?' asked Summervill.

'Just answer my questions or you will suffer for it.'

'I don't know anything about it,' Summervill squeaked, 'other than what I gathered from normal intelligence after it happened.'

'You are lying.' The eyes were black as coal and totally menacing. One hand clamped firmly over his mouth while another grasped the side of Summervill's neck. The pain

205

was excruciating and he could not even scream. 'Now answer.'

'Go to hell,' he gasped wondering how much more of this treatment he could take. Again the pain. This time he passed out momentarily and, when he came to, his assailant was holding a hypodermic syringe in front of his face. 'Pentathol?' he croaked. 'Doesn't work on me,' he lied.

'This is a new truth serum,' the other said. 'It will surely make you talk before I even inject you.'

'That's crazy,' gasped Summervill.

'Not so crazy.'

Despite his predicament, Summervill's natural instinct to seek out intelligence set his mind working. 'Hey, you're an American, or at least you sound like one.'

'You might say so.'

Again the hypodermic was waved in front of his face. Summervill noticed the content was a dull red. Certainly not pentathol.

'What the hell is it?'

'Very simple.' The man paused apparently enjoying Summervill's confusion. 'It's five cc's of ordinary human blood.'

'So what?' asked Summervill automatically, and as he asked he knew and shuddered.

'It's blood drawn from a dying man. A man suffering from the terminal stages of full-blown AIDS.'

'Oh, Christ,' moaned Summervill.

He felt the needle touch the skin of his shoulder and tried desperately to wriggle away to no avail.

'Well?'

'This is bloody inhuman.'

'I'll give you three seconds and then I run out of patience. One...'

'Okay, okay,' shrieked Summervill, 'take that filthy thing away from me. What do you want to know?'

The girl gave a little sigh as if of disappointment. Summervill looked at her.

Bitch and double bloody bitch, he breathed to himself, hating her with every fibre of his being.

'You can start at the beginning and run through the whole lot. Whose idea was it? Names, places everything.'

He heard the whir of a tape recorder start up. He blabbed the lot or almost. He told them about the CIA and Al Craddock, the head of Bangkok station. He mentioned Harwood's aliases, Mayo and Rothnie, but for some indefinable reason, perhaps to keep an iota of his pride more than anything else, Summervill kept back Harwood's real identity. He told how he'd used Ching-hua. He mentioned their whereabouts as well, although Jacob already knew this through Marshall Chau's organisation. He also described how to locate Hung, the pro-democracy gang leader, and how Jacob's mother had been pushed off the eighth floor of the psychiatric hospital in Kunming by an agent of that organisation. Lastly he described the activities and appearance of Kwan Yue Ming, the pro-democracy activist who had brought him much useful information.

Jacob Lee listened in grim silence. At the end he slapped the gag back on the desperate man. 'It's a coincidence that this is the eighth floor, isn't it?' he commented wryly.

Oh my God, they're going to chuck me over the railing; Summervill moaned in his throat at the thought of it.

Jacob snorted at his obvious terror. 'We won't make it that easy for you, you filth,' he said. The two of them moved toward the door. 'We're leaving now, and someone will be told to come and release you in a few hours' time.'

Summervill almost swooned with relief. They weren't going to kill him after all.

'One last thing.'

The MI5 man was all attention.

'I've forgotten to give you your injection.'

As the needle sank into him, and he saw the blood level dropping as it was pumped into his system, Summervill thought he would go out of his mind with shock and self revulsion. They left him alone then to think about his predicament. Summervill had never known such dragging misery in all his life. Later, when his doctor confirmed him as HIV positive, the last flicker of hope died.

The day after New Year, Summervill rang. 'Harwood, I have news for you. Bad news, I'm afraid!'

Harwood's stomach felt as if a large lead ball had lodged there. For the last two months or so they had begun to relax and look to the possibility of a future away from this confinement. Nothing had happened in that period to arouse suspicions and Harwood had let the tension drift from his mind; his conscious mind, that is. He supposed it would always lie there, like a frightened cowering thing in a dark hole, waiting to emerge when and if circumstances warranted it.

'Well?' he asked. He didn't want to say more for fear of losing control of his voice.

'Someone in our organisation has spilled the beans.'

'You mean...?'

'Yes, the whole damn thing. He was put under great pressure.'

'You're talking about torture?'

'That's right.' Summervill's voice didn't sound right. It was obvious he was under considerable pressure himself.

'Go on.'

'Well, they now know what happened at Mengwang, the CIA's part in the affair. Names, places, etc.'

'Meaning my assumed name, and where I am?' Harwood asked. He sighed heavily. ''Fraid so, except for one thing. They don't know your real name.'

'Well, I suppose that's something. Thanks for letting me know.'

'I couldn't not let you know; it could be alright, but I had to tell you, just in case, so you could keep a look out.'

'I suppose we'll have to keep constantly on the move from now on,' Harwood said bitterly.

''Fraid so but knowing those tenacious buggers I doubt it'd do you much good.' He sounded so despondent. Not his usual unpleasant, ebullient self at all.

'Are you okay?' Harwood continued, trying to show some interest in the other man's problems.

'Not really but that's not your worry.' It was left at that.

Ching-hua tended to down play the news. When Harwood first told her she went pretty quiet and thoughtful but then she said: 'I've got a few powerful friends in the local Chinese community myself. Members of the overseas pro-democracy Party. Most of them are on Beijing's hit list but they seem to survive.'

He nodded his head. 'Maybe, but I doubt if their offences were quite so heinous as ours.'

'True,' she replied, 'but let me make a few phone calls anyway. I reckon our minders could use a bit of help.'

The upshot was that her friends arranged for some of their own to keep on eye on the pair as well.

'They can't provide a hundred per cent security,' Ching-hua admitted, 'but at least if anyone unfriendly does scout around, they'll know we are on our guard.'

The MI5 boys soon cottoned on and made a bit of a fuss about these unofficial reinforcements, but there wasn't much they could do about it. After all they'd shown themselves to be pretty vulnerable.

* * *

'Marshall Chau has confirmed that with the information you have obtained from the English MI5 agent, he will have Hung picked up and disposed of without much trouble.' The professor steepled his fingers and looked over them at the tense young man before him. 'The marshall has also said that he thinks your handling of Summervill is quite the most malevolent act he has ever heard of.'

Jacob frowned. 'I regret it that the marshall disapproves. I considered it an excellent way to ensure Summervill's deterioration and eventual demise could not be proved as due to an act of ours. After all, who would believe the wretched man if he were to be so foolish as to tell anyone?'

'No, no,' protested the professor. 'Marshall Chau approves wholeheartedly. In fact, I wouldn't be surprised if he tried

209

to offer you a job. He cleared his throat, leaned forward. 'Of course, I'm not serious.'

'I'm sure you weren't, Professor Wu.' Jacob stood up to go then sat down again as a thought struck him. 'As regards Hung, I wonder if the Marshall would consider it an imposition to let me face him when he is arrested. I want him to know who was responsible for his capture. And also I trust the evil person who murdered my mother is dealt with as well.'

'I will see what I can do,' Wu said.

'Thank you. My sincere hope is that you will remain patient with me.'

The older man laughed. 'After the quality of your recent, most useful, paper, I am convinced this secondary occupation of yours is in no way affecting your work unfavourably. Therefore if it keeps you happy I will continue to support you in any way that is possible for as long as is reasonable.'

'That is most reassuring, sir. Perhaps you would care to hear of my plans for the immediate future in regard to this secondary occupation.'

'Fascinated, I'm sure,' said Wu with considerable sincerity, 'and by the way I can tell you I have heard good reports about your progress in regard to the other matter you are working on. Your initiation will take place at the end of this month. Prepare yourself well.

Hsiao T'un, China

Jacob stared fascinated by the scene about him. The great circular amphitheatre, open to the moon and stars, with marble walls and floors reflecting the brilliant flickering light of a thousand flaring torches, produced a scene that was totally awe-inspiring. Around him there were many hundreds of members of the brotherhood, dressed in plain white flowing garb and behind him, similarly attired, hand on Jacob's shoulder, stood Professor Wu.

There was not a sound. Not a shuffle of a foot changing

position, not a clearing of a single throat, or sniff or cough. Total silence except for the stertorous breathing of the writhing, gagged, tightly-bound object of sacrifice, laid upon the slaughter stone beside him. The slaughter stone, with its hollows and runnels, was ready to receive the blood and body fluids of the victim.

Before him was the heavy solid marble altar to which the body, after preparation, would be transferred. Beyond the altar, on a raised dais, sat a shrivelled little monkey-like man, his bald dome glinting in the torch light, his alert eyes peering keenly at Jacob through slanted slits among folds of parchment-like skin. His mouth was a tight, lipless line and yet he was communicating with Jacob. Communicating as freely as he would have with normal speech and Jacob understood every point and command the sinister ancient was making, as did all others present, with the exception of the sacrificial girl child.

'Now,' came the silent command.

Jacob raised his right arm in compliance and turning, plunged the knife he held into the child's naked belly. With the other hand he immediately delved into the wound, pushed under the rib-cage, and ripped out the still-beating heart, holding it aloft so that his head and upper body was sprayed in blood.

A collective sigh from the onlookers rose about him. The high priest nodded his satisfaction, his lizard like tongue darted out and about the slit that comprised his mouth, then was instantly retrieved.

The professor squeezed Jacob's blood-covered shoulder in approbation. 'It was well done,' he breathed. 'You are now one of us and the secrets of true power will be granted to you.'

Bangkok

Alfred J. Craddock loved Bangkok. He always described it as a city of smells, sex and snakes. He was brought up in the rites of that strange American sect, prevalent throughout certain desert communities of the south-west, who took the bible literally and included in their religious rituals the handling of rattlesnakes.

Al Craddock had, as a youngster, indulged in this fanaticism without being harmed but having once witnessed another worshipper writhe into an agonised death as a result of being bitten he had turned his back on such practices. Nevertheless snakes always held for him a fascination and fearful revulsion that he could not explain. He frequently dreamed that he was helpless and beset by snakes and awoke sweating and screaming, to the considerable fright of whatever little Thai girl he had taken home for the night from one of the local bars.

No doubt a psychoanalyst would have given him any number of Freudian reasons for his snake dreams but he never bothered with that sort of crap, and in a perverted way probably rather enjoyed them. For a person of his strange propensities, the Bangkok Pasteur Institute was complete delight. There, one could safely lean over the wall round the large snake pit and watch, some six feet down, a mass of banded krites, cobras, pit vipers and other deadly serpents slither around in a manner that would send a shiver up the spine of the most indifferent onlooker.

Al was totally fascinated and, being his own boss, came virtually every day. He always chose to arrive in the late afternoon. The keeper, a slim, elderly man with a great sense of showmanship, clad only in shorts and vest, would enter the pit armed with a forked stick for pinning down the snake of his choice. He also carried, in a bag over his shoulder, a few small glass dishes, each with a diaphragm stretched tightly over the top. Carelessly kicking the various snakes out of his way with his bare feet he would trap the one he required in the fork of his stick, then lift it by the back of its head until the fangs were clamped on the edge of the dish, piercing the diaphragm and causing it to eject its venom. For good measure, he would hold the gaping evil mouth up for all to see, the drips still clinging to the fangs and glittering in the bright sunlight, then casually fling the brute aside and go in search of the next donor.

Occasionally he would poke one or other with his stick, causing them to rear and hiss angrily at him just to show the onlookers that they were not as somnolent as they might appear. At the edge of the pit was a beehive shaped construction some three feet high, and four or more in diameter. For a finale, he casually put his bare arm through the dark entrance hole, and after some fumbling dragged out a huge king cobra that duly reared and menaced him with darting tongue as if to order.

At this Al would invariably find himself with an erection, which embarrassed him not one bit. God how he wished he could do what that skinny little gook was doing. It wouldn't take much to blow into his pants the way he was feeling right now. He was so excited he hardly felt the slight prick of the spring-needle-hypodermic on his right thigh. Dizziness overcame him. He found his actions becoming totally unco-ordinated, and leaned heavily over the wall before him.

The young Eurasian beside him made a grab for his collar to try and save him but it was too late. With a choking gargle, he rolled over the barrier and fell, with a solid thud, head first into the pit on top of a nest of vipers who took strong exception to his unannounced arrival. By the time the keeper got to him, the CIA man had been bitten at least half a dozen times on the face and neck and was deeply unconscious, his breathing failing.

The Thai doctor who was supposed to carry out the autopsy saw no reason to query the pronounced verdict of death by misadventure as a result of snake bite. Closer investigation might possibly have located a minute trace of curare but in any case the manner of dying is not dissimilar.

* * *

Jacob looked at the pathetic broken creature lying in his own filth and wondered why they bothered to manacle him.

213

It was obvious he could barely raise his head let alone create trouble. For a few seconds he felt a touch of pity then he noticed the blaze of pure hate in Hung's eyes, which stirred his resolve. He turned to the security man beside him.

'Has he identified my mother's murderer?'

The man nodded affirmatively.

'It took a long time though before he broke. He was a tough one. Real tough.'

'And?' asked Jacob.

'It was a nurse at the hospital. She has been shot – without publicity.' Then he added. 'A pity in a way. She was very attractive too.' The security man's tastes ran to women of generous proportions.

'She was a subversive killer!'

'Of course,' the man agreed hurriedly. 'Shall we leave now?' Obviously the stench was getting to him.

'What about him?' insisted Jacob pointing at the captive.

'He's been sentenced to death as well. We were just trying to get some more information about other members of his gang before we finish him.'

'When will that be?'

The security man put a handkerchief to his nose and retched quietly. 'Sorry, I have a very acute sense of smell.'

'That's alright,' said Jacob and then repeated the question. 'When will the sentence be carried out?'

The other man shrugged his shoulders and looked at the subject of their conversation in a disinterested sort of way. 'In a couple of days but I doubt he'll last that long. His kidneys have been battered to a pulp.'

As they left the bundle of rags stirred and a croaking whisper carried across to them, low but quite clear. 'Freedom will come one day despite anything you can do.'

After the door of the cell had clanged shut behind them the security man said: 'Funny that, it shouldn't be possible.'

'Why not?'

'On his final interrogation this morning we crushed his larynx to stop him making such a noise.'

Jacob's hand automatically went to his throat.

17

The old man, for the first time since Jacob had known him, was acting out of character. Overbearing and impatient.

Maybe I was away too long this time, he thought, but I did return as quickly as possible and my work did not actually suffer. Surely he understands that. 'I am sorry, Professor Wu, that you feel I am perhaps spending too much time on my own pursuits. It is of considerable importance to me, as you appreciate, and my work had reached a stage where a great deal of consolidation was required before I could proceed further.' Jacob shrugged, motioned with his hands. 'Consolidation that could quite easily be done by others and just as well too.'

Professor Wu was by no means appeased by this explanation. 'I disagree with you. Others may be able to synthesise your theoretical research into practical formulae but' – and here Wu wagged an admonishing finger – 'but not as satisfactorily as you and certainly not so quickly.' He sat back with an air of finality, brooking no argument. 'Have you yet satisfied your thirst for vengeance? Is your quest at an end? It has been going on now for quite some time.'

No, thought Jacob. No. No. No. There could be no question of a swift conclusion. The Englishman must know the agonies of mental as well as physical torture. The terror, the relaxation, when danger seems to drift away, then the sudden return of all his worst fears with the continual desperate uncertainty, until he is sent gibbering to his grave. The fact that I shall take his woman must surely be the sweetest revenge. I really do want her to the extent of fantasising about her. I must watch that. It is a weakness which I cannot allow to be exploited by an enemy. His thoughts raced on: God how I hate these people. No way can I back away from my utter determination to destroy them, no matter what Wu expects of me. When I think of the madness inflicted upon my mother and the callousness of her murder! My father went in a flash of light and, had I cared to keep my mouth shut, in a blaze of glory. But my mother – how terribly she must have suffered. The tears had forced themselves unbidden to his eyes as his thoughts raced on.

The professor, while appreciating Jacob's apparent re-morse, totally misconstrued its reason and hastened to mollify his protégé. 'I have perhaps been somewhat hasty, Jacob. I do realise how very valuable your work is but I am getting old.' His shoulders slumped convincingly. 'I cannot wait too long, as you appreciate, and every minute you are away now seems to be a minute wasted.'

This was a complete reversal of his previous attitude. Before Wu had virtually encouraged Jacob's desire for vengeance.

'Professor, I had gathered you did not disapprove, but now ...'

'So now I do,' said the other with the petulance of the old and powerful. 'And,' he added hoarsely, 'I have recently had an operation to cut out a cancer in my buttock.'

Jacob was shocked. 'I did not know, sir. I am so very sorry.'

'By the gods, so am I.' The old man shifted uncomfortably in his chair and cackled wryly. 'It's damned sore, I can tell you, and even though they tell me it's all been taken away, you never know when the foul thing's going to rear its head again. Do you now appreciate my viewpoint?' The professor was staring at him, waiting for his answer.

'Completely, professor, and please rest easy. I will work my hardest to ensure your objective is reached. My personal aims will have to wait for as long as is necessary, although I

216

trust you will grant me some leeway.' He leaned forward smiling in as winning a way as possible. 'After all, professor, this quest of mine for vengeance brings with it much satisfaction which leads on to creative thinking, thus improving the quality of my work.'

The Professor was not entirely impressed. 'What you're saying is that if you aren't happy you won't do such a good job for me.' He mused for a few seconds and said wryly: 'Sometimes the lash works, Jacob, but willing workers make the best workers, I suppose. Remember I'm sixty-one already and,' – he leaned forward and spoke more quietly – 'between you and me, Jacob, I have great plans for you. If all goes well you will be my successor one day and that, my boy, must be sufficient incentive for you.'

Indeed it is, Jacob mused, but there would be a grim grind ahead of him to accelerate the completion of the project sufficiently in order to satisfy the old man. But then, he thought, I will have the power and authority to carry out my personal plans without hindrance. With enormous effort it was possible.

He rose from his chair and smiled. 'I'll get on now, sir. There is much work to do, and thank you for your faith in me.'

The old man nodded at him approvingly.

18

Harwood hadn't heard from Summervill for a couple of months. Then a letter was hand-delivered to him from London. It was short and to the point.

'Dear Mr Harwood, I regret to inform you that a short time ago Brian Summervill died at his own hand from an overdose of sleeping pills. I enclose herewith a personal note that he left you, which you should destroy after reading. As this is a security matter I had to inspect its contents before dispatch. I was Brian's assistant so I am fully aware of the details pertaining to your case and will pass on any pertinent information that might come to hand. Yours sincerely, James Petersham.'

Cold, precise, factual. What more could he expect? Summervill's letter was somewhat different.

'My dear Derek, I feel I owe you a further explanation to my brief telephone call in January telling you that the opposition had garnered a great deal of information concerning our affairs. The party who provided the other side with information of your involvement in the episode was, I confess, myself. I will not go into over-much detail, suffice to say the pressure was considerable but is as nothing to the deep regret I feel at betraying you in this way. As I understand it there has been no attempt, as yet, upon your person and I sincerely hope there never will, but you must know that Al Craddock, the Bangkok CIA station chief, died in most unpleasant and, to my way of thinking, suspicious circumstances, from snake bites, and Hung, who co-operated with you in China, has been taken, and for all I know shot, as has his agent in the hospital. So far as I am personally concerned, they have been ruthlessly vindictive, whoever they are, and have infected me with AIDS, which will suck the life out of me. It has been hell and I am afraid I am not strong enough to withstand any more, so I will take the only way out and put an end to it. Before I close, I want to apologise for exploiting you in the way I have. I admit it was shameless, but my sort of work has always been dirty and the operation in which you were included was no exception. In a way I will be glad to escape. I would commend to you my colleague, James Petersham, who will, to the best of his ability, assist you in any way he can with information and advice. I hope you do not think too ill of me. Farewell and good luck. Yours, Brian.'

There was a post-script: 'One thing that I found very strange: the party who extracted the information from me spoke fluent English in a strong American accent, but with a slight Jewish flavour, yet happened to be Chinese. A strange combination. I know many Chinese do have an American intonation in their speech but this man's came to him in a totally natural way. Most of the Chinese that speak like that have Taiwan connections, if they are not born in the USA, and are not mainland Chinese. This man, when he spoke Chinese to his colleague, used the Hokla tongue and definitely came from the south. Perhaps this small detail may be of use to you but I leave you to draw your own conclusions.'

Harwood was shaking when he'd finished reading the letter and actually felt sorry for Summervill. There was no question that, despite the time which had passed, they were not secure. This was not the tactics of an organisation so unimaginative and blunt as the Guojia Anquanbu. The Guojia might be involved peripherally, but the sort of carefully planned, almost inspired, horror introduced into the destruction and elimination of Summervill and Craddock came from a single, highly fertile, yet twisted, mind, bent on the most dramatic retribution. And he and

219

his girl were next in line. They had to be. Who else was there?

He was unashamedly scared for them and driven to distraction by the constant need to move from one safe-house to another. Would it never end? And how long would they be able to rely on MI5's cooperation and that of Ching-hua's Chinese friends to shield them? He was sitting at his desk, in a daze, with the letter before him, looking out of the window at the garden which looked pretty damn bleak at this time of the year, in keeping with his mood. Then it came.

It had to be young Jacob Levinsky.

It had to be him. He had spoken with a totally American voice using the same phraseology and vocal mannerisms as his father. Even though he was only a youngster if one closed one's eyes it would be difficult to tell them apart. Also there had been the venom in Jacob's parting threat: 'The day will come when you may regret your woman's benevolence.' It made Harwood wish he'd finished him off after all, but Ching-hua would never have countenanced it. How the hell he could achieve the power to carry out a personal vendetta on such a scale was beyond comprehension. When the two of them discussed the possibility, Ching-hua came up with the probable answer.

'After all,' she said, 'they must have considered him the son of a heroic martyr who died because of an act of sabotage.'

That put it in a very neat nutshell but it still didn't ring quite right. Whatever, it did seem the only tenable proposition, and Ching-hua tended to agree, so at least it would appear they had identified their enemy, which was satisfactory in a dubious sort of way.

19

Jacob was 22 years of age. He could, among other subjects, philosophise learnedly on both versions of the anthropic principle, and whether there are many different universes or many different regions of a single universe. He had also, most importantly, recently provided his mentor, after months of grinding work and very little sleep indeed, with a decisive paper on the quantum theory of gravity for which the world had long been waiting.

It had gone out in Professor Wu's name, but he generously gave Jacob the main credit, which he felt he deserved, and now that the Herculean task was finished the opportunities were endless. To start with, a lengthy sabbatical had been promised, and upon his return Jacob was to be given a position nearer the hierarchy. Any doubts of the powers-that-be accepting such a young person Wu brushed aside, with the comment that the decision was his alone and would not be gainsaid.

Jacob's youth had, to a certain extent, passed him by. He had given up everything for his work, except sex, which had been provided courtesy of the state. And why not indeed? But never had he felt any element of affection for the women proffered. Just excitement and then the blessed relief of jangling nerves after the event. He wondered what a genuine romantic attachment must be like. If of course there were such a thing. Would the Englishman's woman fill that rôle for him? Did he feel love for her or was it just lust, or perhaps both? He was confused about such things.

Now that China was dipping her toes into the pool of democracy without its wholesale acceptance, as had proved so disastrous in the USSR, things had become somewhat more relaxed. The China of two roads functioned quite well. If one wished to relax in the bourgeois flesh-pots or become involved in genuine capitalism, it was easy enough to go to Hong Kong or Sham Chun or even Taiwan, which was approachable from the mainland if one knew how to go about it.

After short sojourns in such a frenetic atmosphere, Jacob found it a delight to return to the more measured way of life of Beijing, particularly in academia. And yet he longed to explore the outside world at his leisure. Not to just snatch a few days here or there but to linger, live and experience. He felt he was due such a privilege after the hard labour he had put in, with such stunning success.

He had been told by a delighted Professor Wu that they had both been honoured by the offer of fellowships in the Royal Society, a most scholarly English organisation and had been invited to attend special investitures in London at the end of the year. The professor, now, unfortunately, too infirm to travel such distances, had persuaded Jacob that he must go, as if persuasion were needed.

The marshall, surprisingly, had expired the previous month, and since he had heard nothing from the Ministry of State Security concerning Mayo or Rothnie or whatever he now called himself, Jacob intended to ascertain for sure what the situation was. To this end he had arranged a meeting with the marshall's replacement to find out what was happening with regard to his project.

* * *

'Ah, Lee Xian Sheng nin zao.' Mr Gao Shu Leung's initial welcome seemed friendly enough. The old marshall's place had been taken by a rather dumpy little civil servant, who owed Professor Wu precisely nothing.

Strange, thought Jacob, that such an unprepossessing,

222

middle-aged technocrat should be the second, if not *the* most powerful man in China. But one must be careful of small men. They have an inordinate lust for power. One only had to recall the revered leader Deng Xiaoping.

'I understand from Professor Wu that you wish to ascertain the whereabouts of an old enemy of yours, by the name of Mayo or Rothnie,' Gao enquired easily.

'An enemy of the state,' answered Jacob, perhaps more sharply than was necessary.

Gao's slit eyes flashed behind the rimless spectacles and the initial friendliness dissolved. 'I am very aware of those who are, or were, enemies of the state,' he intoned coldly, looking straight at the younger man. The implication against Jacob's father was ominously apparent. He was on dangerous ground and hurried to a safer footing.

'I must admit, for reasons undoubtedly well known to you, sir, that I have taken up this matter as a personal challenge and intend...' He got no further.

'I know that you have taken a great deal upon yourself in the past, with the apparent connivance of my predecessor, which frankly surprises me.' Gao touched a file that lay on top of his large desk, obviously Jacob's. 'You have meddled in matters in a way that could have caused acute embarrassment to the government, and left mayhem in your wake.'

'But, sir.'

'Things have moved on, Lee. The world is full of intelligence agents who only did their job according to their lights. If everyone started paying off old scores on their own initiative the situation would become untenable.'

Jacob was sweating now, with rage and surprise at this totally unexpected and, to his way of thinking, unmerited attack.

But Gao was remorseless. 'When I took office I studied the Mengwang incident in some depth and I can assure you the cold facts are that either the explosion was caused by an accident or, as you have drawn to Professor Wu's attention, a traitorous act, neither of which can be proved beyond doubt as the work of any foreign intelligence service.' He paused, leaned back in his chair. '"Prove" is the operative word, Lee. We only have here the fantasies of a traumatised young boy.'

Jacob leaped to his feet in a boiling rage ready to do the unthinkable, but the little man had the measure of him. 'I suggest you control yourself, Lee, and immediately, otherwise you are totally and absolutely finished,' and the palm of his hand smashed down on his desk top with a crack like a pistol shot.

That drew him up short. He turned as if to walk away presuming the meeting had concluded.

'Sit down and hear me out.'

Jacob sat, shaking as if in a fit. He was kept waiting for a minute, till he had calmed.

Then the security chief continued: 'Since I took over, I instructed our people in London to lift the surveillance on this man, so if he has moved recently we have no knowledge of his whereabouts, nor frankly do I care. We cannot afford to waste money on the personal vendettas of individuals.'

The young scientist said nothing. There was nothing he could say.

'If you wish to follow up this matter on your own initiative and at your own expense, Lee, so be it, but I warn you that you are completely on your own. We would disown you if anything were to come out. He raised a finger. 'You must appreciate that we have good relations with most of the world now, or at least with those that matter. As far as the USA is concerned we hold most-favoured nation status, and in no way must this be placed in jeopardy.'

At last Jacob felt he could control his voice. 'I understand,' he said. 'I suppose it all really boils down to money.'

That was pretty cheeky but the sarcasm appeared to be lost on Gao. 'Exactly,' he said. 'Whether we like it or not, we all live in a predominantly capitalist world.' He looked at his watch denoting the meeting was over. As he did not proffer his hand, Jacob stood up again and turned to leave.

'Thank you,' he muttered.

'A bit of advice,' said Gao, as a parting shot. 'I recommend you see a good psychiatrist to rid you of this murderous obsession of yours.'

About the only light on Jacob's horizon at the moment was the investiture by the Royal Society. He was looking forward to visiting London and to hell with Beijing. Why not seek pastures new where he might be better appreciated? he thought.

England

In the dark she lay, eyes open, grieving for herself and the man that lay beside her. Something had to be done, and soon, to get away from this suffocating supervision and the constant restrictions they suffered.

Ching-hua now accepted that her relationship with Derek no longer held the same fire she had come to expect, and it was a genuine shock to her when she had to admit that, frankly, she was bored. The fault was not his. It was the dreadful dragging circumstances under which they were forced to live. They made love frequently and enjoyably. He was a masterly lover and she was an enthusiastic partner, but her body did not really feel right. She was a ballet dancer of prima quality, and as such her whole being ached with the need and freedom to dance.

Harwood had arranged for a barre to be set up for her and she exercised frequently. But without companions of her own following – yes, and even that old bitch of a ballet master she had been trained by for years, whom she freely hated but admired for his skill – without such people what she did now was mechanical and uninspiring, and anyway where would the end result be displayed? The ecstatic adrenalin-rushing delights of the dance, the enthusiastic reception by cheering audiences and the sick terror of possible failure, yes even the last, was the very stuff of her existence. Without them life was not worth living.

And more even than this, and in a most contradictory

225

way, she ached for a child with all the fervour of the motherhood instinct instilled in her blood throughout 5,000 years of Chinese civilization. Harwood would not consider it. Having a child when they were never sure what catastrophe might strike without warning was irresponsible. It was crazy. She knew he was right but she also knew that if she was frustrated in all her needs then, surely as night followed day, she would rebel and perhaps hurt her beloved unbearably.

The impossibility of her situation overwhelmed her so that a great uncontrollable tearing sob broke involuntarily from her breast and the floodgates opened. A strong comforting arm came around her. She continued to weep until his soothing quietened her.

'Darling, sweet love, we will leave this place and take a chance on the outside world.' He gently tightened his grip. 'I know what you are going through, believe me, and I cannot bear to see our relationship slowly destroyed like this.'

'You think the risk is worth taking?' she asked tremulously, hopefully.

'It has to be, my darling. Carrying on in this way we will be destroyed anyway, which is just what our enemy wants to happen.'

'When do we go?'

'Soon, very soon. We must decide first where to go and how we arrange things. I will contact Summervill's colleague, Petersham, tomorrow, and see if he can give us any advice and useful information. After all he did say he would help us.

Petersham himself pre-empted them. It seemed that fate had taken a hand. He rang first, and gave a potted history of Jacob Levinsky, now apparently known as Lee Win Sie, and amazingly enough a high-flyer in the Chinese scientific establishment. So much so, in fact, that his successes had caused him to be honoured by the Royal Society with the offer of a fellowship. There was to be an investiture in London early in the new year when Levinsky would attend in person, using the name Lee Win Sie, and read a paper on his subject, whatever that was.

Harwood was sure he had identified their antagonist. Now he would be able to locate his whereabouts on his own home ground. The hunter would become hunted in his turn. Petersham seemed to understand their attitude entirely, although in true civil service fashion he impressed the dangers upon them and stressed the fact that his organization could no longer accept responsibility for their safety if they left. Harwood didn't tell him that they were planning to take on Levinsky. That would have caused all sorts of consternation, and anyway, Harwood had no idea at all how he would go about it yet, or even what he was going to do to the cocky young bastard if the opportunity arose.

As if reading his thoughts Ching-hua said: 'We both think we will have no peace until he is dead, so I suppose there can be no option.'

'Maybe, but it's easier said than done,' Harwood replied.

'You have reservations?' she asked.

'Of course I do, darling. I can't just walk up to him and kill him.'

'You are saying you have no moral objections?' She looked enquiringly at him.

'Not really,' he replied, getting in deeper. 'If he's done what I think he has, to Summervill, to Hung, and to Al, then he deserves what's coming to him.'

'And how about what we did to him?'

'Look,' Harwood said, a trifle exasperated. 'I'm not particularly proud of that episode but what would you have done? Do you reckon he's guilty or not?'

She sighed. 'I don't know, that's the problem. One minute it seems completely clear that he's got to be disposed of, then the next I wonder whether we are utterly sure that he is the ruthless killer we make him out to be. What if we killed him and whoever it is still kept after us?' She paused, and fluttered her hands. 'He seemed to be just a pleasant young man under tremendous pressure when we last saw him. And who can blame him?'

'Really what you're saying my love is that we can only make sure by confronting him in some way and that immediately gives him the advantage.' He looked into her eyes, but something seemed to have shut down behind them. 'Are you going soft on him?' Harwood asked. He kept his voice low because he didn't want to give the impression of jealousy.

'Perhaps. He seems so very young,' she said.

'He's only a year or so younger than you, darling.'

'There is young and young,' she replied enigmatically.

He was a trifle disturbed as to what might be going on in that profoundly Asian mind. People talk, half in humour, about the inscrutable oriental, and that was precisely what she had become. He didn't like it but he did appreciate that no matter how one loves a person, their right of withdrawal into themselves must be respected, and he comforted himself with the thought that whatever she was dreaming up was to their mutual betterment.

If he'd known the truth then he would probably have insisted they stayed where they were in a safe-house under guard.

20

Ching-hua, despite her tough revolutionary ideals, was a girl of strong traditional principles. She simply could not have Jacob's death upon her conscience without definite proof of his evil doing. They had abducted his father, blackmailed him into killing himself and then arranged for the murder of his mother in a most brutal way. Now they were considering the elimination of the son, the young genius, purely on circumstantial evidence suggested by Summervill, because of an unknown's voice and accent. This was democracy?

Her claim to be a member, and an influential one at that, of the pro-democratic party surely precluded her from such an act. She had killed in her time, that was true, but for reasons she considered acceptable in the struggle they were undertaking, or in self defence. This time she had to be very sure.

And yet again, she thought, were her reservations because of high-minded principles or might it be, might it just be, because she was drawn to this brilliant young man? This remarkably beautiful young man whom she had seen running so lithely with his father among the southern mountains. This young man who had kissed her hand and fervently thanked her for his life. How could she take it away from him after that? Only if he were the essence of evil, as was suspected, and if it was his intention to destroy her darling barbarian, then there could be no doubt of how she would act.

Whatever happened it was clear they could not go on living as they were, and therefore Jacob must be confronted by her and the truth extracted from him in any way possible. That was precisely what must be done. Derek was not to be involved, as that would only bring about a premature flash-point that would hide the truth in blood and destruction of one or the other. She would do it her way, by herself. Derek might disagree violently, but he would understand in the end.

February 1992

They made their decision, and left the safe-house routine behind them to live in a lovely isolated Wiltshire village. Harwood had hoped she would now be happier, but she was still jumpy and any mention of the plan to face up to Levinsky seemed to be side-tracked. He still kept his gun close to hand, but the feeling of imminent doom had begun to fade somewhat.

Then one day, as she opened the paper, he noticed her hand begin to tremble. 'What is it my darling?'

She passed it over without comment. There at the head of a special science report was a photograph of their quarry, smiling cheerfully at the camera, and, so the article said, showing modest delight at the honour to be bestowed upon him by the Royal Society in London on 10th March. Whilst in London he would be staying at the society's private quarters, and hoped to have many discussions with his Western peers during his stay.

'Right,' Harwood said, determined that there would be no more prevarication. 'We know where he is going to be, and when. How do we go from here?' He leaned earnestly toward her putting his hand on hers. 'We must talk about it, sweetheart. I really do need your co-operation.'

She stroked his hand nervously and kept her eyes down. 'Me, not us,' was what she said. She was nervous but her voice was quite firm.

'You've lost me,' he replied, genuine in his confusion.

She looked him straight in the face now. 'Do you trust me?' she asked.

'With my life,' he said without hesitation, 'but that doesn't mean I don't want to know what's going on.'

'I have made some telephone enquiries about him through my London contacts.' And in case he didn't believe her, she said quite strongly, 'We have them you know, in the inner councils of the party.'

Harwood sat there without saying anything. He didn't know whether to be furious or to praise her, so kept quiet except to say, 'And?'

'We have an ardent supporter, a mole, who sits reasonably close to Gao Shu Leung.'

'And who's he when he's at home?'

'The new head of Chinese state security,' she said casually. That grabbed Harwood's attention for sure. 'He says the file on Lee Win Sie is so secret it is kept in Gao's personal safe and no one, but no one, else has access to it.'

'So what can your friend tell you?'

'Details about Levinsky which can be ascertained from keeping close observation on him, but nothing pertaining to his work or certain jobs he appears to have carried out at the behest of Marshall Chau, the previous head of state security. Also he cannot tell us what the official attitude might be pertaining to us, which is a pity. However there is something else about Levinsky that needs to be taken into account. He is an ardent student of Chè Gów, the Chinese equivalent of the black arts, and I've also learned that he does not touch alcohol or smoke. He works out in a gym four times a week. He is lusty sexually and takes advantage of party courtesans offered him, but has no close relations with any woman. He is an excellent shot, and most important he is a sixth Dan in judo.'

'How does this paragon find time for his work?' Harwood asked jokingly, but he was worried. He knew about Chè Gów and tended to take it seriously, as he'd seen some pretty strange happenings in his time when Chinese soothsayers set about their business, and as for being a sixth Dan, that made the lad a real menace.

'He only needs two or three hours' sleep in twenty-four. Frequently less,' she added grimly. Harwood was about to ask another question or rather several but she interrupted him. 'There is no proof whatsoever that Lee did what we think he may have done to Summervill and the others, therefore I intend to find out by contacting him myself, and I am sure I can get him to take me into his confidence.' She looked at him entreatingly. 'You, my dearest, who trusts me, will leave this to me. Not only can I do it more easily, because he is half in love with me – don't ask me how I know, I just do – but because for you it would be too dangerous. Strong man though you may be, he would demolish you, darling. You must know that.'

In his heart of hearts, Harwood realised, his SAS training notwithstanding, she was right, but felt as if he had been emasculated. 'You would go all the way with him to get to the truth?' he asked hurtfully, hating himself for saying it.

'To ensure your well being it would be a small price to pay,' she said calmly.

'And if you satisfy yourself that he deserves to die how will it be done?'

'Ah,' she said, head on one side. 'Then both of us will keep well in the background. I have many friends who will delight in avenging Hung.'

If she could arrange all that, who the hell was he to stick in his oar just to try and satisfy male chauvinist pique? 'You'll be going to the investiture, I suppose.'

'Yes, darling, and I was lucky enough to get the last invitation, too.' That was certainly one way of making it clear that he would not be coming along with her.

'God, I hope you know what you are doing.'

'I can look after myself and I will have someone keeping an eye on me, I promise you,' she said, rather too complacently he thought.

'And I will be one of them,' he said firmly. 'And don't think you can stop me.'

'Please, my beloved, don't, I beg of you, alert him to the fact that you are after him. You are not a professional, and if he spots you that's the end of the operation and possibly me as well.'

'Won't your Chinese friend, the one keeping an eye on you, tend to stand out somewhat, too, if he stays close enough to protect you?' Harwood asked.

'Not really. Jacob's expecting to have certain security people from the embassy watching over him.'

'And one of them is loyal to you, I suppose?'

'Absolutely right,' she said.

She had an answer to everything that girl, and she could twist most men round her finger. Harwood was willing to bet that the Levinsky boy would be no exception, as he clearly remembered the look of adoration on his face when he kissed her hand at Mengwang.

'Please, darling,' she entreated, 'it really would be best if you stayed here so I could contact you when I need you. I'll let you know soon enough, believe me.'

'If he allows you to,' he muttered, realising that by such a simple statement he was more or less acquiescing to her mad-cap scheme.

'Don't call me I'll call you, right?' he said bitterly, jealousy boiling up in him like a maelstrom. And then he momentarily lost control and, grabbing her shoulders, shook her hard. 'I love you like crazy,' he shouted, 'and I should never let you do this but I don't see another way. If anything happens to you I'll kill the bastard without pandering to your high democratic principles.'

The tears started to slide down the cheeks of her lovely face then, so he hugged her close, gently now, and begged her forgiveness, and she kept whispering in his ear: 'It must be this way, my darling, it must be this way.'

Maybe so, he thought, but at the back of his mind, squatting, grinning obscenely to itself, was the green-eyed god and it wouldn't quite go away.

10th March 1992

Jacob was delighted to go to London for many reasons. Prestige was, of course, one of them. To rub shoulders with Western scientists and hopefully pick their brains, as he was sure they would endeavour to pick his, would be enormously stimulating. Now that he would no longer receive assistance from that arrogant little bureaucrat, Gao, he had to arrange matters on his own. Somehow he would find this man Mayo, and killing him after such a search would be particularly satisfying. That, and particularly the taking of Mayo's woman, with his knowledge. He therefore had to make the beast come to the trap, and to do this he had courted publicity ever since he had known of the invitation. He was to be the lure that would draw Mayo inexorably to his miserable end and he could not even consider failure in his present euphoric mood.

He was quite calm, awaiting his turn to be called to the platform for the introduction before reading his paper. After all, he had unlocked one of the great secrets of the universe and, despite his youth, was the equal, probably the superior, of anyone here. All about him were men, and a few women, of serious mien but all were congratulatory and obviously eager to hear what he had to say. Where he was presently seated, in the front, his vision was limited to those nearby, so he could not fully comprehend the vastness of the hall and the multitude of his potential audience. The chairman called his name and requested him to come and join them on the platform.

He rose and, in memory of his father, muttered a silent prayer to his god, Yaweh – a Yaweh in whom he did not really believe. He walked up the steps and the chairman shook his hand warmly. He was ushered to a chair next to the lectern and then introduced in the most complimentary terms. He was given a moment for contemplation while the chairman rambled on, and his eyes wandered around the audience. There must have been several hundred upturned faces, but suddenly he saw her, as clearly as if a searchlight had been turned on her beautifully-boned face.

Even though she was ten rows back from the front, she stood out like a golden chrysanthemum among the pale, uninteresting ovoids about her. He looked for Mayo but the beast was not present. Levinsky's heart leaped in his chest. She had come in secret, so that she could see him, just the two of them, in private. Might he be making too much of this? he wondered. He didn't care. First he must have her. She is the key. How did she get in among this throng of greyheads? But she was here, and that was what counted. He gazed at her intently. She knew he had picked her out. A slight movement of her head showed him that.

There was the sound of clapping. The chairman ushered him to the lectern. He rose easily to his feet, smiling, and, taking his notes, laid them carefully before him, then pushed them gently to one side. He knew what he was going to say by heart. He fixed his gaze upon Ching-hua and talked as if to her. Caressing her with his eyes, he made love to her throughout his detailed and fluent discourse on the quantum theory of gravity.

The effect on her was obvious. She leaned forward in her seat, eyes fixed on his as if hypnotised, her full lips slightly parted. She understood hardly a word he said but that was of no import. It was evident she wanted him. He was sure of that.

When he came to a conclusion there was dead silence for a full twenty seconds. The audience sat there, rapt, and Jacob came close to knowing how the deity feels at times of divine pronouncement. Then the clapping started, a polite ripple at first, led by the chair, which gradually built up to a thunderous ovation. He stood quietly, smiling acceptance of their appreciation, then gazed again at that exquisite creature, whom he was sure was his for the taking, willing her to come to him. She rose gracefully from her seat, walked sinuously down the aisle, heads turning as she advanced, then stopped and stood at the bottom of the steps before him. He put out his hand and she came up to him, grasped it, and stood beside him.

I have her now, he gloated inwardly.

* * *

He has seen me and gazes at me so intensely it is embarrassing, Ching-hua thought. She nodded her head to confirm contact. He was smiling now and relaxed and wondrously handsome. No one else seemed to have taken note of their communion. She watched him stand and move easily over to the lectern, pushing his notes to the side, and beginning to talk.

His accent seemed American, but without any harshness or twang, and his voice was deep, well-modulated and demanded attention.

His face recalled to her the look of the young Gregory Peck, with a slightly Oriental touch. With a shock, she suddenly realised she was totally in his thrall. She could not have looked away from him, even had she so desired, which she did not.

Ching-hua could barely make any sense of what Jacob was saying, but it did not seem to matter. His voice and look continued to hold her so that she found it difficult to breathe, not wanting to miss something.

Oh, my darling, hairy barbarian, she thought. When you said this man was dangerous you did not know the half of it. He is seducing me, stripping me naked, doing what he will with me in front of all these people.

She pressed her knees together, squirming in her seat, feeling the moisture slide between her thighs. I don't believe this, she thought, wildly. I am coming. Yes, actually having an orgasm. She seemed to twitch and shudder for an age, but no one else appeared to notice. Was he doing this to her in her mind? She couldn't tell.

He had finished speaking, and the applause was mounting and wildly enthusiastic for such a reserved gathering. Jacob nodded slightly in acceptance, then stared straight at

Ching-hua, eyebrows raised, so that she felt herself commanded to rise and go to him. Flustered by the stares, she stopped below the platform, looking up at him. He beckoned her up, and putting out his hand, took hers. His touch was sensuousness personified, so that she felt quite weak with desire for him. He smiled reassuringly, but for an instant behind his eyes she saw a flash of cruel perversion and a desire for total domination of her mind and body. Despite this, she somehow wished to be overwhelmed by him, to enjoy or suffer any sensation or humiliation he might wish to inflict upon her.

It is madness I know, my darling, was Ching-hua's last thought, but I cannot draw back now. May the gods help me.

21

Ching-hua felt as though she were in a dream, quite unable to change the course of events. She realised that his control over her was more than simple charisma, and whilst frightened by it, it was a delicious form of terror that made him totally desirable to her. After the formalities, they returned to the seclusion of his impressively luxurious apartment with hardly an exchange of words. He introduced her to no one and no one seemed curious as to her identity. Or else they were too polite to ask. Jacob simply took her by the elbow and steered her away to his waiting chauffeur-driven car as if it was the most natural thing in the world.

Once they were alone, there were no preliminaries. He immediately started to undress her, slowly piece by piece. She felt his touch all over her body, sensual yet with tremendous latent strength, so that she knew he could handle her physically in any way he wished and she would have no option but to be completely malleable.

First her blouse, his long powerful fingers undoing each button, touching her breasts, teasing them out from their silken covering, sucking at the nipples, hurting her just a trifle with his teeth. He was impatient with the skirt, tearing it a little. His first sign of human frailty. He stepped back then and looked at her in her underthings as if perusing a painting. His eyes glistened.

'I have dreamed of this ever since Mengwang,' he said, and coming towards her brutally tore the rest of her clothing away, then flinging her back on to the bed stood over her, legs astride.

She cowered below him and tentatively reached out to touch the protuberance at his crotch. He groaned and indicated she should strip him. She complied eagerly, anxious to please.

Naked he was magnificent but with the impatience of youth he wished to take her immediately. She stopped him, kissing and fondling him about his body, which was as taut and well-moulded as only a finely trained athlete's can be. With enormous effort he controlled himself, apparently appreciating what she was doing, and began to search her out in return, his mouth exploring every nook of her, his teeth and tongue holding and tasting her flesh so that she quivered with pleasure. Their mouths melted into each other's seeking out their sliding tongues. Finally they could no longer wait and he took her, without further delaying the ultimate pleasure, which came upon them in a flash of shuddering ecstasy, tearing through both their bodies.

He lay quietly, still within her, exhausted, vulnerable, cheek against hers and she could feel his heart pounding upon her breasts so that an overwhelming affection, almost motherly, for him swept over her.

She had enjoyed the lovemaking greatly but felt terrible guilt, even though she had known that this happening would be inevitable if she were to get at the truth. She was convinced her darling barbarian, inwardly, also knew and would, she hoped with all her heart, accept the situation. She could not bear to contemplate losing him despite what she had done.

Jacob stirred, raised his head and gazed into her eyes, his breath hot upon her face. 'That was the most wonderful thing that has ever happened to me,' he said simply, and she felt him harden again within her until he was once more rampant, swelling with lust.

Gently his hands begin to move about her body, searching for where her sensations were gathered. He waited for her to respond, realising by the slightest tremor, when his fingers touched, where she wanted him the most. Her skin was now so sensitive to his every caress that it seemed charged with electricity.

From an unknown depth of her body there came a burning fever that would not spend itself nor could it be assuaged by mere sexual gratification. She wanted more: to devour him, to take him wholly into her. She wrapped herself violently about him and felt his teeth bury themselves in her shoulder as she bit hard into his neck.

She convulsed with erotic excitement and then the taste of blood on her lips dragged her back to reality and she pulled her mouth away, shaken by the madness that had come over her, yet desperate for more, contracting violently, letting him mould and push and almost tear at her to suit his rhythm. All of a sudden he cried out, as if in agony, head raised, eyes rolled up, the blood dripping from his neck upon her breasts. He exploded within her then collapsed aside with a groaning sigh.

'I adore you,' he whispered, and fell almost immediately into sleep so deep as to approach insensibility.

Would he confide in her now, she wondered. Most men talk too much in the throes of a passion, or so they say, but how could she bring up the subject without arousing his suspicion? And if she were to convince herself of his innocence of these ghastly murders or his intent to kill Derek, what then? She could not help but feel something for this beautiful young man. What woman wouldn't after what had passed between them?

He stirred, and opened his eyes. They were incredibly bright. He smiled gently, stretched luxuriously, then casually fondled her breasts. Was he insatiable, this man?

'Mengwang,' he said, and her heart jumped with excitement.

'What about it?' she enquired, coolly.

'Did you really persuade Mayo to say I could go free no matter what my father did?'

240

He was going to talk and this was no time for the truth. 'Indeed I did.'

'Why?'

But it was a time for flattery. 'You were completely innocent, too beautiful to die, and I think I was already attracted to you even then.'

'You felt that even though you were Mayo's lover?' he asked naively.

She knew the answer he wanted. 'Yes,' she said, lowering her eyes modestly.

'And do you now?' He took one of her nipples between his teeth and nibbled it. It was almost a threat.

She winced then gave a little shiver of genuine desire. 'Yes,' she repeated. 'And you?'

He continued to nuzzle her and she felt her nipples harden. He raised his head and looked at her in a way that touched the heart.

'What is happening between us is the only decent thing to come out of Mengwang.' He was speaking louder now, sitting up, gesticulating, his voice full of emotion.

'The horror of it was almost more than I could bear, and there was only one way to obtain relief from the pressure of the hatred I had building up within me.'

'And that was?' she asked.

'Is it not obvious?'

He looked at her slyly for a second or two, from the side of his eyes. A glance full of meaning, of questioning, as if he were wondering whether or not to commit himself further to the relationship. Perhaps take a step which would be irrevocable. And then he obviously came to a decision.

'Revenge,' he said loudly. Almost a shout. The word hung there, seeming to echo round the chamber.

'In what way?' she asked ingeniously.

'There is only one way,' he said, taking a deep breath. 'Eliminate those who deserve to die for the crimes committed.'

She could understand his feelings completely but she was not doing this to discuss the moral issues. She simply wanted to know how involved he had been, if at all, in the

241

deaths of Summervill, Al and Hung and more importantly now, was it his intention to go after Derek, or perhaps even herself, in murderous fashion.

'How can you, a scientist and academic, carry out such acts?' She smiled in a slightly condescending manner that obviously irritated him. 'You are not a killer. You would need considerable resources and the assistance of professionals to do such things.' She shook her head in feigned disbelief and said, 'I know from my own sources that Hung and our Chinese minder in England were killed by the Chinese security services, the Guojia Anquanbu, but the others who were responsible...' She shrugged her shoulders continuing, 'Summervill killed himself because he had AIDS, and Al died in a snake pit in Bangkok. Surely these things could not be your doing?' She wrinkled her nose at him in a teasing manner. 'You may know the universe intimately but here on earth you live in a world of fantasy. In fact, you probably never even knew their names before I mentioned them, so how would you have been able to identify your targets, other than perhaps Mayo?'

He was furious at her patronising manner, furious to the extent that he did not know whether to strike her or tell her everything, just to show her. He did both. He had professed to adore her but in that second the psychopath took over.

The slap came with lightening speed to the side of her head and whilst it seemed to be a mere flick of his wrist it was delivered with such power that she was virtually stunned. The next second he was all over her, the tears starting in his eyes, begging her forgiveness, crushing her to his chest so that she could barely breathe. Her efforts to release herself were completely unavailing. She opened her mouth to scream. He placed his mouth over hers. The strength of the man was overwhelming. She sagged in his arms. Immediately he released her, soothed her, stroked her hair, pleaded with her to forget what had happened. Promised never to maltreat her again.

'You promise?' she asked, as if talking to a small boy.

'I promise,' he replied solemnly.

She could almost envisage his fingers crossed behind his back but nevertheless, for the sake of survival, she said, 'Then I forgive you,' and gave him a gentle kiss on the cheek.

He perked up immediately, smiled delightfully, then taking her hand in his, kissed her fingertips and held them up before his face. Looking over the top of them, and completely out of the blue, he said, 'I did do it, you know.'

'Did what?' she asked, praying he would not incriminate himself in her eyes.

'I killed Summervill by injecting him with AIDS-infected blood.' He grinned in self-satisfaction at the recall. 'His name was given to me by the Guojia Anquanbu after I told my mentor the truth about what happened at Mengwang.'

'You told them about your father,' she said gaping, 'and they did nothing to you?'

'I had proved my value by then,' he replied proudly, as if the matter required no further explanation.

She said nothing. She could not say anything.

He was amused and gratified by her expression, which he evidently took as hero-worship and approval of his cleverness. 'The Guojia Anquanbu gave me a good lead. I was permitted, no encouraged, to follow it up on my own initiative, which I did, with, of course, complete success.'

'Of course,' she echoed hollowly.

'Under the threat of the needle, Summervill told me everything. Names, places, the lot. You'd be amazed at how easy it was.'

'And then?'

'And then I injected him anyway.' He laughed out loud at the memory. 'You should have seen the expression on the miserable fool's face.'

'I suppose you injected Al Craddock with snake poison too?' she enquired, looking at him with adoring eyes and sick to her stomach.

'Not quite, but close,' he said, smiling charmingly. 'Curare actually, to make him feel dizzy and then I toppled him in among the krites.' He looked at her to see what effect his narrative was having.

She kept a glassy-eyed look of appreciation on her face. 'So who's next?' she asked. 'The heads of the CIA and MI5 as, after all, they bear the ultimate responsibility?'

'I like that,' he said, chuckling happy. 'You're beautiful and you've got a sense of humour too.'

'Thank you, my darling,' she replied, and the last word was the most difficult she had ever had to say in her life.

'No, not them.' He was all serious now, and she could see his jaw muscles working and the artery throbbing in his neck with the strength of his feelings. 'Just one more directly guilty party and that, my beautiful one, is where you come in.'

He turned looking directly at her. She knew what was coming but she still did not wish to believe it. 'Your ex-English lover, Mayo or Rothnie or whatever he calls himself.' The 'ex' was strongly stressed with an enormous amount of gratification. 'He will die knowing you were the willing bait that drew him to his death.' He paused, looked at her quizzically, took her by her hair, pulled her hard against him and whispered in her ear: 'You are willing, are you not?'

She nodded assent as much as she could with his hand now clamped like iron round the back of her neck.

'That's good,' he said, easing up the pressure a trifle. 'We are two of a kind, you and I, and from now on you will not leave me. That's how much I need you.' He smiled at her as if they had been passing the casual pleasantries of lovers, not murderers, then kissed her brutally, pressing her back on to the bed, his hands gripping and kneading her flesh so that she jerked and flinched, and yet could not resist the rising tide of excitement his rough caresses brought her, despite her, now very genuine, terror of him.

'Can you not do this without me?' she asked huskily, trying hard to restrain her feelings and to keep him talking. 'Can't the Guojia Anquanbu do the dirty work for you?'

He stopped mauling her at that. 'Those bastards. I spit on them. They have told me I am on my own and they will no longer have anything to do with it now that Gao Shu Leung has taken over from the old marshall.' He clenched his fist and she drew back but he had no intention of hitting her again. 'Do you know that gutless bureaucrat had the temerity to accuse me of lying about my father's death, and said nothing about Mengwang could be proved as being instigated by any foreign intelligence service.' He shook his head, amazed by such idiocy. 'Oh no, the Chinese government is no longer interested in following up the perpetrators of that foul act, so I am left completely to my own devices. They have washed their hands of me in this regard at least.'

To Ching-hua it was an enormous relief to know that Chinese state security were no longer after them. Now at least they knew without doubt who their enemy was and what must be done. She looked at Jacob, and wished with all her being that this beautiful creature should be allowed to live, but in her heart she knew it was impossible. She felt almost as if the problem was solved now that she could see their way clear.

'Did you hear me?' he asked irritably, gripping her chin. Her mental meandering was brought swiftly back on track. 'What were you thinking about?' he asked, staring at her. His voice had a sinister note now.

They were both still naked from their lovemaking and she felt horribly vulnerable. 'If you really want to know, I was thinking how fine your body looks,' she said truthfully. It was the right thing to say. He was monstrously vain. 'Anyway, what was it I missed?' she asked.

'I was saying we must discuss plans about Mayo.' She was totally alert now but made a non-committal sort of noise waiting for him to take the lead. 'First of all I want you to write down his address and telephone number on this.' He handed her a pad and pen from the bedside table.

As she wrote she could feel his eyes on her, boring into her as if gauging her trustworthiness. Initially she considered giving a false number and address but that would only delay the inevitable. When she finished he snatched the pad away from her and scanned it quickly.

'Where is this Wiltshire?'

'To the west of here, two to three hours by car.'

'Ah yes,' he said, eyes half-closed. 'It is the dark province.'

He was right, she thought. Wiltshire was reputed to be the darkest county in England, and also the one with the highest rate of incest, illiteracy and witchcraft.

She laughed nervously. 'The villages are far apart so it does seem dark, or so they say, but how do you know?'

He said nothing; he just looked at her, and in those piercing eyes, that seemed to see into her very innermost consciousness, there leaped a light of triumph.

He tapped the pad with his finger. 'I know now how we will bring the beast to his death.'

She had to contact Derek and put him on his guard. But would she ever be left alone long enough? She looked nervously around, seeking a phone.

'What are you looking for?' he asked, a quizzical expression on his face.

'Nothing really,' she said lamely, praying desperately that a chance would arise for her to get a call through to her beloved. He must be warned before this psychopath could get at him.

He asked her if she would like to take a shower. She feigned exhaustion. 'I think I'll lie here and rest for a bit; I'm tired.' She smiled at him. 'You're quite a lover you know. You'd wear any woman out.' He liked that and accepted the flattery happily. 'You go ahead,' she said, 'I'll come in after you, okay?'

He swaggered off, pleased with himself, and she waited for the noise of running water, then got off the bed and slipped into the sitting room. She breathed a sigh of relief. The phone was there. An old fashioned one with a circular dial. It took an age to call the number but thankfully it was not engaged.

Come on, darling, she urged, silently. Hurry up please, please. She nearly put the phone down in despair, then all of a sudden his dear voice came over the phone.

'Darling, is that you? I've been worried sick. I can't stand thinking of that bastard laying his hands on you.'

'Enough, enough, my love,' she interrupted him. 'I have only seconds. Please listen.' She took a deep breath. 'The man is totally mad and very dangerous. You were so right, darling. Just watch out for him, please, he's desperate to get at you, but at the moment he thinks he's in love with me. I must admit he has incredible charisma but I see through him completely now.'

'Tell me where you are I'll come for you right away.'

'No, no. Can't you see if I stay with him I can learn how he's thinking and keep you forewarned. Sorry I can't stay on the line or he'll catch me. Just keep alert at all times. I'll get back to you I promise. I love you, darling.' She was babbling now and full of panic. She put the phone down hurriedly and, whether or not it was her imagination, she thought she heard a click, as if an extension had gone down at the same time.

She hurried back to the bedroom, feeling sick with fear, and literally hurled herself onto the bed. A minute went by and she began to breathe easier. She lay, pretending to doze, and then opened her eyes sleepily as she heard him come out of the bathroom.

'What a sleepy girl you are, my darling,' he said and, coming to the bed, he leaned over her, put his mouth on hers and ran his hands gently over her belly and breasts.

She could not help it. She felt herself becoming hot for him, stirring restlessly under his touch. She put her arms round his neck and drew him down but he disengaged himself and said: 'I've left the shower on. You can step right into it. He smacked her bottom as she obediently got off the bed and moved to the bathroom.

She pulled back the shower curtain and, as she stepped in, out of the corner of her eye, she saw the telephone extension on the bathroom wall. Please don't let him have listened in, she prayed. Surely if he had heard her he would have given a sign. Perhaps even strangled her on the spot.

'Calm down girl,' she said to herself firmly. 'You are imagining problems that don't exist.' But she felt weak with fear.

Jacob's disappointment was overwhelming. He'd really thought she was with him. He had forced himself to smile at her so she had no inkling that he knew what she was about, the treacherous bitch. It was as well to lull her into a false sense of security for as long as possible. He could not understand how she could prefer her middle-aged lover to him. He had so much more to offer her. She had not even waited until he got into the shower before betraying him.

If she knew for sure that he had listened in she would undoubtedly be more difficult to handle, so he had to turn his knowledge to his advantage and utilise her as best he could despite herself. When he finally faced her with her treachery she would be truly devastated, and with good reason. How dare she say he was mad. Dangerous maybe. Charismatic he agreed, that was plain from the behaviour of those around him, but mentally unstable, no way. He was close to penetrating her thought processes but not entirely, as it required great concentration, and at present she was too agitated to be receptive.

She appeared naked and still slightly damp from the shower. So beautiful, so very beautiful. It is terrible that he would probably have to destroy her. He put his arms about her and could feel her tremble. Was it fear or desire or perhaps a mixture of both?

'You're trembling, my darling, what is it?'

'You seem to have this effect on me,' she said, her face against his chest.

He held her at arm's length. 'You will phone Mayo tomorrow and tell him that if he ever wishes to see you alive again he is to meet us at a time and place of my choosing.' She started to sag in his arms, her eyes and mouth wide open, consumed by terror. 'It is only a ploy, my sweet, to get him where I wish him to be, a place where I will hold the advantage and be able to dispose of him at my leisure, with you by my side.' He put his hand under her chin and lifted it so that she was forced to look at him. 'It is what we both want, is it not?'

'Yes,' she whispered.

'So relax my dearest, and get some sleep.' He paused, and looked at her with a lecherous grin. 'If I leave you alone long enough, that is.'

11th March 1992

Harwood was reading the science editor's column in the *Times*: 'There was a most delightful happening yesterday at the august premises of the Royal Society when all those present, including the writer, were enraptured by a youthful Chinese genius, Lee Win Sie, who brought our knowledge of the universe forward a great stride with the reading of his paper on the quantum theory of gravity. One of those particularly affected was a fascinatingly beautiful Chinese girl who, obviously at the young scientist's behest, joined him on the platform to share the tumultuous plaudits of the gathering after the reading finished. From the way they were looking at each other it appears obvious theirs is no ordinary relationship.'

Harwood didn't need a journalist to tell him that. He'd seen the short TV extract of the reading on the late news the night before, and also what had occurred at the end. The cameraman had obviously not been overly excited by the affair until Ching-hua had appeared on the scene. He'd immediately zoomed in on her face, almost to the exclusion of everything else, for at least ten seconds, and then a quick flash to Lee, then back to her.

The jealousy and hatred that welled up in Harwood was overwhelming. No one could act an expression like that. She was dying for him. It was bloody obvious. How could she be like this and he be stupid enough to trust her? She had warned him. He had to admit that, but he couldn't believe she would be so blatant about it. 'To ensure your well being,' she had said, 'it would be a small price to pay.' She appeared to be willing to pay it now and with obvious relish. He hated the bitch. No, he didn't, he loved her and was worried sick about her and the devilment young Levinsky might be practising upon her. And there was bugger all he could do about it but hang around waiting for her to call, if she ever would.

Then the telephone rang. It was her and she was terrified. His suspicions were correct and it sent him mad with frustration to know that she was the captive of a homicidal maniac and he could only stand by and do nothing. He should never have let her go in the first place. More fool him.

Bringing in the police would produce even more frustration. 'Officer my girlfriend is in the hands of a murderous nutcase, to whom she went voluntarily when his scientific achievements were being recognised by the Royal Society, and I want you to find out where he is and take her away by force.'

Such an approach would be met with blank incredulity, particularly as Lee Win Sie would probably become a household name in the UK as a result of his appearance on TV and for that matter Ching-hua was now pretty well known too. A young, handsome genius with a beautiful young girl and this middle-aged geezer comes along claiming she's his and is being held against her will. Furthermore, and get this, he wants the police to get her back because she's in imminent danger. He could just see it.

No. He'd have to take action himself, whether or not she wanted it. It shouldn't be too difficult to find out where they were. A call to the Royal Society should do the trick.

He walked toward the phone, his mind made up, to ring the Society. It rang just as he reached for it, making him jump. It was her again.

'Where are you my love,' he shouted, anxious to get it in first.

Her voice was very low. He could hardly hear it. 'No time for that, Derek.' She sounded strangely formal and this time must have been speaking under duress. 'If you wish to see me alive again you must –' She gave a squeal and broke off, as if someone had wrenched the phone out of her hand.

250

'You recognise her voice, Mayo, or Rothnie, or whatever you call yourself?'

It had to be Levinsky. He exploded, shouting obscenities, threats, giving full vent to his rage. The phone was slammed down. He stood there shaking with hate, the phone in his hand. Slowly he regained control and put it back. It rang again immediately. He took a deep breath, steadied himself and picked it up. This time, for her sake, he had to listen.

'No more histrionics, please. I will give instructions as to when and where you will go and will follow them.' A pause. 'If you don't, you know what will happen.'

'I can guess,' Harwood said.

'No police, no accomplices. Just you and me, Mayo, and of course Ching-hua who will be there to witness your total degradation at my hands.'

'When?' Harwood asked, refusing to be drawn.

'That's better, Mayo.'

He waited.

'This coming Friday, the thirteenth, a day of ill omen for Englishmen, no?'

'Time?' he spat out.

'At four-thirty in the morning.' He kept Harwood waiting again, before giving the destination. 'The place is well known to you, Mayo, and conveniently nearby.'

'Thoughtful of you,' Harwood said, but the sarcasm went right over the top of the other man's head.

'Stonehenge,' Jacob continued. 'Within the ring of sarsen stones.' Harwood couldn't help himself. 'For Christ's sake you're mad,' he burst out.

There was a cold silence, then Jacob continued as if he had not been interrupted. 'In front of the altar Stone which lies on the surface of the ground towards the apex of the horseshoe. It is a single large slab some five metres long. You can't miss it. The night will be clear, well-lit by the stars and a quarter moon.'

'I wish to speak to Ching-hua again,' Harwood demanded.

'You will be able to speak to her soon, and remember, bring no one, or she will suffer.' The phone went down.

251

'If he thinks I'm going to turn up for some medieval duel to the death with a sixth Dan and not take any precautions he's got another think coming,' muttered Harwood to himself. He reached in the drawer of his desk for the Browning and the phone rang yet again.

'No weapons, either,' the voice said, and this time there was a slight snigger as the line was broken.

Harwood started to sweat. The bastard's got into my bloody mind now! What in God's name is he doing to my girl?

* * *

'That was well done, my love. He will come now, for sure. The cry of distress you simulated as I took the phone away from you really convinced him.' He grinned at her, hugely pleased with the way things had gone, and the light of madness in his expression was now glaringly obvious. He'd really hurt her wrist wrenching the instrument away, but she gave a tremulous smile in return and backed away from him, anxious to avoid any further contact.

'There are a few things to do before we leave, but there is plenty of time for that, and right now I find you completely irresistible.' He moved nearer and, picking her up without the slightest apparent effort, carried her toward the bed. She was too terrified to resist him. She was not even sure if she wanted to, even now.

22

Thursday 12th March 1992

Tim McGilligan was an oddity. He was a throwback, an Irish tinker – not the type of highly suspect character that goes by such a description these days, but a genuine Irish tinker of the old school, who carried his tools on his back and turned his hand to any odd job to earn a living, mostly honest, except for the acquisition of the odd chicken or two, if perchance it strayed into his path.

He mended pots and pans, did a bit of carpentry, sharpened knives, would turn over a spinster's vegetable garden and, if called upon, might provide additional services as well. There was a considerable number of sturdy, green-eyed children in the area with carrot tops, who bore a striking likeness to him and also bore witness to his popularity, for he was a well-set-up man, big and muscular, and despite the fact that he lived rough he was always clean enough by country standards. Suffice to say, he harmed no one, was welcome in the isolated villages where he plyed his trade, from County Wexford, his place of origin, to the reaches of south-west Britain. He followed a fairly regular timetable on his circuit, so work was kept for his return, which meant he had a reasonable income, there being no contact with the Inland Revenue, and he never applied for any social benefits because he didn't need them.

It could be said that he didn't really imbibe, not in the way that most of his countrymen did. The only time he had been in trouble was when he had taken a few too many. Quite a lot too many, actually. It was in his character to be excessively protective of the fair sex when the poteen was running strong in his veins. And it was then his sense of fair play tended to become disproportionate. He was a romantic at heart, as are a great many of the Irish, and he firmly believed that the age of chivalry was not dead, not if he was around anyway.

It was while he was entertaining a lady friend, in a quiet decent way, in a quiet decent pub, that a large loutish local yokel, emboldened by drink himself, and backed by several equally loutish companions, had started to cast aspersions on McGilligan's relationship with the lady in question, in a loud and most uncouth manner, so that she blushed and began to snivel into her handkerchief.

Very calmly, McGilligan put down his drink, unfinished. He put his left hand on his companion's shoulder and ushered her out of the pub, to the drunken jeers of the lady's persecutors. In his right hand he carried his black-thorn cudgel, which never left him. It was a warm summer's night, so he seated Alice, for that was her name, on a pub bench, and placed his shillelagh just outside the pub door. Then with a beatific smile on his face, he re-entered the public bar and invited the loud-mouthed one to come outside. He also advised that his companions would be welcome to join him as well. McGilligan then turned and went out into the darkness.

After a moment's hesitation, and under the misconception that there was safety in numbers, they lumbered out through the narrow doorway in single file, led by the vociferous one telling the world what he intended to do to the fucking bogtrotter, which was a bad error of judgement. McGilligan was not a bellicose Irish patriot. He was not upset by the inherent racism of the man's threats, but by the language in which he couched them in front of Alice.

This added venom to his arm, and when his victims came, temporarily blinded, one by one, and obligingly stood there blinking in the darkness, the principal culprit received a

254

blow on the shin that cracked the bone, the second a vicious jab in the solar plexus that completely winded him, and the third ran howling into the night before any further damage could be caused. Tim then escorted his partner back to their drinks and, having drained them, they both went quietly on their way.

He'd had to go up before the beak, as he-of-the-cracked-shin lodged a complaint, but he was let off with a mild warning as nearly a dozen occupants of the pub, and that included the landlord, all swore on oath that Tim had not been the aggressor and had acted in self-defence and on behalf of Alice. From that day onward, he'd promised himself to keep as low a profile as possible. Appearances in court were something to be avoided, no matter how innocuous the outcome, as they tended to give one what his mother would have called a name, and that could be bad for business. Next thing you know they'd be calling him a terrorist or some such nonsense and him who had taken the Queen's shilling. He had in fact done an honourable term in the Irish Guards, as had so many others of his country-men, and thought her majesty a dear lady, especially on pay-days. Nevertheless it was probably that experience which had set him to go on the road, free from any restrictions other than a keen sense of responsibility to his fellow man, particularly if it was a woman.

Anyway, fate had, that evening, chosen for him to be on his way up from Fugglestone St Peter, near Salisbury, in a general northerly direction, heading for the army camp at Larkhill, where he expected to pick up some work through acquaintances from his service days. As he came over the brow of the hill which started the final stretch of six or seven miles to his destination, he saw looming up the familiar, if somewhat eerie, outline of Stonehenge in the descending gloom a mile or so on. It was familiar in as much as he had frequently sheltered there, as had many travellers over the centuries. If one knows where to go there are several nooks within the sarsen trilithons beneath the lintels or in the eroded earthworks circling the structures, that when packed with a generous amount of bedding such as bracken, which is in plentiful supply, makes for a comfortable and reasonably dry shelter.

Tim stood and looked about himself. He could easily have reached Larkhill. Walking across the fields in the dark didn't worry him at all, but a quick sniff of the wind told him there was rain in the air and he saw no reason to get wet if he could avoid it. He nodded to himself and made the decision to stay. As he approached the monstrous structure he crossed himself and bowed his head respectfully to the gods of the old religion, thus covering himself with all parties.

A tin of beans, a brew of tea, and he settled down comfortably for the night on his bracken bed. In his hand he clutched a bottle of Jamesons to which he had treated himself earlier in the day. After all he could hardly get into any trouble out here on his own. He took a deep swallow from the bottle and rolled the whisky sensually round his tongue.

'This is the life,' he muttered to himself, and lay back listening to the rain beginning to patter on the lintel above.

23

Friday 13th March 1992

Well, Levinsky had certainly got the weather forecast wrong, the bastard. So bloody sure of himself, he was. 'It will be clear and well lit by a quarter-moon,' he'd said. It was belting down now, with the sky obscured by cloud although the night had started clear and bright, he had to admit. As far as Harwood was concerned there would be no question of going unarmed. Levinsky's fighting skills already stacked the odds against him.

As the moon had first come up in a starlit sky, Harwood had gone out in the field behind the house and, with the silencer on his pistol he'd banged away for over an hour at selected targets, gradually lengthening the range. His accuracy had increased significantly and some of his old confidence returned. He had plenty of ammunition and intended to carry out further practice on the site of the expected action.

He'd no intention of getting there at the prearranged time either. That would be asking for it. A good two hours to scout out the land was what he reckoned on. Nor did he intend to approach from the nearby A360 road. He'd use the A303 which had traffic at all hours, and he intended to park a mile or so to the west and approach over the fields. Never do the expected. He'd thought about bringing in a few ex-SAS friends but there wasn't time, and anyway they'd probably be fat and married, 'out of condition' and understandably reluctant to get involved.

He was dressed very warmly in his old black SAS fighting gear and had clipped the Browning 9mm to his belt after checking that all the eight rounds were there. He had more ammo in a pocket of his outfit and just for good measure an issue grenade he'd purloined from his service days, as a souvenir. He felt it necessary to eat just sufficient to keep the energy requirement up to standard but had to choke it down all the same, because he was strung so tight. One big advantage he did have, and that was night vision glasses. Surely his adversary wouldn't have those.

It should take 45 minutes to get to Stonehenge. He decided to give it an hour and leave the house at 1.30 a.m. for the 4.30 rendezvous. He was shivering with tension but he'd been through similar experiences in the past, albeit a long time ago, and as he got going the old adrenalin rush started up and the feeling of fatalism began to take over.

* * *

Jacob Lee was looking at an AA road Atlas.

'Found it in the car,' he explained, and smiled smugly. 'It should be easy enough to find Stonehenge.' A pause. 'Ah yes, here it is. Clearly marked.' He seemed very calm and confident about the whole exercise. 'We will leave in reasonable time for the meeting. I suggest you get some rest, you will need it.' He took a small phial from his pocket. 'You will drink this now to ensure you relax. There are no side-effects and I want you alert when the time comes, as I may need your co-operation.'

There was no question of argument at all. Ching-hua drank it as instructed and immediately felt as if she were drifting into a delicious languor. Her body was totally relaxed, yet her eyes remained open and she was still perfectly capable of following what was going on, as if he had administered some form of hypnotic drug. She could not talk and was apparently incapable of movement. He bent over her, looked into her eyes, and appeared satisfied with the result.

'I am going out for a short time to arrange certain matters, but I will be back soon.'

She heard the noise of the door shut behind him and tried desperately to move, but she might as well have been bound and gagged. Is he really trying to get me to rest, she wondered, or is it that he no longer trusts me and is ensuring my compliance? She lay waiting and completely helpless. It seemed only a short time before he returned but looking at the wall clock she saw it had been nearly two hours. It was 1.30 on Friday morning.

He did not even bother to look her way for a few minutes but busied himself with packing certain items into a small overnight bag. She could not see what he was doing as he covered his actions with his body. No weapons, indeed; I'll bet he's taking something with him, she thought. She willed herself to move in an agony of desperation so as to do something that would frustrate this man but it was useless. Quite useless. He stopped packing and turned round.

'Right, we are ready to leave,' he said brightly. He came over, put his hands on her shoulders and said: 'You've had enough rest now. Time to get up.'

It was obviously some unnatural influence that gave him such dominance over her, as she rose like an automaton and awaited his further instructions. She could now move in a strangely bemused sort of way, as if wading through water, but she was unable to talk. He smiled and took her firmly by the elbow. How she now hated that ready smile which had certainly lost its charm. In his other hand he carried the small bag.

They stepped into the corridor and moved towards the exit. On a sofa in the entrance hall sat two Chinese security men from the embassy. Both were fast asleep or unconscious, or perhaps even worse. One of them was supposed to be looking after Ching-hua. What a mess.

They went outside. The car was waiting. The chauffeur stepped out and opened the door for her to sit in the front. Strange. Then it became clear. The chauffeur ran round and opened the driver's door for Jacob, who climbed in, threw his small bag on to the back seat and drove off with a casual wave.

He's certainly organised, she thought.

Jacob stole a look at her profile and truly regretted that things had turned out this way, for to him she was the essence of beauty and would have been a perfect partner. Now he would make her creature kow-tow to him in the most humiliating manner, with her as a witness of his shame, then offer both of them in sacrifice, as had been done before at Stonehenge and elsewhere over the surface of the earth, for more than ten millennia, long before these other usurping heresies arose. Hatred surged strongly in him.

I must calm myself, he thought, and forget this minor disappointment, for now is the time to concentrate completely on what is to come, to generate the great power the teaching had instilled, the power that would enable him to communicate with the spiritual entities extant about the stone ring, so that he could call them to his aid and ensure the destruction of his enemy.

Once outside London and well along the M3, he stopped at an empty lay-by and sat silently by the immobile, speechless girl. He thrust his mind back to the amphitheatre of Hsiao T'un, giving himself up to the experience of his initiation. He could feel in his hand, as if it were there, the pulsing heart of the girl child sacrifice, and he called upon the ancient patrons of the cult, long past, to guide and protect him.

In a flash of time he felt upon his shoulder the hand of his mentor. 'Go, but with care, my son. Those who are there are expecting you.' And then he was back to the closed car with the rain beating on the metal roof.

* * *

It was 3 a.m. exactly and Harwood sat in his car, well away from the site, sipping hot, sweet coffee from a thermos. It seemed funny how calm he felt, now the dénouement was inevitable. He wanted his woman back, no matter what might have happened to her or what she may have done, and he knew exactly how he was going to do it. By killing the bastard and to hell with the consequences.

It was still tipping down and the wind was blowing from the north-west, causing the car to rock occasionally during the stronger gusts. He had not taken the opportunity for further practice shooting, as in this weather it would be impossible to ensure he was on his own. He hunched his shoulders unhappily at the thought of having to leave the warm, dry cocoon of the vehicle but he had to make a move now in an endeavour to take a tactical advantage, if it was possible.

The great stones of the ancient Druid monument were surrounded by earth works consisting of an outer counter-scarp, a ditch and then a bank. The whole area was fenced with barbed wire. The wire was really no obstacle to a determined intruder, particularly if there were no security staff in support, which there never were at this hour, apart from during the summer solstice period to stop hippy travellers invading the place.

His plan was to make it to the top of the North Barrow, a raised mound at the edge of the outer sarsen circle, where the ancients had buried their dead, and from there recon-noitre the situation. If Harwood could identify Jacob's position without being spotted himself then he would have the advantage.

* * *

Jacob had decided not to come too early. Let Mayo reach the place first, and get himself soaked and in a state of high tension by the time he arrived with Ching-hua.

With his heightened perception and the protection and help of those who had gone before, Jacob was confident he would sense his antagonist's presence, locate his where-abouts immediately and take the necessary action. He was

261

beginning to feel something already, an emanation of mystic enquiry from the direction in which they were travelling, as if the elemental spirits awaited with interest the coming of one of their fraternity from the orient, and mixed in with the sensors reaching out to him was a subtle vibration of warning that an interloper was in their midst.

So he was there early anxious to place himself before my arrival, Levinsky thought. He smiled gently to himself and turned to Ching-hua. 'He is there already,' he said, 'lying in wait for us.'

He was not yet prepared to let her talk, but she turned her face to him with a look of such agonised entreaty that he physically felt the pain within her and had to turn away quickly to retain the thread of his concentration.

The dashboard clock showed 4 a.m. as they topped the hill that overlooked the stones and, as he knew it would, the rain ceased and the clouds dissolved to show the moon and the constellations in a clear night sky. Jacob nodded his head in appreciation to the powers-that-be who had ordained such a setting for his final act of retribution.

Despite the darkness, the trilithons stood starkly clear and menacing in their blackness, with the slaughter stone sprawled by the entrance causeway, seeming anxious for its due.

* * *

Harwood looked at his watch. It was 4 a.m. and suddenly the rain and the wind stopped abruptly and the clouds disappeared as if by magic. Clever trick that. In fact it must be magic or something worse. What the hell am I up against? Harwood asked himself.

A car came over the crest, lights blazing. It stopped at the bottom of the hill and took the right-hand fork to the A360. Would it turn into the site car park or go on elsewhere? It stopped, its right indicator flicking, and turned into the car park. It must be him. The bloody nerve of the man. No attempt to show caution.

Harwood pulled out his glasses, focused them on to the vehicle to assure himself of the occupants.

He found moisture dripping in front of his eyes and took it to be rain, but it wasn't. It was sweat, and the temperature wasn't much above 5° centigrade. Hardly sweating weather.

His night vision glasses picked out two figures, one a woman. It was them, alright. Making no attempt to hide themselves, they walked across the road to the site. There were a couple of snips as the man casually cut the wire, and they stood at the entrance to the causeway.

Harwood examined them from his position on the North Barrow, keeping his head well down. Projections stand out clearly on the skyline on a starlit night. They were the best part of 200 feet away. A great deal too far for a pistol shot.

Jacob's head twisted slowly in an arc from right to left then back again, in a searching motion. Ching-hua stood beside him, motionless. His left hand was holding her elbow. Then suddenly his head stopped turning and he looked directly where Harwood was lying. Quite casually he moved behind Ching-hua, interposing her between them.

How the hell does he know where I am, let alone that I am even here? So much for the advantage of my night vision equipment, Harwood thought disgustedly.

'We are glad to see you have come early,' Levinsky called out. Ching-hua still stood looking straight ahead, saying nothing.

Harwood kept quiet and still.

'Our arrangement was to meet before the altar stone, Mayo. We are moving there now.'

They walked slowly across Harwood's front from left to right towards the altar stone in the middle of the circle. At all times, Jacob ensured Ching-hua was between them. There was no doubt now that he had sensed Harwood's presence accurately by some means which the latter didn't even like to contemplate. What the hell had he done to Ching-hua? She was behaving like an automaton. Not much help could be expected from her.

Harwood sighed. He wouldn't get anywhere lying up here like a log and out of pistol range. He moved quietly backwards down the Barrow, then doubled noiselessly around the outer Sarsen circle, using the ditch as cover, until he was directly across from the causeway and virtually behind where the couple should presently be placed. He moved up the bank and tried to focus in on the altar stone, but it was not in a direct line of vision. Some fifteen minutes had elapsed since their arrival.

There seemed to be no sign of movement from where Levinsky and Ching-hua should be. Harwood gritted his teeth, pulled his Browning from its clip, and came over the top of the outer bank in a rush, making for an upright blue stone within range of the altar.

He pressed against it to make as small a target as possible, as he was damned sure he was not the only one carrying a weapon, and peered round it. The quarter-moon lit the scene in profiles and shadows to an extraordinary extent. Levinsky stood on the other side of the altar. He was stripped to the waist, his naked torso shining in the cold light, his arms up-raised and, on the stone itself, lay Ching-hua, draped entirely in black, her hands crossed upon her breasts. They were both perfectly still, like a black and white photograph of a satanic ritual.

* * *

Generally a few sips of Jamesons ensured a good night's rest for Tim McGilligan, but something, he couldn't define what, was making him very restless, so much so that he found he'd lowered the level in the bottle by considerably more than he'd planned, although there was still nearly a half left.

He finally drifted off but the unexpected noise and beam of headlights from a car turning into the car park brought him wide awake with a rush. He peered upwards at the sky. It had stopped raining and he could tell from the position of the quarter-moon that it was several hours before dawn.

What the devil would anyone be doing in this deserted place at such a God-forsaken hour? Something profane, he was sure of that, and a prickle of apprehension twisted in his belly so that he took another quick swig to calm his fears and reached for his cudgel.

Peering cautiously out of his cover, he could just make out two vague shapes approaching the wire fence at the causeway. He clearly heard the cutters being used to gain entry. This confirmed to him that they were strangers to the site, as there were several easy ways of gaining access elsewhere, which did not require such measures. Or maybe they just didn't care.

His eyes were getting more used to the moonlit scene now. One was a woman, small, neat and, from what he could see, Asian in appearance. The other was a man, who seemed to be guiding her with unnecessary firmness towards the centre of the circle. McGilligan's protective interests were immediately aroused. And then the man started talking to someone. Someone called Mayo. Now if that wasn't an Irish name, he'd like to know what was.

He turned his head to look in the direction where Mayo was, and out of the corner of his eye he saw a black clad, hooded silhouette move like a wraith round the outer Sarsen. For a second the moonlight glinted quite clearly on the pistol he held in front of him. McGilligan swallowed hard and fervently prayed that he had not landed himself in the middle of something political, for he knew about such things.

His immediate reaction was to withdraw from the scene, keeping very much under cover, but the instinctive curiosity of the man forced him to stay and watch the drama which was unfolding before him.

* * *

Even in the strange light Harwood could see the reflection of Jacob's eyes boring into his and glinting like an animal's. The desire to kill him was overwhelming. He raised the pistol and aimed at Levinsky's chest. He could not miss from that distance. But Harwood's hand locked rigid as if it were made of stone. He could not pull the trigger.

'Come here, Mayo,' Jacob commanded.

He moved slowly forward, arm still outstretched, until they stood across the altar stone from each other. Harwood still held the pistol at Jacob's chest, over Ching-hua's inert body, and noted that her eyes were open although there was no sign of life in them.

The younger man's hand reached out, took the pistol from Harwood's grasp, and flung it behind him. 'I said no weapons,' he said flatly.

'What have you done to her?'

'She will be perfectly capable of witnessing your humiliation before you both go to your final agony together.'

It was the total lack of emotion in his voice that made Harwood's flesh crawl.

Jacob bent over and lifted Ching-hua off the altar so that she stood beside him. She looked at Harwood, and for a second he thought he saw a flash of emotion cross her face, but it was instantly suppressed. He was desperate to touch her and put out his hand, but she made no effort to reciprocate and simply stood and stared.

'Now, Mayo, are you ready?' Jacob moved around the altar and stood within a few feet of Harwood. He was quite relaxed, his arms hung loosely at his sides.

Harwood's old training sergeant had drilled into him that the man who gets in the first blow generally wins, so Harwood turned away as if to make more space and then, without warning, back-heeled with all his strength at the level of Jacob's groin. To his intense satisfaction he felt his foot ram home with a solid thud that jarred his stiffened leg right up to the hip. He spun round, poised to follow up, and to his total amazement the other man was still in the same relaxed attitude as if nothing had happened.

Harwood stood in shock. Jacob, eyes ablaze, came at him.

Harwood evaded the first charge, turned and unashamedly

fled. Another piece of wisdom that had been imparted by Harwood's training sergeant was to totally ignore the thought of fighting against impossible odds but to forget one's pride and get to hell out of it, in order to seek a more advantageous position for future action. Yet another injunction had been, never fight fair if fighting dirty could bring matters to a satisfactory conclusion more rapidly.

It was not as simple as all that, but at least it was worth trying. Whilst Jacob was collecting himself from his initial bull-like rush, Harwood slipped round one of the inner sarsen stones that made up the horseshoe of trilithons about the altar stone.

What he needed now was time. Time to overcome his initial amazement at the way his enemy had so easily taken his weapon from him and then followed up by withstanding what must have been a truly devastating back-heel kick in his groin.

So began a deadly game of hide and seek around the huge stones towering over them. Harwood realised that no way was he up to a face to face encounter. His only hope was to work round to recovering the pistol that the younger man had so contemptuously tossed away. He knew for sure that Jacob had used the arts of Chè Gów to render him powerless at the crucial moment. It had to be a type of mental control which could surely be overcome by avoiding eye contact. If he could get the gun he would know what to do next time. If there was a next time, he thought grimly.

He stood pressed against a stone column, his black fighting gear making him practically invisible, his ears straining for the slightest sound of his opponent.

Nothing. He had to move now while it was still dark, with a waning moon. In the East there was the faintest tinge and in daylight he would be far more vulnerable. He tensed ready to go for the neighbouring trilithon and practically jumped out of his skin as a low chuckle sounded almost in his ear.

'You have to make a move some time Mayo.'

Levinsky had to be only feet away round the edge of the

stone. For the first time since the confrontation Harwood felt anger, as opposed to diffidence at the other's ability to seemingly block his every move. Now was the time to hit back. Somehow he had to give himself a head start to reach the gun.

He sidled even closer to the stone's edge, closer to where he reckoned Jacob was standing. He braced himself and produced what sounded like an involuntary clearance in his throat.

He had gauged the other man's reaction correctly. Eager to bring matters to a conclusion Levinsky rushed it yet again and came round at Harwood like greased lightning. The speed of his reaction caused him to come a most dramatic cropper, over Harwood's rigidly outstretched leg. Harwood gave a grunt of satisfaction. At least the bastard isn't invulnerable, he thought as he stamped the heel of his boot hard down on the back of Levinsky's knee.

It was a blow that would have disabled any man but Harwood wasn't waiting to check out the result of his action. He was off after the gun without a second's delay. He knew roughly where Jacob had thrown it.

A moment's hesitation. Yes there it was, the slightest reflection in the grass. With a triumphant yell he literally dived for it arm outstretched. His fingers grabbed the butt and in one fluid motion he rolled over and began to point the weapon in the direction from which he could expect his opponent to come.

And that was as far as he got.

Before he could even sight the gun Levinsky was on him. A crunching bare foot kick to his right wrist sent the automatic spinning away beyond his reach and he was back to square one. How Jacob had bounced back so quickly he could not understand but there he was, standing over him, legs straddled, hands on hips, arrogantly challenging him to stand up and fight.

'You've provided some interesting sport so far Mayo, now get up and show us,' he bowed to the still impassive Ho Ching-hua, 'what you are really made of.'

Harwood, climbed wearily to his feet.

'Finish me off if it pleases you but for pity's sake let her go.'

'Pity?' snarled Levinsky. 'What pity did you show when you sent my father to his death and hundreds of others, including my mother?' He spat on the ground at Harwood's feet.

'Don't you dare talk to me about "pity" you bloody murderer!'

For a moment Harwood wondered if it would be worth-while to explain that if Levinsky senior had called his bluff no one, except Peng Kiong of course, would have died, but he dismissed the idea as soon as he thought of it. The young man wanted blood and would never listen to him. Levinsky slid forward in a fighting crouch.

'Stop your whining and get on with it.'

Harwood defended himself to the best of his ability and once or twice was even able to set Jacob back a trifle, but he was completely outclassed and finished a bleeding, helpless, dazed mess on the ground at Jacob's feet.

Harwood raised himself on all-fours and stared through puffy, half-closed eyes at Ching-hua, but there seemed to be no pity in her expression. Not even interest. Levinsky put his foot on the small of his beaten opponent's back and jammed his face down on the ground so that Harwood lay before him in kow-tow position. 'See, my dear, how humble your foreign lover is. How penitent, for the murder of my father and my mother.'

But she could not hear him. She could take no more and had apparently sought refuge in robot-like insensibility, where Harwood would have dearly liked to follow her. In his frustration, Jacob kicked his prostrate victim viciously in the ribs and, even though his foot was bare, it was as hard as rock and Harwood could hear the bones crack.

He screamed and, rolling over, pulled his knees up to his stomach in an endeavour to protect himself. It was then he felt the inflexible hardness of the grenade digging excruciat-ingly into him, the ace he had kept as his very last resort, to be played only when Jacob was motionless and unaware, if ever.

Levinsky sneered in grim satisfaction, and grabbing him by the hair heaved him up and dragged him over on to the slaughter stone.

Harwood lay on his back groaning but, through the mist of his agony, his fingers twisted and fumbled desperately for the grenade. It was the only thing still going for him. Jacob, fully confident that Harwood was no threat, turned back for Ching-hua. Picking her up, he carried her over and dumped her roughly upon Harwood, then stood back and gazed at the two offerings awaiting the sacrificial knife, which he now carried in his hand. The sky suddenly lit up with distant flashes, followed by a deep rumble of thunder. Levinsky raised his arms and face to the stars, the knife glinting in the moonlight. Ecstasy upon him!

With Jacob's attention elsewhere, and hidden in part by Ching-hua, Harwood hesitated no longer. The grenade was in his hand, the pin out. His fingers gripped the firing lever tightly closed.

24

Very quickly, McGilligan identified that the girl was in deep trouble, and that the lunatic fellow who had divested himself of his upper garments was the villain of the piece. He had beaten the shit out of the rather ineffective man in black, who's gun had apparently failed him at the crucial moment, and now, for God's sake, the murderous madman was waving a knife around with deadly intent. She was such a pretty little lass too. No way was this going to be allowed to continue.

His chivalrous instincts now fully aroused, McGilligan took a final pull at his virtually empty bottle, gripped his cudgel firmly in his fist and advanced purposefully towards the back of the unsuspecting Jacob Levinsky. The latter was so immersed in his own ego trip that his profound awareness had slipped, and it was not until the Irishman was practically upon him that he sensed an alien presence and swung round.

Even with the split-second left to him, Levinsky might have been able to regain control of the situation in the same way as he had been able to render Harwood powerless, despite being at the point of a gun. Then, he had used sheer mental authority, but McGilligan, by virtue of breeding, or a touch too much Irish whiskey, or perhaps both, was on a completely different wavelength from the usual run of the mill. This time it was Levinsky who was temporarily paralysed, by a crack on the skull which would have put most men out of the picture for several hours or more. He flopped down on his face and then everything seemed to happen at once.

Levinsky had been standing by the slaughter stone looming over the two of them, his arms raised, the knife in his hand poised for the killing strokes, when the distant rumble of thunder and flashes of lightning had drawn his gaze to the sky. It was then that Harwood, close to insensibility, could see no way out but to go for broke. He had nothing to lose.

He released the firing lever and rolled the primed grenade over the edge of the slaughter stone so that it dropped the couple of feet to the earth, coming to rest between Levinsky's legs. That should spoil his day, thought Harwood grimly.

The technique of using a hand grenade was all in the timing. Dispose of it too quickly, once the firing pin was released and there would be time for the recipient to throw it back at you. This particular grenade had a ten-second delay built in. An awful lot could happen in ten seconds. And it did.

Harwood had intended to count away the first five seconds, then roll himself, with Ching-hua in his arms, off the opposite side of the slaughter stone in the hope that it would protect them from the explosion while it blasted Levinsky to perdition. Despite Harwood's shattered physical, and decidedly fuzzy mental, condition, the whole plan still depended heavily on there being no glitches, but McGilligan's totally unexpected arrival on the scene completely changed everything.

With Levinsky dazedly trying to get his own head together, his control over Ching-hua evaporated. Now with a mind of her own, she began to struggle wildly in Harwood's arms, not really knowing where she was but desperate to get away in any direction, even the wrong one. Harwood simply wasn't strong enough to hold her and if they stayed where they were for too long there was no doubt of the consequences. If he let her go the way she was presently headed she would be right over it when it blew. The only one of them capable of constructive action was Tim McGilligan.

Tim's experience in the élite regiment of guards meant that he recognised instantly what he was looking at. Also he knew he had no time to bugger about. Grabbing the hapless Levinsky round the waist he flung him, without a second thought, face down, spreadeagled over the deadly object, and turning away, used the remaining few seconds to put as much distance as possible between himself and the danger zone, hurling himself flat in the process.

The explosion, albeit somewhat muffled, was concentrated powerfully on Levinsky's belly and chest and lifted him clear off the ground. Ching-hua and Harwood were blown off the stone and landed behind it, well protected from any shrapnel. Harwood came to, his ears buzzing, and with a lump on the back of his head where he had hit the deck. Otherwise, he felt fine, not counting cracked ribs and numerous other scrapes and bruises inflicted on him by his enemy. Seeing Ching-hua squatting beside him, looking perfectly normal and highly concerned, was the best medicine in the world. He put his arm out and hugged her. She hugged him back, which made him squeak with the agony of his bruised body and broken ribs. She kissed him gently, then burst into tears. He held her again, not caring about the pain. He'd got her back and this time he was never going to let her go.

The air was full of the stench of blood and cordite. They went round to the other side of the slaughter stone. Harwood tried to turn Ching-hua away from the sight. Jacob Levinsky lay half on his side, his entrails torn out of him, his fists clenched as if in fearsome effort to strike back at something or someone. And yet his face, in contrast, was hardly damaged and bore an expression of eerie tranquility.

'You know, he looks as if he has found peace,' said Ching-hua.

'I must have imagined it,' said Harwood, changing the subject, 'but I could swear I saw a wild-looking fellow with red hair a second or two before the world blew up.' He shook his head in bewilderment. 'He was carrying a rather wicked club and looked intent on using it on Levinsky.'

Ching-hua laughed nervously. 'You must have imagined it, or rather it was wishful thinking.' She looked around somewhat apprehensively. 'He would have stayed to receive our grateful thanks if he'd been real wouldn't he?'

'I suppose so,' said Harwood, and then, raising his voice; 'Whoever you are, or whatever you are, we are forever in your debt.'

McGilligan, badly battered, cut about, and covered in blood but miraculously not seriously damaged, watched the entire performance from behind a strategically-placed blue stone in the outer ring. 'I might take you up on that one day,' he muttered to himself, but for now, as all seemed well, he intended to slip away and avoid all the ensuing complications which were bound to arise. After all, as his blessed mother would have said, it might give him a 'name', which is not good for business.

'And what do we do now?' asked Ching-hua.

'We go home and work out what we are going to tell the police, as no doubt they will find their way to us. His vehicle in the car park will lead them back to the Royal Society and someone must have seen you leave with him.'

* * *

They told the detective who visited them that Jacob had brought Ching-hua home to Wiltshire and had left very early on the morning in question. Evidently, as far as they knew, curiosity had caused him to stop at Stonehenge on the way back to London.

After much investigation, the official verdict was that Lie Win Sie had committed suicide while the balance of his mind was disturbed. No one could provide a reason why a man who had been so lionised should take his own life in such a dramatic way but the caretaker who had found the ghastly sight when he turned up for his duties that morning expressed the opinion that there was no rhyme or reason to what foreigners get up to, which more or less echoed the private thoughts of the coroner.

The Chinese authorities, and Professor Wu in particular, complained bitterly at the loss of one of their favourite sons, but the matter was finally dropped as no one could prove any misadventure, and in any case Gao Shu Leung, the head of Chinese state security, wished the matter to be suppressed. He knew continued insistence on following it up might have opened a Pandora's box that would have been most embarrassing for his department.

As for Tim McGilligan, although Alice doubted his tale that he had been blown up by a stray piece of ammunition left on the Salisbury Plain firing range by a careless trooper, she was happy enough that he'd decided his roaming days were over.

With the death of Jacob Levinsky and the knowledge that the agents of China's State Security were no longer on their trail Ching-hua and Harwood were at last able to settle down to a normal life. To put the seal on their happiness Ching-hua became pregnant and whilst the boy was somewhat premature he was born lusty and loud.

'My goodness he's a little tiger,' exclaimed the midwife. 'And he must be terribly hungry too with the noise he's making.'

'Give him to me,' commanded Ching-hua eagerly stretching out her arms and taking the infant to her breast.

He found her swollen teat without hesitation, tearing and tugging at her so that she cried out with the unexpectedness of it. Startled by the noise his mother had made he paused for a second and turned his head to look at her.

For a long second their gaze locked and she found herself transfixed by the knowing eyes of Jacob Levinsky.

Startled but mesmerised she stroked the back of the baby's head. 'There, there my darling,' she soothed, and smiled contentedly.